Dirt Sailors

Navy Seabees in Vietnam
A Novel

Raymond Hunter Pyle

This story is a work of fiction. Names, characters, places, and incidents either are the product of the author's imagination or are used fictitiously, and any resemblance to actual persons, living or dead, business establishments, events, or locations is unintended and entirely coincidental.

ISBN: 9798772552407

VIETNAM COLLECTION
BY
RAYMOND HUNTER PYLE

<u>Marines in Vietnam</u>

The Gunny

Bullets and Bandages

Master Guns

The Beast

<u>Army in Vietnam</u>

Jump Wings and Secrets

<u>Navy in Vietnam</u>

Walking on Water

Dirt Sailors

CHAPTER 1

1965

New Castle, Delaware.

The old guy who lived in the little green trailer down on Tenth Street was called Popeye. Hank and Toby had known him for as long as they could remember. Popeye was a retired Navy Chief Petty Officer. He had been a Navy Seabee in WWII and Korea and had his twenty in and was partially disabled before the current war in Southeast Asia fired up. Popeye tried to get back on active duty for the new war, but the Navy wouldn't take him. His right leg was missing below the knee.

Hank and Toby Tucker were big boys, Hank being the biggest and oldest. They had stopped by Popeye's trailer for a cold drink coming back from snapping turtle hunting in the marsh since they were small. Popeye always had time for them and usually had good advice when they had a problem, and if the problem was one of their bikes, Popeye could fix anything. That's the way it was in the fifties. You knew your neighbors from the time you learned to walk and probably married one of their daughters when you grew up. Helping out was just part of being neighbors, part of getting by in a blue-collar neighborhood.

Grown now, Hank and Toby had served their apprenticeships and were hard workers. Hank was a master carpenter and Toby was a heavy equipment operator. They still occasionally stopped by the old trailer to visit with Popeye and partake of his wisdom and occasionally his sea stories. Popeye always had a good war story to share, over a beer now that they were both of age, and when they brought a six-pack with them. Hank had a particular reason for stopping this day.

"Pops, are you in?" Hank called at the door.

"Where the hell else would I be? Come on in."

When Hank came through the door Popeye was already moving to the fridge to get a couple beers.

"I need some advice, Pops."

"Well, I got plenty of that and it's all free. Take a load off. What's the problem?"

"I think my number is coming up at the draft

board. You were in the Seabees, right?"

"Best time of my life," Popeye said.

"Take a look at this flyer. The business agent at the union hall gave it to me. What do you think?"

The flyer explained a program the Navy was offering to experienced construction tradesmen and it was supported by the AFL/CIO. Instead of entering the Navy as a recruit, journeyman in construction trades could enter the Navy at advanced enlisted grades depending on their experience.

"It sounds a lot better than going in the army as a recruit," Hank said.

"Brings back a lot of memories," Popeye said. "Back in Willie-Willie Twice when they first started the Seabees, this is how everybody came in. There weren't any construction rates then and they needed to build airfields and warehouses and all kinds of stuff all over the Pacific in conditions no contractor would work in. They had to get experienced construction men in fast, but most construction men were exempt because they were doing critical war effort jobs already like building liberty ships. We had men wearing chief hats that hadn't been in the Navy more than a week. Damndest thing you ever saw. They brought construction men in, trained them like Marines, and sent them to the islands to build the airfields. They had to make construction men who could fight and build so they didn't have to tie up Marines and soldiers guarding the construction sites. They had to be able to drop their tools and grab their rifles to defend themselves."

"Looks like they're doing it again for Vietnam," Hank said. "What do you think, Pops? Does it sound like a good deal?" I have ten years of experience and a good job, but I sure as hell don't want to get drafted. I had an apprentice deferment and then I had a defense contract deferment, but the contract is up and I'm all out of deferments now. The man at the draft board said my name is in the hat."

"Talk to the Navy recruiter. See what they'll give you. With your experience it's got to be better than recruit. I'd do it in a minute if they'd let me. Hank, you're a big, strapping young man and you got a good attitude, always did, but I'll tell you something. That war over there is going to change you. This one is a nasty one and I can't figure out why we're even over there. Never even heard of the damn place, and the last time I looked, they weren't attacking America. If you could find a way to stay out of it all together, that's what I'd tell you to do. But if you have to go anyway, the construction battalions are the way to go. Best damn outfit in the military."

"How do you figure it will change me?"

Popeye didn't answer right away. He looked away and took a deep breath.

"Jungle wars change a man," he said. "I don't figure this one will be any better than the ones we fought."

CHAPTER 2

August 1967
Dong Ha, Republic of Vietnam

Dong Ha was a big Marine base about as far north as you could get in South Vietnam. It was in northern I-Corps near the DMZ with a lot of red dust in the dry season and a lot of red mud in the wet season. The base housed a little of everything military. Some Army personnel who rotated out to Con Thien had their own area. A load of Marines, of course, since it was a Marine base, but some of everything the Corps had was there, recon, infantry, artillery, ordnance, Marine air, communications, supply, the whole enchilada. The Navy was well represented with the Navy Support Activity Detachment, Seabees, and the supply activity. Even the Air Force had a detachment of air and forward air controllers on base.

After getting off a Navy landing craft called a Mike Boat at the Dong Ha ramp, Hank Tucker, Builder First Class (BUL1) and his brother Toby, Equipment operator Second Class (EO2), stacked Hank's cargo at the top of the ramp. While he was in Danang waiting to escort equipment up to Dong Ha, he made good use of his time and money. Danang had a great PX at China Beach, and not knowing what to expect at Dong Ha, he stocked up on gedunk, as much for trade as personal use.

It hadn't taken him long to pick up on Navy-speak. Gedunk was a general name for all the junk food and goodies you couldn't get at the chow hall. By the time the mike-boat was ready, he had about four hundred pounds of jerky, Vienna sausages, pogey-bait (candy), instant soups, jars of hot peppers, hot sauce, A1 sauce, etc., and his prize, a case (1000 commercial sized packs) of popcorn, popping oil, salt, and a popper kettle. Hidden away and shock protected he also had six quarts of bourbon, vodka, rum, and a gallon of moonshine that closely resembled vodka but took your breath away.

It was hard to almost impossible to get bonded spirits if you were a Navy enlisted man in Vietnam, but Hank was a natural trader and had access to things officers needed. They had access to spirits.

While waiting in Da Nang to move north, Hank pulled a public works job at the Army Special Forces camp out at Marble Mountain. He liked the Special Forces troops. Those guys lived by the trade, but you had to be careful. They'd make it one-sided if they could. He worked out a deal with an SF captain to build a bar and bar cabinets in their club on the sly in exchange for the booze. He drew the materials from the Navy and built the SF a bar. He got the booze which he shared with the materials Chief. Everybody was happy.

Toby was the younger brother and the serious one. When Hank decided to join the Navy Seabees instead of taking his chances with the draft, Toby was right on his heels. It had been that way since they were kids. Both of them were big men and both of them had extensive experience in construction.

Hank's stash was palletized and banded and he needed to get it to the builder's shop in the CBMU 301 camp. Toby took care of it. He had to move the equipment off the boat anyway so he used a forklift to move Hank's pallet to the camp. The Tucker brothers had each other's back.

When the important stuff was off-loaded from the boat, Hank found his way to the Seabee area on foot and stopped dead as he turned onto the old French Road that separated Camp Barnes, the MCB11 compound, from the CBMU301 camp.

There near the equipment yard stood Tubby Long, Steelworker Third Class (SWF3) with his back to Hank. In front of him stood two Marines, two very pissed-off looking Marines. Now, Tubby was five foot seven inches tall and weighed all of 140 pounds soaking wet. He also had a pot belly no amount or work or PT back at Davisville and Port Hueneme could work off.

Tubby's mouth was running as Hank approached from the rear. One of the Marines was moving forward with a balled fist and Tubby was squaring up for a brawl. Like a lot of little men, Tubby was fearless, and he hated Marines. For some reason, their very existence seemed to be a challenge to his manhood. How he had made it out alive from weapons training at Camp Lejeune was a mystery to Hank. Didn't matter. Tubby was Hank's and Toby's buddy.

Hank stepped up right behind Tubby quietly and lifted his big fist and just shook it silently looking straight at the young Marine who stopped suddenly five feet away from Tubby. The Marine was bigger than Tubby, most men were, but he wasn't even close to being in Hank's class.

Hank just pointed down the road and the Marine got the idea. He tuned to his buddy and said, "Come on. This little shit isn't worth the trouble."

Tubby didn't notice the Marine was looking over his head. He taunted the Marines until they were out of sight. Feeling ten feet tall, he spun around and jumped when he saw Hank right behind him.

"Where the fuck did you come from?"

"Nice to see you too, Tubby. What are you doing standing in the middle of the road shaking your fist at the air and cussing? You talking to ghosts?"

"Hell no. I just backed down two Marines. Didn't you see them?"

"I come around the corner and all I see is an empty road and you talking to yourself.

Tubby squinted at Hank for a moment and then he grinned.

"Yeah, you're shitting me. I can always tell. How long you been here behind me?"

Tubby waited just a moment for an answer knowing he wasn't going to get one. "Glad you got in, Hank," he said "I've been watching for you. Where's Toby?"

"He's moving Equipment to the equipment yard."

"Did you get our stash up here okay?"

"Yeah, Toby is dropping it off at Charlie Company. Now, if you can point me to Admin and point out where I can find operations, I can get checked-in."

"Hell, everything is still being moved around, but go on down to the gate, then take the first left when you're inside. The Headquarters CP is just off the road, near the fire lane. Admin is further east near the Navy Supply Detachment camp. There's a few SEA huts up, but we're mostly in tents right now."

"Thanks, little buddy," Hank said. "Where's Charlie Company CP?"

"Charlie Company shop is down a little further from HQ, next to the tent we're using for the EM club. You can see it there on the other side of the supply yard. Like everything else, the club ain't much, just a tent to have a beer in when they got it."

"Thanks," Hank said. "I better report in. Take it easy, Tubby."

"Anyway I can get it. See you at the shop."

If anyone else had called Tubby little buddy, or little anything, it would have been general quarters, but Hank was big enough to call anyone little. Tubby was a DPPO like Hank and went through CBMU 301 pre-commissioning at Port Hueneme with him. As opposites often do, they became buddies early on and Hank had been bailing Tubby's ass out of trouble ever since. Since Tubby was Hank's buddy he automatically became Toby's buddy. They were dubbed the terrible trio among the DPPOs at Port Hueneme. Tubby was a journeyman sheet metal worker in civilian life, and a good one too. With his experience, he should have been given Second-Class Petty Officer (PO2) when he joined, but life isn't always fair, especially to loud little guys who can be obnoxious sometimes. Maybe that's why he was obnoxious sometimes.

Hank and Toby enlisted in the Navy as DPPOs. DPPO stands for Direct Procurement Petty Officer. Only the Seabees had such a program. A construction tradesman with extensive experience could enter the Navy at advanced enlisted grades depending on his experience. Due to expansion because of the Vietnam war, the Navy Seabees were hurting for experienced tradesman and the Navy Department reactivated an old WWII program to fill manpower and leadership needs for new construction battalions. Hank was a master carpenter with ten-years-experience in light and heavy construction and qualified for first-class petty officer (E6) in the builder's rate. Toby, being younger and starting his trade later, was a journeyman and had six years in heavy construction and qualified for second-class petty officer (E5) in the equipment operator's rate. He could run every piece of heavy equipment known to the trades including batch concrete plants and asphalt plants.

Hank didn't make it ten steps before a siren started wailing and Tubby sprinted to a sandbag bunker fifty feet away. Hank just looked around wondering what hell was going on. He knew what the siren meant during the night from the time he spent in Da Nang but hearing it during the day was new.

"Hank, get your ass over here!" Tubby yelled.

Still in no hurry, Hank started toward the bunker, but an explosion from the direction of the airfield got him moving. He dove over a sandbag wall protecting the door opening and landed hard on his shoulder.

"What the hell was that?

"That was the sound of more work for the runway crew," Tubby said. "Sounded like a rocket hit the runway again."

"Again?"

"Yeah, it's happening pretty regular now. This is the first time it happened during the day though."

"Any of them things ever land in the camp?" Hank asked with his eyes narrowed.

"Not our patch of ground, so far, but the Marines get hit a lot, usually at night. The big ones are 122-millimeter rockets, but they aren't accurate. The VC just kind of point them at us and hope they hit the base somewhere."

"How'd they know to sound the siren? Can you see them coming?"

"Not hardly. The Marines have what they call a rocket net going. They got one channel on their radios reserved for rocket notices. If any of the units in the field, especially out by Con Thien, see a rocket launch they get on the rocket net and yell. "rockets, rockets, rockets." All the security CPs have one radio they keep up on the rocket net. If they hear the rockets call, they hit the siren. It's hard for Charlie to get a rocket off without some unit out there seeing it launch. That usually gives you a few seconds to get to a bunker. You never know where the damn things are going to hit, so head for a bunker as soon as you hear the siren. Sometimes you don't get a siren, but that's rare if it's rockets. If it's artillery, the people out at Con Thien can usually hear it firing and we might get a few second warning."

"Damn. Is it safe to go now?"

"Yeah. I doubt we'll get any more incoming today. That's the way it's been going. If they try more than one launch, the Marines will have artillery on them before they can get away."

CHAPTER 3

He had a chance to see most of the camp on his way to Admin. Tubby was right. It was pretty raw. A lot of equipment and supplies had arrived, but there weren't any buildings to put the stacks and stacks of supplies and parts in. Some SEA huts were standing and more were under construction, but most of the materials were on the ground and covered with tarps. The tents he could see looked old and worn and probably wouldn't last long. There was a whole lot of work ahead just getting the camp finished. Toby caught up with him at the Personnel office.

"Word is they got a job for you out in the mountains," Toby said. "My Chief won't let me go with you. See what you can do."

"What have they got you doing?"

"Runway crew here in Dong Ha."

"I'll ask, but I don't have any pull with

Alpha Company. You free right now?"

"Yeah. The Chief gave me the afternoon to get checked in."

"Did you get a hooch?"

"Four racks, just you and me in it so far."

"Come on down to Operations with me. Maybe we can get them to shake you loose."

After turning their orders in at the personnel office, Hank and Toby walked down to Operations to see what was on the schedule for Charlie company. Hank was getting used to the Navy now, but he was still just a civilian in uniform. After his time at Davisville, he finished out his first year on the east coast and then requested and was granted assignment to the Thirty-first Naval Construction Regiment at Port Hueneme, California so he could be with Toby. As soon as he reported-in, he was assigned to a unit performing pre-commissioning activities for CBMU 301, a new Construction Battalion Maintenance Unit scheduled to be deployed to Vietnam. Toby was already there. They deployed in June.

One of the differences between a Mobile Construction Battalion (MCB) and a Construction Battalion Maintenance Unit (CBMU) was how they were homeported. MCBs had permanent homeports in the states and rotated to and from Vietnam, and other places, as a battalion. They also had an eight-month tour of duty in-country with a four to six month refitting period at their homeport before returning to Vietnam for another eight-month tour. The CBMU was homeported in Vietnam and individuals were rotated in and out of the CBMU on twelve-month tours. CBMU 301's homeport was Da Nang, Vietnam.

Charlie Company was the general construction company for the battalion and consisted of builders and steelworkers. Anything built with wood, steel or concrete or any combination of the three was the work of Charlie Company. The builder's rate was split into three specialties: BUH - heavy, BUL-light, and BUR-concrete and included carpenters, plasterers, concrete finishers, masons, roofers, brick layers and cabinet makers, pretty much a solid general construction crew. The Steelworker's rate had two specialties: SWF- Fabricators, and SWE – Erectors.

Coming out of civilian life straight into petty officer ranks with no background and little use for the Navy's rank structure, Hank and Toby had reputations as mavericks, but also as men who knew what they were doing and got things done. But hell, most Seabees were mavericks compared to fleet sailors, so they were doing okay so far. As far as Hank was concerned, a man's status on the job depended on his mastery of the trade, not on how many stripes he wore on his sleeve, or bars on his collars for that matter. The Navy didn't always see it that way though.

Some of the Civil Engineering Corps Officers could get a little stuffy and military now and then, but most of them were more concerned with getting the job done and done well than with formalities of military title and etiquette. There was always more work to do than Seabees to do it. And hell, they were engineers. Enough said.

Even the Marines got used to the Seabees pretty quick and made allowances. Hank liked the Marines. They weren't bashful about anything and they weren't afraid of hard work. They'd make good concrete finishers, every damn one of them.

Except for addressing Chiefs and officers, nobody used rank or titles. He was a petty officer, but he was just "Tuck" to everybody including the chiefs and officers until Toby arrived. Having two Tuckers caused some confusion until they were finally just called by their first names.

Hank's mastery of his trade had gained him respect quickly at Port Hueneme and his willingness to pitch in wherever needed and for as long as needed had gained him a lot of friends. The plumb-bob and framing square symbol of his own rate was a comfortable badge to wear. He had used the term "plumb and square" since he was a boy, to signify anything done right. Toby was the serious Tucker and a hard worker himself with loads of road and heavy construction experience. Weighing in at over five-hundred pounds between them, the Tucker boys tended to get respect, even if DPPOs in general didn't.

"Tuck! Hey Tucker, hold up."

Both Tuckers stopped and turned.

Chief Murphy caught up. He had called Hank "Tuck" since the first time they met back in Port Hueneme. Murph had taken Hank under his wing during the commissioning period in California. Hank was a good carpenter and a strong foreman, but even after eighteen months in the Navy, he didn't have any patience with what he considered Navy bullshit. Murphy saw Hank's value quickly and had him work directly for him and provided a buffer between him and some of the old Navy men in the unit who didn't like the idea of instant petty officers, one of the nicer names they used for DPPOs.

"Hey, Chief. What's going on? Sounds like you're all tuckered out."

Toby nudged him with his elbow and grinned. "Good one. Out of Tuckers."

It went right over Murph's head. "I wanted to talk with you before you talked with the company commander. Hello, Toby. He's got a detail out in the boonies he wants you on. It's at a Special Forces camp in the mountains south of here. The job is mostly fortifications and hardened bunkers. Look, you don't have to take that detail. I can work it out to let you have some time here in Dong Ha getting the builder's shop up."

"Any reason I shouldn't take the detail. Sounds like an adventure."

"Well, it's out in Indian country. You could get shot. That a good enough reason?"

Hank rubbed his jaw for a moment.

"He's got a point," Toby said.

"If I don't take it, somebody else will have to. If that happens, the regular Navy guys won't let me have any peace. Besides, one of them rockets could land on us here. Did you hear those explosions a few minutes ago?"

"You'll get used to it," Murphy said. "I just think you need some time here in camp getting to know the crews and a little about Vietnam before you go out on projects like that one. Up to you though."

"Thanks, Chief, but I'll see what the Lieutenant has to say."

"Okay. But if you want a little time to settle-in, I can work it out."

"Thanks, again."

Hank realized he probably should listen to the Chief. Murph had a lot more experience than he did but working out in some Special Forces camp did sound kind of exciting. He was ready for an adventure and he didn't plan on experiencing war more than once.

Murph was one of the better Navy chiefs in the battalion. The Chiefs he had met and worked with so far were a mixed bag, in Hank's opinion. All of them had a lot of technical knowledge and a lot of Navy knowledge, but it was book learning knowledge. He guessed they needed it to pass the tests getting to Chief. But their practical knowledge was specialized and kind of narrow. As the Navy saw it, a Third-Class PO was equivalent to a third-year apprentice, Second-Class was equivalent to a journeyman, and a First-Class petty officer should be a master mechanic with at least seven-years' experience, qualified in every aspect of the trade. Chiefs ought to be master mechanics able to perform every aspect of a foreman's duty. That's how they recruited DPPOs so that's how Hank judged his peers. They didn't always stack up.

Some of them and a lot of the first and second-class petty officers resented Hank and Toby and the other DPPOs. They had spent years getting their crows (The eagle on a petty officer rank symbol) and had a hard time accepting anyone could be a civilian one day and an instant petty officer the next. He could understand the attitude and didn't let it bother him. If a contractor in civilian life brought in a crew from out of state while there were still men in the hiring hall, the local guys would walk-off and shut the job down. Construction men weren't much different anywhere they were. The Navy guys didn't have a union though and had to settle for resentment.

DPPOs were reserves and like in all services, the regulars looked down on reserves. Everybody needs someone to look down on, it seems. Hank remembered one gate guard at Port Hueneme who couldn't control his mouth after Hank, Toby, and Tubby passed through in dress blues. He was a boot-ass E3 seaman and the Tuckers and Tubby were petty officers, but he was regular Navy and somehow felt like that made him superior or something. Just after Hank and Tubby passed through, the seaman said, "Fucking titless waves," just loud enough for Hank to hear. That was one of the names regulars used for reserves to let themselves feel superior.

The DPPOs were easy to spot in dress uniform. They were the only senior petty officers without any hash marks, the stripes on the arm indicating years of service. DPPOs didn't have any because they came in as petty officers. The Tuckers and Tubby returned to the gate and proceeded to give that stupid ass a lesson on proper military courtesy, something they, themselves, often ignored. Before they were done he had barricaded himself in the guard shack and called the shore patrol. Murph got them out of that one.

The pet name for DPPOs with some of the regulars was dipshits, a take on the DP (direct procurement), but it stayed under their breath mostly. Hank's size tended to mitigate any confrontations even though his nature was gentle. He was six feet, four inches tall and weighed two-fifty-five, very little of it fat, and with hands like hams. Toby was only slightly smaller. Besides, there wasn't a damn one of them any better at his trade, and damn few as good.

Of course, the DPs had their own names for regulars and their own ways of getting their digs in. Regulars were lifers, a seemingly innocent term just referring to the amount of time they had to serve, but the way it was used wasn't lost on the regulars. The implication was people too dumb, incompetent, or lazy to make it on the outside. When coupled with how soon the DPs would be getting out and how much money they made on the outside, those digs probably caused as much resentment as the dipshit and titless wave comments coming the other way. DPPOs signed up for a thirty-month tour with the Seabees and then returned to civilian life.

Except with a few who probably didn't have the skills to make it on the outside, most of the adolescent, petty shit disappeared when the work started. Demands of the work, twelve-hour shifts, and six and a half day schedules soon pulled teams together and submerged petty resentments. The only thing that mattered was if you could pull your own weight. The Tuckers pulled their own weight and then some.

CHAPTER 4

The Seabees were originally conceived as Marines who could fight and build and were organized into regiments, battalions, companies, platoons, and squads like the Marines. The organization could be confusing to a regular Navy sailor. It was all Hank knew from the beginning though, so he was okay with it.

Lieutenant Blake was in his office when Hank reported in. Blake was a full lieutenant in the Civil Engineering Corps with railroad tracks on his collar like a Marine captain. A lieutenant Junior Grade (JG) was equal to a first lieutenant and an ensign was equal to a second lieutenant. Working with both Navy and Marines had made it confusing at first, but Hank was used to the ranks now.

Lieutenant Blake was trying to find something on the big map on the wall.

"Afternoon, sir. That flat-bottomed thing they call a Mike boat finally got us here."

"Hello, Hank. Did the equipment get off-loaded?"

"Far as I know, sir. The equipment operators took over and I didn't hang around."

"Okay. I have a job for you. How about giving Tucker a quick overview, Chief? Then send him over to the shop. Hello, Toby. You still hanging out with this reprobate?"

"Yes, sir. I try to keep him from losing the family fortune."

"How's it going, Hank?" Chief Kelly said. "Step over here and look at the map. The Army Special Forces are building an A Team camp at a place called Bu Duc near the Laos border." Kelly put his finger on a spot on the map and stepped back. Hank took a look.

"What all do they need?"

"Site clearing, a large, reinforced command bunker, perimeter bunkers, revetments constructed, ordnance storage points and hooches for the CIDG troops. It's a good-sized job for a small team . I want you to run the detail."

Hank looked closer at the map.

"I don't see any roads," he said. "How are we getting our equipment and supplies out there?"

"The Army is providing heavy lift helicopters out of Phu Bai to move as much as they can to the staging point at the base of the hill. You'll move the equipment up the hill and clear an LZ to get materials in. Get settled in a hooch for now, but don't get too comfortable. You won't be here long. Check in at the builder's shop. Chief Murphy will work with you to put together the detail."

"Well, I'm ready to get back to work. Is an officer in charge?"

"We're stretched to the limit, Hank, so it's your team. You are the leading petty officer, (LPO)."

"Okay, Chief. That's the way I like it. Do we have a departure date?"

"You've got a couple weeks to plan and get your materials and tools assembled. The plan is you'll arrive at the site on the 15th with an Army escort."

"How about an Army contact?"

"He'll be in touch. Sergeant Stout is flying in to work with you."

"One more question. Can I have Tubby and Toby?"

"You'll have to talk to Chief Murphy about Tubby, but I don't have any objections. Toby we need here though. Sorry, Alpha Company isn't going to release him. We're hurting for EONs (construction equipment operators) with his experience."

Operations had already analyzed the Army's specification and developed sketches and a man-hours and materials estimate. Chief Murphy introduced Hank to his crew. He had a mechanic (CM), three equipment operators (EO), six builders (BU), a steel worker (SW) and one electrician, but not all at the same time. Initially, an Engineering Associate (EA) would be attached for the surveying and soil testing, but he would be released back to the CBMU when the job was laid out.

The CBMU was stretched thin already with runway maintenance and public works at Dong Ha and three permanent details off-site, so Hank would have his team manned as the skills were needed and had to release them back to the main body as construction phases were complete. He'd have to manage a tight schedule. The CBMU was like a large construction company with multiple jobs running at the same time and was the hiring hall for all the trades too. Running the detail didn't bother him. He'd been a foreman on big jobs for several years.

He spread the prints on the table and waved the crew over. He studied the bunker layout on the sketches for a moment and studied the topology from the map for a bit more and then shook his head. Then he looked at the materials order.

"Is this our design or theirs?" he asked.

"Ours," Murphy said. "We're using the same plans for a Seabee bunker at Khe Sanh. The Army wanted a bunker like the one we built for them at a place called Lang Vei south of Khe Sanh, but that would take too much concrete. Bu Duc is too far into the boonies to fly it in, and the job isn't big enough to put a batch plant out there. You can use ready-mix for small jobs, but the bunker is too big."

"That's a lot of heavy timbers. How are we getting it out there and where is it coming from? We don't stock anything like that, do we?"

"Not here, but it's used in ammunition storage point (ASP) construction. The Army said they can get whatever it takes."

"How about the equipment? Do we have to move it from here to Phu Bai?"

"No. That's one thing we don't have to worry about," Murphy said. "The Army 8th Engineer Battalion at Phu Bai has agreed to provide the equipment and get it to the site. They already have a delivery LZ chosen but it's not at the building site. First thing you need to do is make a site visit and figure out how you're going to get the equipment from the staging area to the work site. Look, the Army is providing the equipment and materials, and they have to get it to the staging area. They can land materials at the site once you get it cleared. Ask for what you want, Tuck. Don't skimp.

They want this and they got deep pockets."

Hank nodded and studied the prints and materials list again.

"Looks straight forward to me," he said. "What kind of dozer, Thompson?"

"I want a TD9, if we can get it. This is too big a job for a toy dozer. We'll need a cherry-picker crane, a front-end loader, and a rough terrain fork-lift to start with. I'd like to have a bigger dozer, but I'm not sure even a TD9 can be flown in, even if they fly the blade in separate."

"Ask for what you need," Murph said. "They have to get it there."

"We'll need a couple water buffalos, if they're not already on site," EO3 Clark said.

"Hope you're talking about the metal ones," Hank said.

Clark just grinned at him.

"Okay, good thinking. We don 't know what the potable water situations is out there. Anyone else?" Hank said.

"Hell, since it's a wish list, a tractor backhoe would be a help," Clark said. "There's always work for a backhoe. If we don't take one, we'll have to do a lot of hand digging while we ought to be doing other things."

"I'll add a backhoe," Chief Murphy said. " I have to get the equipment list to the Army engineers today. Anything else? No? Okay, let's get the tools and materials plan done, start the paperwork, and decide who will take the equipment in. You guys draw weapons before you go. Draw plenty of ammunition. If you have any trouble with the armorer, let me know. Sergeant Stout is supposed to be landing right about now. Hank, let's head over to the airfield and pick him up."

Hank got Murphy aside and asked him if he could have Tubby. Murph didn't have a problem with it as long as Hank was willing to give up one of the assigned builders. Hank agreed.

One of the things Hank had come to like about the Seabees was the attitude. They just needed to know what, where and when. They knew the how or would figure it out. If they didn't have what they needed and couldn't get it, they made it. Can't wasn't in their vocabulary. Hank didn't get along with all of the regular Seabees, but he admired their ability to get things done. Didn't matter if it was an airfield or a hole in the ground, they'd get it done on time and in budget. He and Murphy waited at the helipad for fifteen minutes before an Army twin-rotor helicopter landed.

CHAPTER 5

A Green Beret Sergeant First Class (SFC) approached the Seabees waiting near the landing pad. Spotting the fouled anchor Chief's emblem on Murphy's utility cover, he went straight to him and held out his hand.

"Name's Stout," he said. "Are you guys the Seabees I'm supposed to meet?"

"Murphy," the chief said. "Good to meet you, Sergeant. The little guy here is Tucker. Are you going to need quarters for tonight?"

"Yeah, Chief, I believe I will. No Special Forces here and I don't feel like sitting-up bullshitting with the regular infantry all night."

"We'll find something for you. We want to pick your brains about the situation out there anyway."

"Hell, you can crash with me and my

brother," Hank said. "We're the only ones in my hooch. There's four bunks and you're welcome to one of them."

"Works for me," Stout said.

As Hank promised, the quarters weren't much, but the tent had net sides, plenty of room and a raised wood deck. The deck had a trap door in the center for access to the mortar hole, a place to shelter when incoming made life unpleasant. The canvas was dry rotted, but so far it was holding up. Murphy said he would let Stout get settled-in and meet him at the builder's shop later. Stout dropped his ruck on an empty cot and sat next to it. Hank sat down on his cot and reached under the mattress and pulled out a canteen.

"Care for a snort?" Hank asked. It was a rhetorical question for him. He had never met a grunt who didn't care for a snort, and he figured the green berets were just grunts with fancy hats.

Stouts eyes opened wider. "Depends on what you got."

"Best moonshine in Dong Ha," Hank said. "It used to be the best in Da Nang. I brought a supply with me. Go ahead. It's pretty good stuff."

Toby flipped the flap back and came into the tent. "Kind of early to be hitting the rotgut, isn't it?"

"Depends what time zone you're in," Hank said.

Stout looked at the canteen skeptically but reached over and took it. He raised it to his mouth and took a healthy pull. Then his eyes got big and started to water as he let out a big breath.

"Smooth, ain't it?" Hank said with a grin.

"You could have warned me," Stout managed to wheeze out.

Hank retrieved the canteen and took a pull himself, then he handed it back to Stout. "Have another."

"Oh hell, why not. It obviously hasn't poisoned you."

Stout took another pull on the canteen and smacked his lips.

"Second one goes down a lot smoother than the first. Thanks. You guys got first names or do I just call you Tucker one and Tucker two.?"

Stout had run into Seabees before and didn't expect a lot of military correctness. Most of them were good troops though and knew how to get things done. Seabees always had something to trade, a trait dear to a green beret's heart. Tucker two was a smaller version of Tucker one.

"Yeah, it's Hank and this is Toby. Seems that's all people call us since we joined the Navy."

"Don't you Navy guys ever use rank?"

"I can't remember anybody ever calling me by my rank," Hank said. "I'm not even sure how they would do it. Petty officer Tucker, First Class

Petty Office Tucker, First Class Builder Tucker, hell I've been Tuck or Tucker or Hank since I came in. I don't know. That Petty Officer stuff sounds silly as hell to me. I ain't an officer and I ain't petty."

"Okay, so you're a first-class builder. Did they just call you Tucker when you were a second-class?"

"Never been anything but a first class. Came in as a first-class petty officer. Toby came in as a Second Class."

"Bullshit! How in the hell do you join the Navy as an E6? It took me six years to make staff sergeant and another thee to make SFC."

Hank took another pull on the canteen and grimaced.

"Shew, that'll put hair on your toenails. I don't believe it can be done anywhere but in the Seabees. The Navy is so short of skilled construction help over here, they revived an old, World War Two program called the Direct Procurement Petty Officer Program. A skilled mechanic can come in with different petty office ranks depending on his experience and how bad they need his skill. I qualified for First Class Builder."

"A skilled mechanic? You mean like an auto mechanic?"

"No, that's just a general term used in

construction for a journeyman in any trade or used to mean that before I came in the Navy.

"That's the damndest thing I ever heard. So how long have you been in?"

"About eighteen months now," Hank said. "Don't let that bother you though. We know what we're doing."

"How much experience do you have to come in as an E6?"

"Officially, I think it's seven years, but hell, I've been around construction since I was a kid," Hank said. "My granddad and my dad were carpenters. I can remember a time when I was real little. My dad was building a house on the lot next to our house. Maybe I was four or five. He gave me a nail pouch. That's a canvas nail holder with pockets . . ."

"I know what a nail pouch is," Stout said and reached for the canteen.

"Okay. Anyway, he wrapped it around me and put some flat head nails in it and let me hammer tarpaper on the side of the house. Could only reach the first row. I don't think I ever wanted to be anything else after that. Had an apprentice card from the Wilmington Carpenters and Millwrights Union when I was sixteen and had my journeyman's card a year out of high school. Ten years later I joined the Navy. Toby never wanted to do anything but drive big machines. He can operate anything on a construction site."

"What made you join the Navy? You'd make a good infantryman at your size. I'd put you on an M60 right away."

"It was the best deal going. Both of us were out of deferments. The business agent at the hiring hall showed me a poster from the AFL/CIO about the DPPO program and I showed it to Toby. To be honest though, I didn't want to get drafted and sent to Vietnam. My number was going to come up soon."

Stout laughed.

"Well, sometimes you get the bear. Sometimes the bear gets you. If they gave you E6 right out of the chute, I figure you must know what you're doing. How long you been in Vietnam?"

"Well, let me see. Two months at the homeport in Danang. A day on the boat coming up here and now a day in Dong Ha. That's about it."

"Every been under fire?" Stout asked.

"Some rockets came in this morning."

Stout watched Hank's face for a few seconds. "Did you fuck-up already?"

"Not that I know of. Why?"

"Well, Bu Duc isn't exactly a place I would send a new man. Right now, it's not much different than here, maybe even a little quieter, but it's going to get hot out there when the VC figure out we're moving in, and I'm not talking about the weather."

"Yeah, they told me about that. If it isn't me, it has to be someone else. I don't figure on skipping the tough ones. How about you? How long you been here?"

"For fucking ever," Stout said. "Six months on this tour, but this is my third tour and all of them have been in I-Corps. I shouldn't even be back here, but I fucked-up in the states, and Vietnam seemed like a safer place than the land of the big PX, at least for me, and I wanted to keep my stripes."

"We're from Wilmington, Delaware," Hank said. "I got a wife back there I'll be glad to get back to. She ain't happy about the money, but she likes being the wife of a Navy Petty Officer a lot better than being the wife of broke Army recruit. She even gets PX and commissary privileges at Dover Air Base and the Navy base at Bainbridge, Maryland. She can use the Aberdeen Army base too. It's a better deal than I figured it would be. Toby, he's single, so the money don't matter to him."

"Bullshit," Toby said.

"Wilmington, huh?" I've done a little drinking in that town. I did a tour as training advisor for the Delaware National Guard at the New Castle airport. Know where that is?"

"Sure. Delaware is a small state," Hank said. "We live pretty close to the airport."

"Ever been in a place called Dutch's Inn on New Castle Avenue just south of Wilmington?"

Hank grinned real big.

"Sure. Used to stop off there for a couple beers on the way home when I had a job on that side of Wilmington."

"Get out of here," Stout said. "I had a girlfriend over there. Well, not quite a girlfriend. She lived close to the Inn. Well, to be honest, she and her husband lived there. Used to meet her at the Inn. Maybe enough said about that. You might know her."

Hank grinned. "Well, I guess some of that goes on everywhere. I married my neighbor's daughter. I might stop for a beer with the crew after work, but I like getting home in time for supper."

Stout just grinned and shook his head.

"Good luck. You're young yet. You had any weapons training?"

"Sure. The Marines trained us at Lejeune. Had more training in California. All Seabees get military training."

"That's good. You may need it."

CHAPTER 6

Plans, Materials, and equipment came together quickly when the paperwork was done. Working with the Army was a lot better than working for the Marines. The Marines seemed to be the stepchildren of the armed forces and were always scraping for funds and materials to get things done. The Army had deep pockets, and with the CIA involved, cost didn't seem to be a factor.

Toby was mad about getting left behind, but NVA artillery and rockets were keeping the runway crew busy and he didn't have time to fret over it.

A big boost to the schedule happened when a platoon of Army combat engineers were assigned to do the initial clearing of the hill-top on the 13th of August. Forty men with chain saws and demolitions went in and took the trees down to just stumps and then blew up the stumps. The work went quickly since all they had to do was drop the trees. Site-prep was heavy equipment work for the Seabees.

The weather was good for construction with hot, clear days that usually ended with a short rain storm. Mornings were foggy but cleared by 0800. That wouldn't last long though. Clouds rolling in from Laos already signaled the transition to the northeast monsoon season was underway. Hank and a utilityman made another visit to the site to evaluate the water supply while the Army was staging the equipment at the LZ. After estimating the flow capacity of the spring on-site, the team flew to Phu Bai to talk with the Army 8th Engineers about piping and pumps.

The equipment, staged at the bottom of the hill, had to be moved up to the site, the site cleared, soil testing done, and surveying completed. Excavation and grading could then begin and materials could be moved and stored on-site. Initial living quarters and defensive positions needed to be built. After the bunker site was excavated, builders could begin construction. The schedule was ambitious and likely to be interrupted by weather and possibly by the enemy, but they were conditions all projects in Vietnam faced.

Hank and three equipment operators landed at the staging area on August 15th. EO2 Thompson brought EO3 Clark and EO3 Kaufman with him.

Dong Ha had been getting rocket attacks almost nightly and the team was glad to get out of there. Tubby came out with Hank. Stout and a platoon of Montagnard Civilian Irregular Defense Group (CIDG) were already in place guarding the equipment. His A Team would land the next day with the rest of the CIDG company. The Seabees would be roughing it that night with CIDG as security.

"How's it look to you?" Hank asked Thompson. "Can you get that crane up the creek?"

"The top looks hairy, but we'll cross that bridge later. I need to get the dozer up there and clear an area for the rest of the equipment. Do you figure anybody is around that might shoot at us?"

"Stout and the Yards did a recon and seems to think the area is secure for now. He doesn't know how long it's going to stay that way though. Tubby and I will stay near you to give you some cover just in case."

"Sounds good. It's going to take a bit. I want to cut away those two banks half way up. Better to do it now than have to come back down to do it later."

Getting the equipment up to the site turned out to be less of a problem than anticipated. With a TD9 bulldozer to assist, the move went quickly except for the cherry picker. That damn top-heavy beast almost toppled even after Thompson cut a Ramp for it out of the creek bed they were using for a road.

Thompson cleared an area large enough to park the equipment and then went to work clearing the rest of the site while Clark and Kaufman brought the rest of the equipment up. The Army engineers had not only downed the trees, but they also used chain saws to break the larger ones up into manageable logs. The dozer, forklift, and frontend loader made fast work of the rubble. Hank waved Thompson down.

"Save everything from ten to fifteen inches in diameter. We can use them for roof reinforcement of the perimeter bunkers. Push everything else off the hill."

Thompson pointed to the forklift. "Tell Clark to stack everything you want. I'll work around it."

By evening, a football field sized area had been cleared to the dirt and the crest of the hill had a ring of logs and rubble circling it. Stacks of logs that would be useful for temporary fortifications were piled at various locations around the site for further use. It was all green stuff, but useful until they could get cured lumber in. The rest of the hill would be cleared the next day providing a clearing the size of two football fields side by side. That area would become Bu Duc SF base camp. Another hundred-yard-deep area would be cleared on the sides of the hill to provide clear fields of fire later.

Stout supervised placement of defensive positions and EOs using the backhoe dug them out while CIDG filled sandbags and began fortifying their new home. By dark everyone was exhausted but had a reasonably comfortable hole covered with ponchos for shelter. Tubby just assumed he'd be with Hank and made the hole big enough for two.

After inspecting the perimeter, Stout stopped by Hank's hole.

"What is it you Seabees say? Can do?"

"Yep," Tubby said. "What do you think, Sarge? Are we okay here tonight?"

"Hell, you never know, but I'm not expecting trouble. Too soon yet. While you were clearing, I was patrolling with the Yards. The only villes in the area are Yard villes and they aren't a danger to us. There's only one within a mile of here. I did a little trading with the chiefs and they have people watching. Yards don 't like Vietnamese, north or south. If Vietnamese move through the area, the Yards will let us know."

"It's been awful quiet," Hank said. "Do you think the VC are watching?"

"If the VC even know we're here, they'll want to see what we're doing without letting us know they are here. It will be a little risky tonight but the rest of the team will be in tomorrow and we can get some wire up. They'll bring communications and heavier weapons. By tomorrow night we'll have a perimeter and a company of Yards for security and radios to call in artillery support."

Hank looked around at the jungle on all sides and shivered a little. "Risky" wasn't a word he wanted to hear.

"So, what kind of watch do you want the Seabees to stand," he asked. "Remember, we're sailors."

"Dirt Sailors," Stout said and laughed. "Hard to believe how much you got done today. The Yards are on fifty-percent alert. Just make sure your troops are locked and loaded. Other than that, rest them up. We have a big day tomorrow."

The perimeter was as primitive as it could get, just a series of foxholes dug in a large circle. Five Americans and thirty Yards in seventeen holes provided a fifty percent watch with one man sleeping in each hole. Stout moved hole to hole throughout the night keeping his Yards alert. He would get his rest the next day when the full A team arrived. Day one had been a productive day and Stout was satisfied.

"Tubby, you take first watch," Hank said. "Wake me up in four hours to relieve you."

"You got it. Don't worry. Nothing will get

by me."

Tubby was in commando mode.

"Okay, but don't go shooting anything. Stout's Yards are all around us."

"You got it."

Hank surprised himself and fell asleep quickly but woke up after a couple of hours with a stone poking his side. He spoke softly with Tubby for a while and stood and looked around the site. The night was calm and cool. Overcast made it a dark night, but it wasn't completely dark. He could see dimly almost to the next hole on the security line. That produced a lonely feeling. It would have been nice to see the rest of the platoon.

The noise that had been just a buzz in his ears while sleeping resolved into jungle sounds, strange animal calls he had never experienced. Hoots, chattering, buzzing, and growling all raised a cacophony that set his nerves on edge, especially the growling. After a few minutes he leaned his back against the side of the hole and tried to get back to sleep.

Later, he knew he had managed to doze off, but Tubby had just elbowed him. Hank sat up. Tubby put his hand on Hank's shoulder, pointed and ducked down.

Two CIDG sized men walked into sight from outside of the perimeter and walked right past their hole to the center of the clearing. The image was dim but he could see they were carrying rifles. They were apparently Yards making rounds or something because they obviously were not Stout or any of the Seabees. Stout must have had them checking things out. Hank and Tubby stayed down in their hole and kept quiet.

After standing in the center of the site for a few minutes and looking around, they continued walking to the other side and disappeared into the night. Hank looked around for a while longer and then laid back down and went back to sleep. It was comforting to know a patrol was keeping their eyes on things.

CHAPTER 7

Tubby woke him up at 0200 and sat in the bottom of the hole to get some sleep. Hank settled back to look around. Most of the jungle sounds had quieted down and the night was peaceful. He relaxed and enjoyed the quiet. It wasn't nearly as scary out there as he thought it would be. Sitting still made it difficult to keep his eyes open, but he toughed it out. At 0400 he stood and stretched, did a couple squats, and rotated his head slowly to get the stiffness out of his neck.

Stout stopped at Hank's hole and kneeled. Hank was trying to stretch the cramps out of his leg muscles without waking Tubby. It was 0430 by the glow on his watch.

"One hundred percent alert," Stout said quietly. "If anything is out there wanting to cause trouble, this is when they'll do it. Did you get some rest?"

"I was a bit nervous early, but after your patrol came by, I felt better and slept some."

Tubby woke up and stretched and yawned.

"What patrol?" Stout asked. "What are you talking about?"

"The two Yards you had moving around last night."

"You saw Yards walking around last night?

"That's what I said."

Stout stared at Hank a moment.

"What did they look like?" he asked.

"Hell, I don't know. It was dark. Just two little guys with rifles. They came from outside the perimeter right there and walked right by our hole to the middle of the clearing and just looked around for a while. Then they walked back into the jungle over there. It was good to know you had people checking things out. I slept better after that."

"Are you sure you weren't dreaming? Did you see them too, Tubby?"

"Sure," Tubby said. "Two guys just like Hank said."

"Okay, show me where they came in when it gets light. Your men can have a fire when the sun comes up. For now, make sure they're awake and locked and loaded."

Stout moved off into the dark along the perimeter. Hank checked with his men and returned to his hole to wait for the sun. His gut was rumbling. It would be a C-Rats breakfast, but right then he was looking forward to anything that would fill the void—and caffeine, any source of caffeine.

The next hour passed quietly and Yards and Seabees began moving around, relieving themselves, and breaking out C-Rats. A few small fires were built and boiling water was soon turned to instant coffee. Civility returned to the team and Stout found Hank.

"Show me where the people you saw last night entered the camp."

Hank asked Tubby where the Yards first appeared. He wondered what was bothering Stout. Maybe the Yards had been screwing-off during their watch.

Stout walked slowly to where Tubby pointed and searched the ground. The surface dirt was loose from the clearing work and took footprints well. He stopped and knelt and then touched something on the ground with his fingers.

"Is this about where they came in, Tubby?"

"Close as I can figure,"

"Come here and take a look."

Hank and Tubby walked over and knelt. Stout was pointing at footprints but they had tire-tread patterns in them instead of the boot-tread patterns Hank's boots made.

"Ho Chi Minh sandals," Stout said. "They

cut up old tires, punch holes in them for straps, and presto, sandals that never wear out."

"Your Yards?" Hank asked.

"No. We provide our CIDG with boots. It wasn't Yards that made these prints."

Hank felt a little chill.

"Who?"

"Appears we had visitors last night and no one but you saw them."

"Come on, Sarge, what kind of visitors?

"VC, NVA, local villagers, hard to tell, but I figure VC. The locals don't go into the jungle at night. Well, I'd say they know we are here for sure now. I'll be glad to see the rest of the team landing. Can you focus on clearing the LZ this morning? We'll police it after you've leveled it. I want to get the company dug in as soon as possible and get a perimeter up."

Hank briefed his operators on the nocturnal visitors and turned everyone loose on the LZ. He wanted his operators to focus on the job and not on the surrounding jungle, but after his story of visitors in the night, everyone was keeping one eye on the jungle. Siting up high on the equipment, they made excellent targets.

Stout worked with the backhoe operator to rough dig fighting holes and bunkers while enlarging the perimeter after digging two latrines.

Several flights were scheduled for that day. The first flights in would be the A Team and the rest of the CIDG company with their equipment and weapons. Then heavy-lift birds would bring in tents, food, ordnance, and communications. On the third day the first bird would bring in AM2 runway matting to finish the landing pad. Hank's builders, another steelworker for the matting, and an EA would come in with that load. Getting the LZ done and matted would be an all-hands effort. The only blessing in that work was they wouldn't need an asphalt base for helicopters, so they wouldn't ruin their greens and boots with asphalt work.

When the LZ was finished on day five, building materials would come in and it would be time for the EAs to get the rest of the job laid out. The SF weren't going to be happy until the main fortified bunker was done.

The company began landing at 1000 and sandbag filling commenced on a commercial scale. A lot needed to get done, but the priority right then was securing the site. Hank built several wedge-shaped pieces of plywood with stud sides. The small end was the size of the sandbag opening. He set them up like sliding boards at each bunker site. One-man shoveled sand onto the chute. Another held the bag at the opening and filled the bag. A third man stacked the bags. The three-man team rotated the positions to reduce fatigue. A company of CIDG can fill a bodacious number of sandbags in a day with that set-up and they did. The frontend loader kept them supplied with loose filler dirt.

By the end of day two and with the help of the backhoe, the fighting holes had become a shallow trench with sandbagged bunkers every hundred feet. The bunkers would get covers the next day. The trench itself had a sandbag parapet two bags deep and two bags thick. A single row of concertina wire circled the entire camp and everything in camp was covered with an inch-thick layer of red dust from the clouds of dust created by the helicopters. Life was getting dirty on the hill and there was no way to get clean.

The spring at the water point was strong enough to feed a good-sized stream and would provide enough water to support the camp needs without being supplemented from the outside. Hank got a message off to Dong Ha to add a couple utilitymen to the schedule to lay in pipe and connect a pump to bring the water to a water point near the site for the main bunker. The team got a lot of work done that day and had tents to sleep in that night, but they still slept on the ground. Hank needed his builders to start erecting the hardback frameworks to get the tents off the ground. Monsoon rain was coming.

After Stout briefed his team on the nocturnal visitors, the SF made sure they had an alert perimeter that night. With a company of CIDG looking for trouble, the Seabees no longer had to man the perimeter and got a good night's sleep, or about as good as they could get in a hole in the ground with hordes of enemy just waiting for them to sleep so they could attack, or so it seemed to men not accustomed to rough camps in the middle of nowhere. They needed sleep. The operators hadn't left their equipment except to eat and crap for twelve hours. Fortunately, no new visitors disturbed the night.

On the morning of day three, the first flights arrived thirty minutes after sunrise. Hank's builder's, two EAs, and two plumbers arrived on the first flight with pipe, lumber, tools, pallets of ready-mix concrete and a gas-powered mixer—and one more pallet he wasn't sure he wanted there.

"How did that get loaded?" Hank asked one of the EAs.

"Chief Murphy said it was yours and he wanted it out of his Conex box. We loaded it up and brought it along."

His gedunk stash pallet had been loaded with the other supplies at Dong Ha and there it sat at the LZ. Now what the hell am I going to do with that stuff out here? He wondered.

The next several flights delivered AM2 runway matting for the LZ and two more flights brought POL (Petroleum, oil, lubricants) just in time. The camp was dangerously low on diesel fuel.

While the EAs and builders laid-out the post footers to support the flooring for the tents and the plumbers analyzed the waterpoint job, the SF began erecting radio antennas and fortifying a temporary command post. Hank set up his own command post and pulled back from the work. It was now time for him to become the foreman. He had to get the measurements for all the timbers back to Phu Bai to get them precut with saws that could handle the massive beams. He had a small team, far flung supplies and materials, and a lot of work to get done. Coordination and scheduling and utilizing outside help when he could get it was the only way to get it done.

By the end of the day, floor-post footers were poured for fifteen tents, the SF temporary command bunker was complete with operating radios, soil was tested at the fortified bunker site and the site surveyed and staked for grading. AM2 matting was stacked next to the LZ. The LZ was leveled and prepared for the matting, and the spring water was collected and samples sent back to Phu Bai for testing. While all that was going on, EOs worked with the CIDG to improve their bunkers and trench line and a shower-point was constructed by the builders and steelworkers using fifty-five-gallon drums as holding tanks. Later, the utilitymen would see about piping water directly to the shower. The final task of the day was enclosing the latrine.

Hank surveyed the team's work completed that day and felt the same satisfaction he always got watching a job go up. His favorite work was custom homes. He loved to see the house come together day by day from a bare lot and set of prints to a completed home that would be someone's dream. Looking out across the camp gave him an immense satisfaction. Three days ago this hilltop had been nothing but a football field sized area piled high with blasted and fallen trees. Now it was a military camp for 220 men, still rough, but a long cry from where it was. Stout and his Team Lieutenant stopped next to him.

"I think we can sleep a little more soundly tonight," Stout said.

"I know I will," Hank said. "I've been spooked ever since you told me about Ho Chi Minh sandals."

Lieutenant Taylor looked around and frowned. "I know it isn't on your schedule, but could you work in some equipment time to help the team get the perimeter finished tomorrow? You guys may sleep well, but I'm not going to sleep well until I know we have something we can defend, and a single coil of wire ain't it."

"We'll make the time," Hank said.

CHAPTER 8

Stout pulled Hank aside.

"You got any of that shine left, Tuck?"

"Sure. I have more than that too. Someone put my gedunk stash on the first flight in."

"What have you got? It will be a while before we can get our good stuff in here."

"Man, I got everything that will rot your teeth. Plus I got jerky, Vienna sausages, soups, canned snacks, damn near everything you can get at the exchange at China Beach."

He started to tell Stout about the booze but stopped just in time. Probably not a good idea to reveal that.

"I got popcorn too, and a popper. I just need to get it all in a safe place."

"You willing to do some trading?"

"Sure. Me and the Seabees can't eat it all."

"Bring the backhoe over there. I'm going to give you some OJT on fighting holes. A bunker is okay, but your guys are going to need individual foxholes too. We'll start with you and your stash."

Hank located Clark and had him bring the backhoe. Stout marked out an outline with his foot and told him how to build his hole.

"Two ways you can go. You can dig two parallel trenches with a connecting trench at the center, or you can dig one L-shaped trench and make the short side of the L wide and deep enough to make a bunker for your stuff and for sleeping. If you do the H, the back trench is covered and the cross trench is covered. If you do the L, the short side is covered."

"I like the L," Hank said. "I can make the room big enough for my stash and frame the door so I can lock it."

It was 1900 and getting dark and foggy by the time the hole was done. They spent another hour scavenging heavy planks and logs for beams from trash piles already building up on the site. They continued to work until the first layer of the bunker roof was on. After a break, Hank brought the Seabees over and explained what he had done and the other option for fighting holes. Together they sealed the roof with plastic and used a frontend loader to cover the roof with two feet of dirt.

Hank planned to add a layer of runway matting and three layers of sandbags later. The hole was done for now and he had a dry place for his stash. The forklift took care of getting it to the hole.

That night while Hank and Tubby were heating cans of C-Rats pork and beans and adding Vienna sausages and a little hot sauce to spice the concoction up, Stout sat down next to Hank.

"Have you noticed the lights over there on that hill?"

"Where?" Hank asked.

"Look high up, right about there," Stout said while pointing.

Hank and Tubby watched for a moment.

"I'm not seeing anything," Tubby said.

"Just watch for a while. The yards spotted them."

The clouds were building up, but a little moonlight was getting through. Hank watched the vague shape of the hill top wondering what Stout was talking about. All the Seabees were heating food or already eating after a long day's work. None of them had been looking around for lights or anything else. After a few moments he thought he saw something, a quick flash of light like a firefly. A few moments later he saw it again and then he saw several of the pinpoints of light.

"The little specks of light near the top of the hill?" Hank asked.

"Yeah. They're hard to see unless you know what to look for. There aren't any villages up there and the people from the Khe villages don't go into the jungle at night."

"What are they?" Tubby asked.

"Probably VC. Not sure what they're doing but it's probably not good news for us. They're not afraid of us knowing they're there. Worse case is artillery or mortars, but maybe it's just an observation camp. We need to get the defenses done."

"You got my attention," Hank said.

CHAPTER 9

On day four, the SF sent out recon patrols, each with two SF and six Yards. The SF were getting nervous. So Far, the perimeter consisted mostly of a single coil of concertina wire with claymores set at intervals. Some fields of fire had been cleared simply as a result of clearing the site, but a lot of elephant grass and trees were still in place offering concealment pretty close to the wire, in some places within grenade range. LT Miller decided fixing all that sooner than later was a good idea. Clark drove the front-end loader to assist the SF and took Tubby with him.

“We were told to make ourselves useful to you guys, sergeant. What do you need?”

“First thing I need to do is get all this wire distributed around the whole perimeter. We’re going to put in a three coil stack all the way around.

We'll stretch a double row and put a row on top. Some places we'll have to take-up the old wire and move the perimeter out beyond hand-grenade range. Can you handle distributing the wire for me?"

"Yeah, sure."

"The Yards can provide the labor. Just drop two coils every fifty feet."

Tubby and two Yards loaded coils in the bucket of the loader and moved wire to places around the perimeter. The coils were more than a yard wide and stretched out about fifty feet like a slinky toy. The SF began stretching coils and securing them with steel posts as soon as the first load was dropped. They had their eyes on the hills and weren't wasting any time.

The Yards were fascinated with Tubby. They were used to towering Americans, but Tubby was just an inch taller than most of them. He directed them with hand signs and they paid attention to him. They chattered between themselves and tried to communicate with Tubby but didn't get much further than simple coordination signs.

When Clark finished delivering the wire, Hank sent the dozer out to begin clearing fields of fire and turning everything a hundred yards out from the wire into an open killing field and preparing the ground out there for a second concertina wire perimeter. Two twin-rotor helicopters landed with wire and fortification materials. A heavy lift helicopter brought a twenty KW generator in on a sling and set it down near the site for the command bunker.

On day five work on the landing pad continued, the builders began constructing frames and floors for the tents, Tubby set about fashioning tin roofs for SF hooches and the SF improved their perimeter. The A team's demolitions man began constructing and burying *fougasse* flame weapons around the top of the hill just outside the first perimeter wire. The SF called them "Foo Gas." They were fifty-gallon drums filled with a mixture of gelled gasoline and diesel fuel with a sealed top. They were fired with the same kind of trigger used for claymore mines called a clacker. When the claymore clacker was closed a thermite grenade ignited the mixture. C4 exploded and propelled the *fougasse* out at an angle and created a wall of burning liquid not a whole lot different than napalm.

The SF were turning-to like Seabees. On day six, a third crew with Seabee help began constructing a double apron barrier well out from the *fougasse* line. The double apron barrier was a multi-strand barbed-wire fence with anchor wires sloping down on both sides. Horizontal wires were stretched across the anchor wires creating sloping barriers, or aprons. Between the concertina and the apron barrier a fourth crew began laying in tangle-foot and antipersonnel landmines. Tangle-foot is a crisscrossed pattern of barbed-wire set horizontally about a foot above the ground. It was impossible to move through it quickly and difficult to move through it at all, especially at night, and with landmines mixed in, it is a formidable barrier.

Seabees distributed the concertina, moved barbed-wire and *Fougasse* drums for the other crews. With the entire A team assisted by Seabees working together, the perimeter became more formidable hour by hour. From the inside all you could see was a triple stack of bright shiny concertina six feet high. From the outside you saw the apron-barrier and tangle-foot and then the concertina. Neither the residents of the base or the enemy outside could see the *fougasse* buried in the side of the hill, or the landmines and claymores under the wire. Hank helped Tubby fashion a steel pipe and barbed wire gate and erected it at the access road.

Everyone in the camp worked twelve to fourteen-hour days and by day fourteen, the 29th of August, the camp had a double perimeter made of concertina wire with tangle-foot and double apron wire and land mine obstacles in the open area between them, all backed up with claymores and foo-gas. The LZ was complete with AM2 matting, bunkers were all covered with timber and sandbags, and tents now sat on raised wood floors. The SF had tin roof, hardback hooches courtesy of Hank, Tubby, and the builders. The amount of work completed in just two weeks was staggering, literally. Everyone in camp was exhausted.

The camp now had a real perimeter barrier and a full company was manning it. With the major components of the perimeter in place, the demolitions man began putting in the finishing touches. Antitank mines were placed in areas that would make favorable avenues of approach for armor. M16A1 bouncing betty antipersonnel mines were planted in open strips between the barriers. M14 toe-poppers augmented the bouncing betties.

Since Hank was available and everyone else was busy, Stout took him out with him to secure the claymores against tampering.

"The VC and NVA's favorite tactic is to sneak in at night and turn our claymores around so the face is pointing toward us," Stout said. "If they attack and we fire the claymores, we blow our own line away. What we are going to do is make that a very dangerous operation for them."

"How?"

"With these."

Stout showed Hank a small munition that looked like a can of chew, smokeless tobacco to the uninitiated.

"These are small mines similar to toe-poppers with a built-in pressure release fuse. When pressure is applied, the pressure-release fuse is armed. If the pressure is removed, the fuse fires the mine."

"Okay. So we install the claymores on them with pressure?"

"Exactly. If the pressure of the claymore is removed, like when they lift it to turn it around, the popper explodes. It probably won't kill them, but they'll lose their fingers and the claymore might explode in their hands. In any case, the claymore isn't likely to be turned against us."

"What if you have to move the claymore for maintenance or something?"

"We blow the whole thing. Once the poppers are in you don't touch the claymore again."

Noise makers and pop flares were installed in the wire. If moved even slightly, they would rattle or fire a flare. Finally, to add insult to injury (for the VC and NVA) the SF added a few personal touches. Partially used spools of barbed-wire, empty ammo cans, fuel cans and other apparently abandoned but possibly useful to the VC junk, containers, and broken tools were booby-trapped and scattered around the perimeter.

The SF would continue to improve their design, but the camp had a perimeter that could be defended now.

CHAPTER 10

Hank was checking off the schedule items one at a time. A lot of work was done and a lot more still had to be done. It would be time to begin the excavation for the main underground fortified bunker soon. He sent a message back to Phu Bai to begin flying the materials in for the bunker.

Tubby nudged him with an elbow.

"Trouble," he said.

A recon patrol was coming through the gate with two wounded Yards being assisted and one dead being carried in a poncho.

"That doesn't look good. Come on, let's see what happened."

Stout caught up with them crossing the camp.

"What happened, Sarge?" Tubby asked.

"One of our patrols ran into an ambush

while inspecting a camp about five miles from here close to the Laos border. Two wounded. One dead."

Hank stood to the side and looked at the dead Yard. It was the first body he had ever seen killed by violence. It was a bloody mess with multiple wounds. He didn't want to keep looking at it, but something morbid in him wouldn't let him look away. He had never seen bullet wounds before. That was a living person this morning, he thought. A living person who lived right here with us. Someone had seen him and killed him deliberately. That though hit him hard. What it meant to be in Vietnam was sinking in. People were out there who wouldn't hesitate to do the same thing to him. And probably wouldn't even feel bad about it.

Stout and his Lieutenant stopped by Hank's bunker later. Hank was still shaking off the shock of seeing the dead Yard.

"Can you step up the schedule for the command bunker," LT Miller asked.

"All the materials are here. I guess we can do whatever you want. Are you sure you want to do that? I'm ready to start the guard towers tomorrow. The bunker is going to take all of my equipment operators to start and then all the rest of the team getting it up. How bad do you need the towers?"

"I think getting underground is the priority, Hank. NVA are moving into this area and there's no good reason for them to be here except us. I'm not sure what's going on and I don't like it. How much will the weather impact the bunker construction?"

"We're not pouring concrete or laying block, so we can handle some rain as long as it isn't bad enough to wash out the excavation."

"We just received a report from Phu Bai to prepare for a cyclone coming in off the South China Sea. We can expect tropical-storm-force winds and torrential rain here, but its forecasted to be no more than a two-day event for us. How's that hurt the schedule?"

"Well, it won't help, but we can live with a two-day delay if you can. I wouldn't start the excavation for the bunker until after it passes though. I'll continue with the current schedule until the storm passes and then we can look at the change. How's that?"

"About as much as we can expect, I guess," Stout said. "If we can get you anything that will help, let me know. I got a feeling we're all going to wish we were underground soon. Let's make sure we are."

The cyclone hit the next morning. Ten inches of wind-driven rain pounded the camp in one day. In one way it was comforting. Nothing could maneuver or fight in that weather including the NVA and VC. That night the wind increased and took out five tents. Then things got exciting.

Hank and Tubby were chowing down on some C-Rats supplemented with instant soup from the stash in the gedunk bunker. The hole and bunker had good drainage and a waterproof roof, and other than smelling like a swamp, was reasonably comfortable.

"We're going to lose some tents tonight," Tubby said.

"We're going to lose more than that. I've never see rain like this. It wouldn't surprise me if half the damn hill washed out. You know, this would be a perfect time for the VC to attack us. They'd be through the inner fence before anybody ever saw them. I can't even see the outer perimeter."

"Nah," Tubby said. "Stout said there ain't nothing going to be moving in this crap, not even the VC."

Just as Tubby finished uttering his ill-conceived words, the first explosion on the perimeter lit up the fog and rain.

"Oh really?" Hank yelled. "What the hell was that then?"

Suddenly, all hell broke loose on the perimeter. Every Yard bunker was firing into the night. Hank and Tubby grabbed their rifles and moved out to the fighting portion of the hole. Hank had chosen the location for his hole well. It sat a little higher than surrounding ground and had good drainage in all directions. He and Tubby had covered the open trench with ponchos tented on poles and the inside was just muddy, not flooded. They saw the SF running for the perimeter.

"Aren't we supposed to move up to the perimeter bunkers?" Tubby asked.

"Not unless Stout tells us to. Just keep your eyes on the perimeter."

"I can't see shit."

Just then another explosion hit the perimeter and streamers of light shot off into the night.

"Damn! Get ready," Hank yelled.

They both fingered the selectors on their rifles to make sure they were ready.

Another explosion rocked the perimeter.

"What the hell are they shooting at us?" Tubby yelled. "That's powerful shit."

"I don't know. I've never done this before."

Then Hank saw the SF walking back from the perimeter through the rain. Another explosion rocked the perimeter further away. The SF didn't even try to get under cover.

"What the hell are they doing? Tubby, this shit is screwing with my head."

Stout cut away from the other SF and walked over to the Seabees positions.

"You can stand down," he said. "It's just the claymores. The rain is washing away the ground and they're lifting off the booby-traps under them."

"Claymores? Ours?"

That was kind of a stupid question, but Hank was thoroughly confused by then.

"The very ones," Stout said with a grin. "Remember the pressure release poppers?"

"Yeah."

"There you go."

"Oh. We're not under attack?"

"Nope. It's going to be like this all night. In the morning, we'll check any that don't blow and replace the others. Try to get some rest."

The rain was unbelievable. Portions of the perimeter washed out. Random explosions rocked the perimeter all night, but no incoming resulted and no movement was detected. That didn't help anyone's nerves though. Every explosion had to be treated as incoming until proven otherwise.

In the morning, the SF inspected the perimeter while the storm still raged. They located several claymores exposed and ready to wash away and managed to repack them and dig channels around them to carry the wash. On that inspection they discovered a large area washed out from under the outer wire. The wash-out tunnel was large enough for a man to crawl under the wire. Seabees turned out and made that repair with the loader. At mid-day Hank and Tubby took a break in the stash bunker.

"This is some crazy duty," Hank said. "I didn't expect this when the CO gave us this job."

"Yeah, but I like it better than doing public works at Dong Ha. Toby is probably bored out of his gourd by now. Get up. Go to work doing the same thing every day. Go back to the hooch. No chance of anything exciting. Just more work."

Hank bit the end of a C-Rats nut cake and chewed for a moment.

"I'm thinking bored might be a good thing," he said. "This is crazy, Tubbs. Freaking explosions, a hurricane, little brown people who want to shoot us, and here we sit in wet, muddy clothes in a hole in the ground eating stuff from a can that was packed in the second world war."

"Yeah, it's great ain't it?"

Hank grinned at Tubby. It probably was great for him. He had been in commando mode since he got there.

The storm continued to rage through the 31st and 1st of September turning everything not covered into thick, sticky mud. Hank tried to get across the open ground to the SF bunker on the morning of the 31st but didn't quite make it.

"Tubby! Give me a damn hand."

Tubby climbed out of the hole to see what Hank needed.

"What are you doing standing out in the rain, Hank?"

"I'm not standing in the damn rain! I'm stuck in the damn mud. Give me a hand so I don't lose my boots."

The strong wind had died but the rain was worse. The rain poured straight down in drops as large as grapes. The red dirt of the camp had turned into foot deep red mud that sucked the boots right off your feet when you tried to walk through it.

"How the hell do I do that without losing my boots?" Tubby asked. By that time Stout was outside with two of the SF team. They were grinning and enjoying the show.

"All right, all right. I'll do it myself."

He yanked his left leg up and sure enough, he left his boot in the mud. He put his left foot back in the mud and worked the boot out with his hands. Then he jerked his right leg up and left his right boot in the mud. When he tried to pull the right boot out, his left foot slipped and Hank fell face first in the mud.

"Any one of you fuckers laugh and you're going to be in here with me." Hank yelled.

Tubby grinned but held the laugh in. He knew Hank would follow up on his promise. Stout wasn't as disciplined. He not only laughed, he bent over and slapped his knee. Hank was moving before Stout could straighten up.

"Oh no you don't," Stout yelled backing up and still laughing.

"Oh fucking yes I do," Hank yelled and charged.

Stout didn't even have a chance. He was a big man himself, but he didn't stand a chance against Hank's size and strength. Hank grabbed him and pulled him out into the mud and then flipped him over and down into the muck. That was just the beginning. Stout's SF buddies jumped in to get Hank and Tubby jumped in to help. Seabees started gathering outside their bunkers and watching. More SF came out of their bunkers and made the mistake of jumping in too and that triggered the Seabees. Soon, fifteen men were mud wrestling and laughing their asses off. The CIDG gathered and laughed and cheered, but they stood back. They weren't about to get between the American giants.

Finally, LT Miller came out and put an end to the match before someone lost his temper.

"Okay. Knock it the fuck off. If you ridiculous adolescents have so much energy, put it to use building some boardwalks between the bunkers."

They looked at each other and had a good laugh. They did look ridiculous covered in mud and soaking wet in a downpour.

"A boardwalk is a good idea," Stout said. "We're going to need it when the monsoon really gets underway. Can't get anything else done today anyway."

Hank agreed and set the builders to building pallet-wood boardwalks connecting all the major bunkers and tents. The SF pitched in and the whole crew worked. Piles of lumber and timbers for the guard towers just sat there. Other than boardwalks, nothing else was getting done in the massive downpour. Well, at least they got a good shower to get the mud off.

Finally on the afternoon of the 1st, the rain eased up and a little sun appeared for a short time. Bands of rain and squalls still came through, but the cyclone was passing. SF, Yards, and Seabees emerged from sodden bunkers and hooches and inspected the damage.

Tubby had a harder time with the mud than others, but he was used to that and dealt with it in the same stoic manner and good humor he dealt with the rest of life. If you're tall and attractive in this life, life itself seems to go out of its way to help you, but when you're short, pot-bellied, and kind of comical, you better be really good at something and have a good sense of humor. Fortunately for him, Tubby had both those qualities.

Hank watched Tubby and Clark shoveling mud away from the base of a hooch and laughing about something. The Yards were pulling damaged tents down. Not too bad, Hank thought. The tents had to be replaced with hooches anyway. We'll start with the damaged ones. He could see washouts on the inner perimeter that would need equipment to fill. The LZ looked okay. Other than having their camp turned into a quagmire of red mud, they had gotten off lightly.

And then he remembered the body of the Yard and wondered how he would feel if it had been Tubby or Toby. Knock that stinking thinking off right now, he thought.

On September 2nd, Stout came to Hank's bunker and shook off his poncho. It was raining so hard concrete footers for the supporting posts on many of the tents were standing six inches above ground after most of the earth under the hooch washed away.

"Hank, You said you had to get somebody to Dong Ha to pick up something for the crane, didn't you? I got you a ride if you have somebody you can send. We're expecting a break in the weather soon. He'll make a stop at Dong Ha."

"Today?"

"Right now. The bird on the pad is just waiting for a break in the clouds. Get your ass in gear."

"Tubby! Over here," Hank yelled. "You're flying back to camp to pick up the terminal gear for the crane." Tubby shuffled over and Hank briefed him on what was needed.

"Get Toby to help you. We need terminal gear to handle the big timbers. Toby will know what we need. Get it and get back here as soon as you can."

"When?"

"Now. You're on that bird on the pad. He's ready to go.

Chapter 11

The clouds lifted that afternoon, but the bird had to fly under the clouds, sometimes only 900 feet above the trees all way to Dong Ha. Tubby hadn't been happy about being sent off like an errand boy, but Hank couldn't spare any of the other builders or EOs and he didn't need any metal work done.

When Tubby entered the MCBU 301 builder's shop, Chief Murphy spotted him.

"You picked a hell of a time to visit, Tubby. The NVA got a hardon for Dong Ha. What are you doing back here anyway?"

Murphy looked worn and haggard, like he hadn't slept in a week.

"I've got to find terminal gear for handling those big damn timbers we're using in the SF bunker and get it back to the job. The Army supplied the crane but claims they don't have the terminal gear. What happened to the camp, Chief? The place looks like a city dump."

"Make damn sure you know where the closest bunker is at all times. Like I told you, the NVA got a hardon for Dong Ha all of a sudden. Probably has something to do with the elections coming up. We've been getting incoming since your crew left. Artillery from above the DMZ too. We got hit this morning. Expect more tonight. What kind of gear are you talking about? I'll try to give you a vehicle to help get it to the LZ and get your ass out of here as soon as a bird can get off the ground."

"That bad, huh?"

"Worse. You aren't getting off the ground today. I'd sleep in a bunker tonight if I were you. Forget the hooches. You got a poncho?"

"No. I just brought a change. I'm already soaked. Been soaked for three days. The damn storm is about to wash Bu Duc away."

"Stop at the storekeeper's hut and pick up a poncho with liner. It's all the heat you'll get tonight. I'm serious Tubby, sleep in a damn bunker."

"I'll do it. Thanks, Chief. I need to find Toby. He'll know what Hank wants."

After describing the problem to the LPO at the EO shop, Toby was provided with the terminal gear needed to use the cherry picker crane for moving the massive 12x12 timbers and lifting them vertical. Knowing the Bu Duc crew was using Army equipment, the LPO threatened Tubby with castration and loss of thirty-day's pay if he somehow forgot where he got the terminal gear and it ended up in Army hands.

Toby and Tubby got the gear assembled, covered, and strapped down on a pallet and moved to the airfield LZ before evening chow. Tubby said he could handle it from there.

The previous night had been scary with a lot of incoming and cold as well and Toby needed to find a bunker to sleep in that night. He was glad Hank was out in the boonies somewhere. Dong Ha was getting pounded. Not constantly, but the random incoming was terrifying.

They managed to catch the storekeeper before he closed shop and got ponchos and liners for the night.

"Let's get some chow while we can and then find a bunker with some room to sleep in tonight. You don't want to be in a hooch, Tubbs. How's Hank doing?"

"You know Hank," Tubby said. "A tank couldn't hurt him. Had some excitement with our own claymores exploding in the perimeter, but we haven't been getting any incoming at all. One of the SF patrols got hit, but that was away from the camp.

What the hell happened back here?"

"The Chief says it's all about the elections coming up. The NVA want to do something big to keep the people from participating. It's not bad most of the time. It's just the random nature of it. You never know when they're going to hit us or what it will be. When that damn siren goes off at night, it scares me so bad I can taste metal in my mouth. But the ones that come in without the siren warning are even worse. That's the artillery. They shoot them from North Vietnam just across the DMZ and we don't get a warning."

"We need to get you out at Bu Duc with us," Tubby said.

"Forget it. They won't let me go. Not now. Too much damage is happening."

After chow they found an underground bunker with 10x10 beams reinforcing the roof. It also had a layer of steel matting and three-deep sandbags over that. It was already crowded with Seabees not wanting to sleep in a hooch above ground, but they made room for Toby and Tubby. The place smelled like a locker room after a hot, tough game with all the wet Seabees packed inside, but the nose soon grew insensitive to the smell as the ears grew more sensitive to incoming on the base.

"Hey, Tubby, you got any empty racks out there in the mountains? I'd like to come out for some R&R."

"Sure," Tubby said. "We could use some help. The damn cyclone is washing away our bunkers faster than we can dig them out, and pouring concrete is a loss, so I can't anchor anything down. A couple of you lard-asses might make good anchors."

"That's better than the fuckers blowing your bunker away with artillery."

Tubby wiggled his ass into the sand to find a comfortable position.

"Yeah, you're right about that. Chief Murphy tried to get me and Hank to stay here when they put me on the detail, but I think I made out getting assigned to the Army job. Bu Duc is a mud pit right now, but at least the VC leave us pretty much alone. Maybe a little sniper harassment, but not much else. I hear it's been pretty exciting back here."

"Yeah, exciting, that's one way to describe it. Those fuckers are throwing some big shit at us damn near every day and you never know where the hell they'll pick for the next one. One thing's for sure. They got a wild hair up their asses for Dong Ha all of a sudden, and don't seem to have any shortage of artillery shells. The Marines say it's hundred-and-fifty-two-millimeter stuff they're tossing this way from on the other side of the DMZ in North Vietnam. If one of them hits us, the bunker won't help."

"Damn!" Tubby said. "I hope they take the night off. I want to get my load on a helicopter and get out of here before they start again."

"Good luck. They haven't missed a day since you guys left. Try to get some sleep. We're safe enough in here unless one lands right on top of us. Oh shit! Why'd I have to even say that?"

That night was one of the rare quiet ones and Toby and Tubby did get some sleep. Toby was learning to sleep in damp clothes on damp bedding—when bedding was available. What he couldn't get used to was the cold. The cyclone brought a mass of cold air with it and nighttime temperatures dove into the low sixties and even fifties at times. He wrapped himself in his poncho and let the liner insulate him. If I can get the moisture up to body temperature, he thought, I won't feel it. He still shivered.

The sirens went off at 0710. Tubby and all the other Seabees were gone and Toby was alone in the bunker. He had to check in with air operations at 0800 to get Tubby squared away, so he decided to get a little extra shuteye. Only seconds elapsed before the rockets struck somewhere on the combat base. Inside the bunker the shock was hardly felt and the noise from the explosion was muffled. He waited to see if more were coming.

No one had rushed to the bunker and no

more explosions occurred for ten minutes, so he gathered his gear and headed for the mess hall to see if he could scrounge up something for breakfast. They were probably secured by then, but something was probably left on the chow line.

On his way to the mess hall, Chief Murphy caught up with him.

"Did you and Tubby do like I told you?" Murphy asked.

"Damn straight, Chief. I slept inside a covered bunker and was still there when the rockets came in this morning. Tubby was with me."

"Say thank you, Chief." Murphy said.

"Thank you, Chief," Toby said and grinned.

"Don't bother about air-ops until 1330. The cyclone is about petered out, but nothing is getting out of here until after fourteen hundred. Why don't you cut between the Marine ammo dump and the Avgas storage facility to get over to your crew on the runway. Check with air ops later. Call me when you have a flight time and I'll send Tubby over."

"Okay. I'm heading over to the mess hall anyway. I'll be glad to get him the hell out of here and back to Bu Duc. At least they ain't dropping artillery on their heads out there."

"Yet," Murphy said. "Their turn in the barrel is coming."

Chapter 12

Toby's Chief had pulled him from the runway crew for the day as a favor to Chief Murphy and Toby decided not to waste it. He took care of some personal business at the personnel office and made noon chow. After stopping to talk with some EOs in MCB 11, he started the hike to air-ops at the airfield at 1345. At 1400 he was almost across Camp Barnes and nearing the ASP and fuel storage facility.

There weren't any sirens this time. Toby's first warning was the weird rushing, whistling sound as the incoming dove in. The next thing he knew, he was rolling on the ground and looking for a hole as the Avgas facility blew up in a massive ball of fire. The Army calls them foxholes. Marines call them fighting holes. Seabees called them mortar holes or just holes. Whatever they were, Toby was looking for one and getting desperate. Even at a distance, heat from the burning fuel began scorching his exposed skin.

Before he could find a place to get underground, two more rockets or artillery shells came in and hit the ammunition dump. Whatever they were, they were big. To Toby, already dazed, it seemed like the whole world around him exploded. Barely able to think, he watched a weird lens-like curling in the air come rushing right at him.

The first shockwave rolled him over three times. Something big and very explosive blew inside the dump almost completely demolishing one ammunition storage point (ASP) bunker and shot hot munitions into the air. The munitions: artillery shells, mortar shells and rockets, began falling all over the camp and many went as far as CBMU 301s camp on the other side of French Road. Some were smoking when they hit the ground. Some exploded when they hit, and they were hitting everything including offices, sleeping hooches, shops, and bunkers.

Toby found a construction hole and rolled in. He wasn't sure how long he watched the ASP cook-off because he was dazed by the force of the shockwaves and sound. Sometime later his senses began to return and he began to look for a way to get safely away from the ASP. The ground was covered with what used to be the contents of the

ASP and more was still being blown into the air. Moving around without cover was dangerous as metal shells and fragments fell from the sky.

He spotted a Seabee throwing his tools on a six-by truck between him and the burning ASP and ran as fast as he could ignoring the duds and live rounds scattered on the ground around him. He had just one thought, get the hell out of there. Rockets continued cooking-off and whistling into the air from the ASP. He had to dive for the ground when a cluster of several pieces of ordnance fell around him, two of them clanging off the top of the truck.

"Can I ride out with you?" he yelled.

The Seabee waved him over and Toby climbed into the cab. The roof of the cab gave him some relief.

"Can we get out over all the explosives on the ground?" he asked.

"Not much choice, unless you want to walk," the Seabee said. "No way I'm walking, but you're welcome to if you want to try."

He didn't seem excited at all.

"I'm happy for the ride. Let's go."

Toby was too excited to even ask the guy's name and he didn't ask Toby's. The ASP was still cooking off and the truck was rocked by a large explosion. It was hard to even think.

"That was demolitions," the Seabee said. "Probably C-four. Fire won't blow it, but a big explosion will. There's a lot of it in the dump. Hope the rest of that shit holds until we can get further away. We have to go right by the damn ASP."

The six-by is rugged and all-wheel drive, but there are some places even it can't go. The only way out of where they were was the road past the ammo dumps and more ammo bunkers were starting to cook off. During his orientation lecture when they arrived, Toby was told over 20,000 tons of munitions was stored there. It was one of the largest ammo dumps in Vietnam. The ride out was going to be an ass-puckerer.

As the Seabee wheeled the big truck past the flames and explosions and began to turn away from the dump, a Marine jumped into the road and began waving his arms.

"Tell him to get in the back."

Toby opened his window, but the Marine sergeant ran to the driver's side.

"I've got a platoon trapped in the ASP in fighting holes. We've got to get them out. Can you drive in there and pick them up?"

"Shit!" the driver said while looking at the flames in the ASP. "Yeah, I'll do it. You going with us?"

"I'll just take up room those guys will need. Straight in. Blow your horn so they'll know you're coming. They're keeping their heads down."

All Toby could see was flames and explosions as the truck turned and drove right at them, but when they got closer he could see an open area surrounded by flame. They would have to drive through a wall of flame to get in there though. The Seabee driver shifted down and pushed the pedal to the floor. The Six-by picked up speed and he started blowing his horn. Toby ducked down in his seat as the flames whipped at the cab.

He got really antsy when the truck started bouncing over munitions that had been blown out of the ASP. Suddenly they were through the flames and in an open area. Everything around them was burning and thick smoke made it hard to breath. His Seabee buddy laid on the horn and gunned the engine. Toby saw shadows in the smoke and the truck slid to a stop.

Marines seem to come from everywhere. They didn't have to be told to get on the truck. Marines climbed over the sides and climbed up the back. Toby opened the door and two Marines shoved inside the cab. He pulled one on top of him and another climbed in and sat on the other Marine's lap. Another Marine climbed in and curled up on the floor.

"Shut the damn door!" he yelled at the Marine by the window.

Marines started banging on the roof of the cab and yelling for the driver to go. One leaned around to the driver's window and yelled, "Go. Get out of here. That's all of us."

The driver had to do a back and forth a couple of times to get turned and the Marines on back screamed for him to go each time. Flames were shooting out of a tunnel in a mound of dirt and making a whooshing sound that was getting louder.

"Go man. Get the fuck out of here. That shit is going to blow."

The Seabee didn't need any further encouragement. He gunned the rpm up to get the turbo blowing hard and slipped the clutch in. The Six-by lurched forward and he banged a gear with the fastest double-clutch Toby had ever seen. He'd need all the speed he could get. Thirty Marines were in the back, hanging on the sides and off the rear, and every one of them were exposed to the flames they had to push through on the way out.

The truck bounced over smoldering rockets and artillery shells almost losing a couple of Marines, but they held on as though their lives depended on it—and they did. The truck hit the wall of flame accelerating, pushing a wall of air ahead of it. The envelope of moving air pushed the flames back and the truck went through. The driver kept the rpms up and the turbo kept that diesel whistling. And suddenly clear air was in front of them. The Marine Sergeant was still in the middle of the road waiting.

Toby's buddy let the gears slow the truck and stopped next to the sergeant. The Marines piled off the truck and out of the cab. Damn if they didn't fall-in in formation. The Sergeant came to the driver's window.

"What unit are you attached to?" he asked.

"MCB eleven. You guys need a ride anywhere?"

"No, you've done enough. We have to secure the area. You ever need the Marines, you just call."

"Will do. I better get the hell out of here now."

As the truck started moving again, Toby realized he still didn't know the guy's name. He was about to ask, but the Seabee spoke first.

"I have to go down to the old French road anyway, so I can take you that far. Better find a bunker pretty quick. This shit ain't over. That stuff is going to cook-off all night."

"Yeah, thanks. I just have to jump across the road to the equipment yard. There's a good bunker there . . . What the hell was that?"

A large explosion rocked the truck from behind. Before either of them could say any more, another explosion erupted a hundred yards in front of them.

"That's incoming," the Seabee yelled.

"We better ditch the truck and find some

cover," Toby yelled.

"Fuck that. Hold on."

Hold on he did. The truck picked up speed and bounced over holes and obstructions. Toby had to grab the seat and dash to keep from jamming his head into the roof and probably breaking his neck. The Seabee drove right at the site of the last explosion. Another explosion erupted a hundred yards past that one in CBMU 301 materials yard.

"You're driving right at the damn explosions," he yelled in panic.

"They're walking them across the base that way. I don't plan to catch them. Hold on. I'm about to cut left onto French road. I'll drop you at your gate. If you try to get in anywhere else now, somebody will shoot your ass."

The truck stopped at the gate and Hank jumped out.

"Thanks, man. It was a hell of a ride."

"Yeah it was. See you around."

Toby stood at the side of the road and watched the Seabee drive away toward his own compound. He still didn't know his name. A loud screeching whistle followed by an explosion shook him out of his daze and he ran to the sandbagged guard shack at the gate. No help there. The guard shack already had six men crammed inside a space designed for two. He took off running. There was a large underground bunker near the Operations office.

The dirt road and the ground everywhere was littered with munitions. Small arms rounds that had been blown hundreds of feet into the air were everywhere. Aircraft rockets with warheads, bombs, mortar rounds, and stuff Toby hadn't seen before was everywhere. Some of it was smoldering and there was no way to tell what was live or when it might explode. When he saw the bunker, he breathed a sigh of relief, but still had to pick his way through a minefield of ordnance that could explode at any time. He kept thinking; I'm going to lose a foot. Sure as shit, I'm going to lose a foot. Another explosion blasted a cloud of munitions into the air at the ASP.

Just before he reached the bunker a shower of small arms rounds fell on him. One or two smacked his helmet and several slammed into his shoulders and left cuts on his arms. He hit the entrance to the bunker running.

Chapter 13

Sheltering in the bunker didn't last long. The officers and chiefs were out in force and directing work even while munitions were exploding around them. Toby found Tubby in the bunker and both of them were quickly assigned to a crew removing munitions from around the operations office. Toby's cuts weren't serious and he forgot about them and got busy.

"Tubby! Leave that smoking shit where it is for the EOD to handle."

"There won't be no EOD help today," Tubby said. "We've got to get this stuff away from the office."

Proving that ignorance is bliss, Toby shrugged and began cradling rounds in his arms and moving them to a hole about fifty yards from the office. Those smoldering rounds were probably as unstable as they could get without exploding.

"Tucker, Long! Get over to the hooches. We've got fire."

Toby and Tubby dropped what they were doing and ran to the berthing hooches. Just as they got to the first row a falling round exploded near a hooch and set it on fire. No way to tell if the round had been incoming or just more munitions being blown out of the ammo dump. It was still cooking off.

"There's somebody in the hooch," Tubby yelled and started running. A chief and another Seabee were closer and didn't hesitate. They ran into the flames and reappeared with their clothes smoking and the wounded man between them.

"Check all the hooches," Toby said.

They ran from hooch to hooch yelling to see if anyone needed help. Near the end of the row they found a man unconscious on the ground. They checked him for wounds but couldn't find anything obviously wrong.

"We'll have to take a chance and move him," Tubby said. "Hard to tell where the corpsmen are. Sickbay or Delta Med?"

"We'll never make it to Delta Med. You get his feet."

They had to take cover four times before they reached sickbay. Explosions in the dump shot fresh showers of munitions into the air and it fell all over the camp adding to the volatile carpet of danger already there.

Seabees all over camp were clearing fallen munitions while more was falling. Men were wounded by explosions and falling metal, but they kept working. Fires had to be put out. Men had to be moved to sickbay. Wreckage had to be searched. That day was the longest Toby and Tubby had ever experienced.

The ammo dump continued to cook-off for the next eight hours, well into the night. By midnight, the major explosions had ceased, but an occasional rocket from the dump would ignite and scream overhead in a wild twisting flight and explode somewhere while still in flight.

Enemy incoming had stopped for the time being, but now the problem was thousands of unstable mortar, artillery, and rocket rounds, some still smoldering. Across the road, Camp Barnes looked like a city landfill had exploded next to a housing project. The area between MCB11 and the airfield, the area where the ASPs and Avgas facility used to be, looked like the aftermath of a nuclear bomb. Everything was leveled and scorched for hundreds of yards. Ammunition for the warbirds was going to be scarce for a long time to come. 20,000 tons of munitions and explosives was either blown up or scattered over several acres.

The unit S2s (intelligence) had been warned to expect the NVA to try something spectacular as the elections neared. Well they did, and they succeeded. Toby wanted to get Tubby out of there because he knew that is what Hank would want. After the day they just went through, an occasional sniper round or mortar would seem peaceful. But no one was getting in or out of Dong Ha for a while.

Chief Murphy found Toby in the Operations bunker at 0500.

"You're not getting Tubby and his gear out of here today, Toby. I need you on a front-end loader."

"I've got to get out to the runway. My crew is short."

I already cleared it with your Chief. I want you to work with the EOD people clearing the ground. Start with the builder's shop. Some duds came through the roof and can't be blown in place. Get a loader and see what EOD needs."

"Is the chow hall operating," Toby asked.

"No. There's a stack of C-Rats in the S3. Take one with you."

"I hope they at least got coffee."

"Yeah, the cooks set up a ten-gallon field container at S3."

"On my way," Toby said.

Everyone in camp was doing whatever was

necessary to clear the camp of munitions and get the facilities repaired, in some cases rebuilt. The morning was overcast with low clouds and fog. The fog smelled like explosives. Smoke from fires at the ammo dump and several burning structures was mixing with the fog to form a nasty smog. At least the cyclone had taken a small break and the rain stopped. Small openings appeared in the clouds and a little sun got through making the day seem a little less dreary and the future seem a little less scary. Toby really wanted to sit down with Hank and talk things over.

It had been that way since they were little, little being relative. Hank had never been little. But Hank was always there if the problem was too big for Toby. No problem seemed too big for Hank, not to Toby anyway. They lost their dad when Hank was sixteen and Toby twelve, and Hank took over the role of dad for Toby, not smotheringly, but being there when problems or bullies got too big or overwhelming. They were always able to talk and Hank always seemed to have answers. With everything and everybody around him in a turmoil, it would have been nice to have Hank there just to talk to.

After eating a cold can of something from a C-Rats box and gulping two cups of foul tasting and almost cold coffee, he got a front-end loader from the equipment yard and drove it to the builder's shop. An EOD Tech was putting small flags on different spots around the floor. Toby dismounted and approached the EOD guy. The guy wore PO1 pins on his collars.

"Chief Murphy assigned me to you. Name's Tucker," Toby said. "What do you need?"

"Hello, Tucker. I'm Crowder. Get some dirt in the scoop to lay these rounds on. Tilt your scoop outward so there's some steel between you and the ordnance. We'll move them down to the rice fields by the south perimeter where I can blow them."

Toby looked at the rounds lying around the shop and frowned. "Are they stable?"

"You think I'd be fucking with them if they weren't. I got to load them. Get some dirt in the scoop and get in here as far as you can."

Crowder explained what he was doing and why while he worked. Three artillery rounds had fallen into the shop.

"None of them are fused so they can be moved. The explosives inside are still dangerous, but without the fuse, they're stable. When we get to the site, you're going to dig us a nice big hole to use when we blow these things."

"So, we're going to pick up all the ordnance laying round and move it to the hole?"

"No. Some of it can't be moved. Anything that is fused has to be blown in place. Rockets are inherently unstable, so they have to be blown in place. You're going to lose more structures today. Can't be helped."

Crowder cleared the shop of ordnance and rode with Hank to a place well south of the camp where a dozer was already pushing trees over and scraping a big depression in the only dry land in sight. Other crews were working with EOD north of MCB11 burying ordnance and building their own pits for blowing what wasn't safe to bury.

Toby followed Crowder around picking up dud munitions and then hauling it to the disposal hole. They had most of the big safe stuff moved by noon chow. Loads of smaller stuff was being buried.

Crowder stayed with Toby to get some lunch. It was C-Rats again. The chow hall kitchen had taken shrapnel through some of the stoves and one large cold storage fridge. Utilitymen were already working to get the kitchen back on-line.

Sitting with Seabees and trading stories over lunch, Toby caught up on the status of Seabee casualties. With his world blowing up around him, he didn't have the time or attention to notice much of what was happening to others unless they were involved in the disaster he was dealing with. With new disasters happening by the minute, acts of unthinking bravery and selfless heroism became commonplace and mostly unnoticed at Dong Ha.

The Seabees simply did what was necessary, sometimes the only thing there was to do. Men were pulled from burning hooches by other men already wounded by shrapnel. Wounded were carried by those able to lift and walk, carried through flying shrapnel and exploding ordnance to get them medical help. A lot of purple hearts would be awarded to Seabees for wounds received that day.

The casualty list was all word of mouth right then. The full list wouldn't be known for days. Walking wounded Seabees were still working to clear dangerous ordnance and trying to put the camp back into some kind of order. Others were on the perimeter preparing for a ground attack if that's what the NVA had planned. Building was only part of the Seabee job description. Fighting was right there at the top.

There were still munitions in the camp that couldn't be moved and the EOD people prepared to blow them in-place with as little damage as possible. Toby and his loader, along with all the other equipment that could scoop or scrape dirt, were needed to build walls of dirt around the munitions to contain as much blast and shrapnel as they could.

"Let's take a break and get some coffee," Crowder said. "My Chief is working out the charges and schedule. We've probably got an hour to relax."

"Works for me. Hop on. I'm not walking

around until you guys got everything that goes bang out of here."

"Yeah," Crowder said. "That sounds good. Can you lift that bucket up close to give us a little cover?"

"Yep. That's exactly what I'm going to do."

Toby took it slow trying to watch for anything in their path that looked like it could go bang if run over. He wished he could call a time-out and everything would just stop for a minute. Too much was going on and he was having trouble concentrating. All kinds of equipment was moving around the camp roads and the dirt was chewed up. It was hard to tell if something had been buried. The problem with duds that have gone through an explosion is they sometimes don't remain duds. Sometimes it only takes a nudge.

He turned the front wheels to follow dozer tracks. Anyplace a ten-ton dozer went had to be safe, he thought.

"Keep looking out front," he yelled at Crowder. "I'm lowering the bucket close to the ground. I need to see better."

He was being careful, but he couldn't avoid what he couldn't see. One moment everything was going great, the next moment the front of the loader was raising up in the air. Toby was caught in a shock wave and envelope of sound that took his senses away.

It was the bucket that saved them. The force of the explosion shot out to the sides, but still lifted the machine off its front wheels. He and Crowder were slammed back. Fortunately, they stayed on the machine and the machine stopped.

The front end slammed back down and it sunk lower than it should. The front tires were shredded and smoking. Toby's hearing was gone and he hurt from head to toe. He was too dazed to even move. Everything had stopped but not the way he wanted. Crowder was bent over and shaking his head. Blood was running from his nose. Toby knew he ought to be doing something but couldn't think.

Fortunately, other Seabees were close enough to help. Two men climbed up on the loader. One pulled Toby upright and looked into his eyes.

"You okay? Can you move? You have to get off this machine."

All Toby heard was buzzing and screeching in his ears.

"Come on, man. I'll help you down."

The other guy was pulling Crowder up and two guys were climbing up that side of the machine. With more help from guys just arriving, Toby and Crowder made it to the ground while men were calling for a corpsman. The corpsman never got there. The NVA wasn't done with Dong Ha or Toby yet.

Chapter 14

Faintly, through the buzzing in his ears, Toby heard the siren. Seabees began shouting, “Incoming! Incoming!” He was pulled to his feet and rushed through the dirt until he lost his footing and then he was dragged to the bunker. The first of the incoming 152mm artillery rounds hit the Operations hut and blew it completely apart. He knew something happened but not what. He was laying in the sand at the bottom of the bunker rubbing his legs.

His head was clearing and he was getting nauseous. Everything hurt. He still had enough sense to know he had to get it together though. He shook his head to clear his vision. That was a mistake. His head felt like mush and the shaking set off a violent headache.

“You okay, Toby?” Chief Murphy asked.

"Not sure," he said. "What happened, Chief?"

"You must of hit a live round with the loader. That sucker is out of commission for a while. Just relax, a corpsman is on the way as soon as we get an all-clear."

He braced his back against the side of the bunker. Fragmented thoughts were flying through his brain making it hard to focus. It seemed like everything he was experiencing was accelerating and life itself was getting away from him. He'd worked some big, dangerous jobs in his time, but nothing like this ever happened in Wilmington. A corpsman arrived at the bunker a few minutes after that. He stuck smelling-salts under Toby's nose. That cleared his head quickly.

The corpsman examined him and poked and bent and twisted things. He had treated men in battle who didn't even know they had lost a leg. Even though Toby appeared to be just dazed, trauma can do strange things to men and Doc was a careful corpsman. Then he checked Toby's eyes with a light.

"Well, I can't find anything broken or seriously damaged. You might have a mild concussion, but I don't think so. You took a pretty good blast though. I'll give you some APCs. That's the best I can do. Take a couple now and a couple more in about six hours. Come to sickbay if it gets too bad."

"Okay," Toby said. "I'm starting to loosen up now and my head's clearing. How long before my hearing returns to normal?"

"You'll have some ringing for a while. Next time you get to Da Nang, get a hearing test to get it in your record. I don't think it is, but you could have some permanent damage. You good to go now?"

"Yeah. Hurting some, but that's about it."

"It will hurt worse tomorrow. Let me know if it gets too bad."

"Will do. Thanks, doc."

Toby spent the rest of the day in the bunker. His utilities were grubby and his body was filthy. That was going to be a common condition for everyone at Dong Ha for several days. Of course, that was a common condition for Seabees anyway, but now there wouldn't be any end of day shower until the shower points were rebuilt.

Tubby checked on him several times but couldn't stay. Every able-bodied man in camp was working to put the camp back together and no one could be spared. Sleep was grabbed in three or four-hour snatches.

In the morning, Toby felt almost human again. He stretched and moved cautiously until he felt like it was safe to move around. Murph said air ops was expecting weather above minimums and to get Tubby to the airfield if he felt up to it.

After a cold cup of coffee, Toby drew his forklift from the equipment yard to help Tubby load and took him to the airfield. Tubby was able to get a flight to Phu Bai almost immediately. From there he could catch a supply bird back to Bu Duc. The pallet with the terminal tackle for the crane had survived the ammo dump disaster.

At 1100, he loaded the pallet on a CH46 and Tubby was on his way back to Bu Duc. Toby wished he was going with him. Instead, he turned the machine toward the end of the runway where his crew was replacing matting damaged in the attack.

Chapter 15

Tubby looked at all the green from the door of the chopper. Landing at Bu Duc was a relief. No incoming and no exploding ammo dump. Just miles of green, a small patch of red dirt, and a lot of activity.

The forklift was parked at the landing pad. Tubby didn't hesitate. He fired it up and moved the terminal tackle to the equipment yard and then found Hank. The jobs were moving along well without them, so Hank and Tubby took an hour and caught up.

"When did you learn to operate the lift?' Hank asked.

"I had to learn a lot of stuff in the last three days. Geeze, Hank, what a damn mess it was."

"Is Toby alright?"

"He got banged up some when something

blew up under his loader, but he was okay when I left. We need to get him out here."

"I tried. Hell, I tried to keep him from coming to Vietnam. Brothers don't have to serve in the war zone at the same time, but you can't stop them if they volunteer. Maybe I should have raised more hell. Well, Toby is a big boy. Even the old man couldn't tell him much."

Stout heard Tubby was back and came by their hole.

"Hey, Tubby. I hear you guys lost an ammo dump."

"An Avgas storage facility too. Dong Ha is a mess. Our S3 office took a direct hit. Blew it to hell and gone."

"Any casualties?"

"Yeah. A lot of wounded but no fatalities, at least in our camp. What's been happening here?"

"Mostly quiet," Stout said. "Our patrols have been finding signs of NVA in the area but no contact since the ambush. We keep seeing those lights in the hills. They want us to know they're here but they don't seem to want any contact yet. Well, that's why we're here. Hank, want to see some of the countryside?"

"How?"

"I'm making a village civic action visit with a patrol later. There's a Khe Montagnard village about four klicks southeast of here. I'd like to recruit them into our network. Maybe we can build something for them. I'd like to have you with us so I don't make any commitments we can't deliver on. I've got to be careful. They use the same word for will, might, and maybe, but they only understand will."

Hank took a sip of coffee and thought for a moment.

"Yeah, I'd like that. Let me get with my teams first and see how the schedule is going."

"I'm going too," Tubby said.

"You got a couple of hours. We'll leave at 1300. Rifles, flak jackets, and helmets."

"Are you expecting any trouble?" Hank asked.

"Who the hell knows? The NVA are out there."

Excavation for the main bunker was underway. The dozer was breaking ground and rough cutting the hole. The site was staked, tested, and prepped. The Forklift was moving the massive 12"X12"X 9' timbers to the site and preparing to move the 4"X12"X10' planking for the sides and roof to the site from the storage yard.

The design was simple. The SF had originally wanted reinforced concrete for the sides and top, but for several reasons including water supply and the need for a batch plant for that much concrete, the alternative timber reinforced wood structure was selected. Hank had no idea where the Army had come up with that much cured and treated lumber that size. It was really quality material. The supporting timbers were massive, virtually whole trees square cut. The only place he knew of it being used was for construction of ASPs and critical command bunkers. Fact was, he hadn't seen timber that massive used anywhere in civilian life. There just wasn't much call for beams that big when steel and concrete were available.

With the entire team turned-to getting ready to raise the bunker, Hank picked up his web gear, helmet, and rifle and went to find Stout. Tubby caught up with him as he crossed the camp to the Yard camp.

The Montagnard CIDG company had their own compound within the camp perimeter. Actually, they had two compounds. The Yard company was made up of Khe and Bru Montagnards and the two groups didn't always get along. They would all take orders from the SF, but they would only take orders from Montagnards of their own tribe. Stout was inspecting a squad of Khe Yards near the gate to the access road.

"Hank, you'll walk behind Tubby. Tubby, you'll be behind me. Let me have a look at your gear."

He inspected the Seabees like he inspected

the Yards. He lifted both canteens to make sure they were full.

"That's water in them, isn't it?"

Hank grinned. "Yep. No shine. Just water."

"Okay. I'll walk fourth in the column. Tubby, you'll walk fifth and Hank sixth. Fifteen-yard intervals. Lock and load now."

The cyclone had departed the area and the sky had cleared. It was a rare, but very much appreciated clear and cool day. Tubby took a deep breath to loosen up. Life had been going at a crazy pace for days. Maybe a walk in the woods would help him slow things back down to normal. They hadn't done anything like this outside the wire since the exercises in California and both of them were excited and nervous, Tubby more so because he was still recovering from his experiences at Dong Ha.

The patrol left the wire at 1300.

Chapter 16

Seabees were trained by the Marines on weapons and small unit tactics early in their career. The CBMU had military training back in California as a group. Patrolling was part of the training. They even "captured" a hill and defended it overnight, with blanks. Hank was wishing he had paid more attention to the lessons.

Seabees assigned to the security platoon patrolled outside the wire regularly at Dong Ha, but this was Hank's first time on a real patrol. He was wishing the intervals were closer. Forty-five feet between him and Tubby and forty-five feet behind him to the Khe Yard following made him feel alone and vulnerable. He kept his mouth shut though. Tubby was in commando mode and looked like he was having a ball. Hank watched Stout closely for any sign of danger when he could see him.

Stout had a PRC25 radio with him, but it was line of sight, which meant, if you could see it, you could talk to it, and he couldn't reach the camp at times. On a break he told Hank not to worry about it. The Village they were visiting was well within range for the radio and the camp mortars.

The village they were visiting was a Khe village and the patrol was made up of Khe Yards although not of this village. The Khe sergeant with the patrol spoke good English though and would be able to interpret for Stout. He was the man directly behind Hank.

The point man was from this area and knew the trails well. He also knew all the creek beds and easy passage areas away from the trails and led them to and through double canopy jungle that was dark but easy to walk through without having to hack away elephant grass and vines. Lack of direct sunlight kept the vegetation in check. That was great for keeping the movement quiet too.

Four klicks, or kilometers, is just about two miles, and normally two miles would be an easy walk, but when you are trying to watch everything around you and expecting an ambush every step of the way, the stress makes it seem like ten miles.

They moved toward the village slowly and quietly with frequent stops to listen. Stout had two scouts out in front providing advance recon for the patrol. When the scouts came in, Stout signaled a stop and signaled for the column too close up.

"We're going to approach the village in a skirmish line, Hank. You and Tubby stay next to me. I want a chance to observe for a few minutes before we go in. When I think the time is right, I'll send our terp in to let them know we're coming."

Hank just nodded and resumed a careful scan of their surroundings with his eyes.

"Relax," Stout said. "It's just routine precaution. I'm not expecting trouble."

"I'll relax when we're back inside the wire at Bu Duc."

"Suit yourself. When's the last time you took a drink? It's time to hydrate."

The village was typical of mountain villages according to Stout. Several small huts surrounded one long community building. All were set on stilts about five feet off the ground. Monsoon season could wash away anything built on the ground.

The large building seemed substantial to Hank's experienced eye. The building methods were primitive, but the structure looked like it would stand up to any kind of weather it might be subjected to in this area. It didn't have to ward off snow or cold, so bulky insulated walls and roof weren't necessary. The area wasn't prone to earthquakes and only rare cyclones like the one of the previous week came through. Mainly, it just had to keep the rain off the people and the jungle animals out.

"The big hut is where the entire village lives," Stout said. "The smaller buildings are just storage huts, and sometimes used by newlyweds for the first two weeks of their marriage. They cook mostly outdoors, but meals are communal and eaten inside. We can expect to be greeted by the chief near the fire pit. We won't be invited inside, but they will probably share a meal with us outside."

"What kind of food?" Hank asked.

"Don't ask and don't look at it too closely and don't try to make points by complimenting it too much. They'll feel obligated to serve you seconds."

A few Yards were walking around the village and others were taking their ease in the shade. The morning was already hot and sticky. Women went about their chores with babies on their hips. Kids ran around chasing each other. A group of boys and a little girl were playing some kind of game the object of which Hank couldn't figure out. Kids are kids regardless of race or country. Let them get bored and they will invent a game. It might not make any sense to anyone else, but they will have a ball with it until something else occurs to them.

"Don't stare at their women," Stout said.

Several women went about the village bare

breasted, but the sight wasn't erotic. These women lived hard lives and were old by the time they were thirty. Sagging was common, if not the rule.

"Don't worry," Hank said and shivered a little.

Stout sent his terp in and waited for his signal. Social rules and mores among the Yards could get complicated, but most villages had had some contact with Americans by 1967 and made allowances. Still, it was important not to be too much of the ugly American. The SF were experts at avoiding cultural faux pas. Hank didn't need to be told to keep his mouth shut. The problem was, he was huge by Montagnard standards. Stout was a big man himself, maybe six foot and 200 pounds, but Hank was by far the biggest man in the group. Everything about him was oversized, even by American standards. When they entered the village, the Yards were fascinated by him.

"The Chief invites the giant warrior to sit next to him," the terp said.

Hank looked around for the giant and wondered who the hell the chief was talking about.

"He's talking about your big ass," Stout said and grinned. "Go on. Sit next to him. You don't refuse an invitation from the chief."

The chief was about 5'5" tall and weighed all of 110 pounds. Hank was 6'4" tall and 250 pounds. When he sat next to the chief, he had to admit he was a giant to these people. The chief didn't take long to get things rolling.

He made a signal with his hands and soon a woman appeared with a bowl of dark, steaming liquid and another with a basket of what Hank assumed was some kind of fruit, although he couldn't identify it. As soon as the bowl of liquid was set in front of him, his mouth began to water. Coffee! Good coffee. Not C-Rats instant coffee, but brewed coffee that smelled like the best he had ever had. Small clay bowls were handed out and the chief dipped one in the coffee bowl and handed it to Hank, taking his small bowl to dip a bowl for himself.

Hank sniffed the coffee. It was fabulous. He took a sip. Wonderful. He'd forgotten what good coffee tasted like. He had to sip it through his teeth to filter the grounds, but the taste was perfect.

"Most of the tribes in this area have worked on French coffee plantations and know how to grow and process it," Stout said. "You won't find any better in Paris. The chief is handing you a piece of cane. Let it soak in your coffee."

Hank took the cane and nodded his thanks to the chief. As soon as he put it in his coffee, it began to lighten. He took a sip. Sweet. The cane both lightened the coffee like milk and sweetened it like sugar. Stout told the terp to say something complimentary about the coffee to the chief.

A tiny little girl completely naked walked up to Hank and held her hands out to be picked up.

"Pick her up and hold her," Stout said. "Having her single you out is good. The village children are important in the mountains and they are nurtured by the whole village. So many die in their first year, and that makes each one that survives even more important."

The little girl snuggled into Hank's arms and then pushed and turned until she was on his lap and facing the circle. Hank grinned.

"Kinda wish she had a diaper on," he said.

"If anything happens just grin and bear it."

Stout got down to business. Hank sat back and let the words wash over him. It felt strange having a tiny little girl on his lap. He and his wife hadn't had any children and all his experience with them was through cousins. That was the best way because when they got cranky you could hand them back. He wondered why the little girl had picked him.

Tubby was using sign language to attempt communications with two Khe men about his own size. Hank could only imagine what the conversation was about and wondered if Tubby even knew. The terp joined in and all four of them wandered off into the village. They all had pot bellies. If Tubby traded his greens for a loin cloth and got a tan, he would fit right in, no questions asked.

Chapter 17

Over the next four days Hank and Tubby returned to the village with two builders to reinforce the village community hut and to build some chests they seemed to like. He salvaged wood from pallets and crating for the construction, but the villagers were happy to get it. Two green berets and a squad of Khe Montagnards escorted the Seabees and helped provide the labor. Chain saws allowed them to salvage tree trunks from the jungle.

Making the patrol out to the village without any challenge helped Hank and Tubby get comfortable with being outside the wire, but the SF didn't let them get complacent. Each trip out and back was conducted as though they were picking their way through enemy infested territory, and perhaps they were, but the VC or NVA, or whatever the hell they were, didn't seem interested in challenging them yet.

The little girl waited for Hank and attached herself to him as soon as he arrived. On the second day several children waited with her. That day he dug into his stash before he left the camp and brought some gedunk with him.

Stout told him not to bring candy. The kids never had it and the lack of refined sugar in their diet along with high fiber in their food kept their teeth healthy. Introducing candy into their diet would have rotted their teeth and who knew what else. The kids loved the Vienna sausages though, and the adults treated the hot sauce he gave them like gold.

On the fourth day he brought a couple packs of popcorn, a kettle, and some oil and salt. He put the right mixture in the kettle and set it on the fire. The entire village gathered around to see what he was doing. It was obviously food, but they weren't sure what he was fixing.

He sat and watched the pot. His little girl reached up for him to set her in his lap. The children gathered close and the adults pushed in closer.

He wasn't prepared for what happened when the corn started popping.

Popcorn wasn't unknown in this part of the world, but it was rare in the mountains. It was just a normal part of his childhood, so Hank hadn't thought about it before bringing it with him.

Pop—pop, pop—pop, pop, pop. The kids jumped up and stared at the pot. The adults backed up. Pop, pop, pop, pop. The corn started cooking off and the kids jumped back. The lid started to rattle and the popping got louder. Hank looked around. The kids were hiding behind the adults and the adults were standing thirty feet away. His little friend in his lap started giggling.

Soon the lid started lifting off the kettle and popcorn started falling out into the fire. He'd put way too much corn in the kettle. The baby's giggling turned into a tiny belly laugh Hank couldn't resist. He started laughing too and hugged her tight.

He reached over and caught a handful of popcorn and blew on a piece to cool it. He put it in his mouth and chewed and then handed the little girl a piece. She didn't even hesitate and popped it into her mouth. She chewed for a moment and smiled.

She was tiny and looked like a hairless monkey, but her little smile melted his heart. Her world was small and safe and she was loved and protected. She wasn't afraid to trust, even a giant like Hank. He was getting attached to her.

The kids were first to return to the fire. Hank pointed at the popcorn. They didn't need more of an invitation. The adults were next. Hank pulled the kettle off the fire and set it where everyone could get a handful.

"It's the salt," Stout said. "Salt can be pretty dear here in the mountains. It's not easy to get. I think you made some friends."

One of the Khe CDIG squad came close to Stout and talked quietly with him for a moment.

"Hank, get your tools together. We have to get out of here."

"I haven't even started yet. What's going on?"

"The Khe say there's movement of some kind on the next hill over. It isn't our people so it's not friendly. Come on. Get your stuff together. We leave in five."

"What about the village?"

"They'll be okay unless the NVA find us here."

The little girl didn't want him to go and she didn't want to be put down. He didn't even know her name and probably couldn't pronounce it if he did. He decided to name her Peanut. Hank finally had to force her into one of the adult's arms. The squad was ready and getting impatient with the Seabees. They left the ville in single file.

Chapter 18

They could hear the machinery from a mile away as they approached the camp. The Seabees were busy preparing the excavation that would hold the bunker when it was ready. The sound of the dozer rattled leaves in the jungle.

Getting back inside the wire at Bu Duc took longer than usual, and for Hank, was a tense process. The camp had taken some incoming from a sniper while he was gone and the perimeter guards were on edge. Stout talked them in and they had to sprint through the gate one at a time for fear of presenting too tempting a target for the sniper. But it turned out okay. They sprinted through the gate without taking a single round of incoming.

The crew had been busy while Hank and Stout had been working in the village. The excavation for the command bunker was complete and the framing and support timbers were stacked around the hole. The dozer and frontend loader had removed the dirt down to bedrock and the loader was being used to level the base with rock and stone. The excavation was the simplest method for producing a hole the depth and width needed. The dozer cut a wide trench between the width markers leaving both ends open. The Loader moved dirt left by the dozer and squared up the sides. Later, when the structure was built between the dirt walls of the giant trench, the ends would be filled in leaving the entire structure underground.

Even though the camp was on one hundred percent alert, the crew had to keep working. No one knew why the NVA hadn't begun harassing the camp with mortars yet. They certainly knew the SF were there. Whatever the reason, the SF and Seabees were thankful for the relative peace to finish the work, but they all knew it couldn't last. They needed to get underground as soon as possible. Hank had a different motive for the haste. He wanted to get his crew the hell out of Bu Duc. Seabees were trained to fight and could fight, but that wasn't their primary calling. He wanted to get out of Bu Duc before the inevitable happened.

For the next three days the bunker heavy work took place and the SF increased their patrolling activity. The sniper hadn't returned, but Khe villagers were reporting regular contact with NVA patrols. Several heavy-lift helicopters brought in ammunition stores and heavier weapons.

A 4.2-inch mortar pit was set up near the center of the camp and the SF and CIDG preregistered multiple points around the perimeter. Two more 81mm mortars were delivered and set up in the CIDG area. Four M2 fifty-caliber machineguns were delivered for the guard towers, yet to be built, and multiple crates of LAW rockets were stacked in the ammo storage bunker.

Hank supervised building the frames for the command bunker. 12"x12"x10' pre-cut timbers were laid out for supporting timbers and fastened between 12"x12"x 24' pre-cut top and base plates. Having them precut back at Phu Bai saved a huge amount of work onsite. Next, the cherry-picker crane began setting up the frames while the crew braced them in place to await the 4"x12" cross laid sheathing that would tie them together. AM2 aluminum runway mating was used for the flooring. The frame was an imposing structure in itself and able to support a prodigious amount of weight. The electrician moved in and laid in the cables for the communications room and strung lighting and outlet wires back to the generators.

Next, the entire structure was sheathed in 4"x12" plank timbers with a double layer cross-laid on the roof. Air vent tunnels were dug, sheathed, and covered again. The roof was sealed with tar and plastic for waterproofing and the sides were tarred for water and bug proofing. The top of the roof was now six feet below ground level surface of the trench.

On the fifth day, Clark on the frontend loader began backfilling the sidewalls with rock and dirt while the dozer moved the excavation dirt back against the ends and created the entrance ramp. With the ends and sides filled up to the roof level, the cherry-picker crane laid in a layer of AM2 matting on the roof. An all hands working party filled sandbags and two layers of sandbags were laid on the matting. Then another layer of AM2 matting was laid on the sandbags. The ends of the trench were built up to the second layer of matting and the backhoe and loader moved a foot of stone on top of the matting.

Next came a feature Hank hadn't seen before. The SF had a load of used brass artillery shell casings flown in and installed them, vertically, on top of a double stack of pallets on top of the stone and filled in with dirt. Finally, two more layers of sandbags were laid on top of the shell casings and the rest of the hole filled with dirt and built up for drainage.

Stout said the purpose of the artillery casings and pallets was to detonate time delay fused rounds and provide an area of lower density where the blast could dissipate to the sides rather than pushing down through the roof.

There wasn't any finish carpentry to worry about, so a week after it was begun, the command bunker was ready for the SF to move in. The interior was still rough and it would take some time for tar and wood treatment odors to dissipate, but they could start installing communications equipment and moving bunks and furniture in. Strangely enough, they moved their small arms armory in first. Well, maybe not so strange at all.

"What the hell is that thing, Sarge?" Hank asked.

Stout had a submachine gun on a sling hanging from his shoulder, but it didn't look like any machine gun Hank had ever seen.

"It's a Russian RPD."

"What did you do to it? The stock looks like it was sawed off."

"Good eye. The stock is sawed off and so is the barrel. Both are modifications our armorers made to make it lighter for patrols and give it better balance.

"How many rounds does that drum hold?"

"This is a fifty rounder, but it has a hundred round drum too. It ejects spent casings straight down and not to the side which is kind of nice when you have to fight next to someone. The Russians make good weapons. They rattle and look like cheap copies of something else, but they have chrome lined chambers and bores and don't jam, and you can drop them in mud and still fire them."

"That's cool. Can I fire it sometime?"

"Sure. Look, if you like it, I can probably get you one if you have something to trade.

That's the opening gambit, Hank thought. He looked at the RPD. It was a really neat gun. He had no idea what the hell he would do with one, or even if the Seabees would let him keep it. He wanted one, and Stout had let him see it for a reason.

"What do you need?" he asked.

"Let me think about it," Stout said.

"I have a lot of good stuff in my stash."

"Hank, that stuff was good stuff as long as we didn't have our bunker and couldn't risk bringing in our own. Now that we have a safe place to put it, we can bring in about anything we want. Believe me, you don't have anything worth an RPD. Let me think about it and talk to the boss. The work order didn't cover everything we'd like to have in this camp."

Ah ha, Hank thought. That was the come-on.

The next day, the NVA provided them with the perfect trade.

Chapter 19

Hank and the Seabees were up and working before the sun came up. Work had to cease as the perimeter was alerted just before sunrise, but the alert turned out to be a false or at least a mistaken report of movement near the wire at the access road.

Hank kicked back at the Seabee firepit near their fighting holes.

"Try this," Tubby said, handing him a canteen cup.

Hank could smell the coffee before it got close to his nose. He took a sip. Absolutely wonderful.

"Where'd you get this?"

"I did a little trading of my own. Turns out the villagers love C-Rats, any kind of C-Rats, even those damn lima beans and ham chunks. The Yards showed me how to grind it with rocks. I got a gasmask bag full of grounds. We're good for a couple weeks."

"Tubbs, you are a wonder. I just might have to promote you to admiral."

"Second Class would do. I got to go. The rest of the crew haven't had any yet."

The job was almost over and the crew could get back to Dong Ha soon. A Seabee mechanic was coming in with an Army engineer to do the final checks on the diesel generators and the army guy would do an inspection on the equipment while he was there and the mechanic would repair anything the Army needed fixed to take the equipment back. There were still two towers to erect, some interior work to do on the bunker and some reinforcing to do on the CIDG bunkers. The final job would be the water system, but that was for later.

While the Seabees sipped their coffee, Stout crossed the open ground between the bunker and the shower point/latrine with just a towel and his boots on. Hank wondered what kind of trade for the RPD Stout would come up with. He had just set his cup down to pour another cup of coffee and bent over to reach the pot.

A tracer went over his head and the sound of a machine gun followed almost immediately. He flipped over the log and looked toward the perimeter.

"Get down! Everybody get down!"

The machinegun continued to fire and the flutter of incoming rounds buzzed just a foot over his head. The Seabees scattered and found cover. Return fire from the perimeter started almost immediately.

Stout started running for the latrine with dust from machine gun rounds kicking up just behind his heels.

Hank couldn't see the origin of the incoming through the perimeter wire, but he could see the tracers coming through the wire. Stout made it to the latrine, but that didn't slow the machine gun down.

Hank wondered if he could make it to his fighting hole. His rifle was there. It was too late to wonder why he hadn't brought it with him. Hell, no one kept their rifle with them. Not even the SF carried their rifles in camp.

The machine gun started taking the wood latrine apart. Chips and splinters started flying as round after round tore into the wood sides. The NVA machine gunner didn't seem to care about anything else in camp.

"That fucker is going to take the latrine apart," Tubby yelled.

"Don't worry about that," Hank yelled. "Get in your holes."

With the incoming focused on the latrine he

and Tubby made it to the hole and grabbed their rifles. It was only a short time before Hank could see light through the wood in the latrine. What the hell was Stout going to do?

One of the 81mm mortars began dropping rounds trying to find the machine gun, but it kept firing and chopping up the latrine. Whole sections of the perimeter were focusing their fire on the area machine gun tracers were coming from, but it kept on firing. The latrine was coming apart.

He flipped his selector to automatic and emptied a magazine back down the path the tracers were coming in on. He couldn't see the gun, so he just tried to put rounds in its general direction hoping to put pressure on the gunner and give Stout some relief.

One whole slat of wood collapsed and the wall wobbled under the impacts of steady fire. All the Seabees were in their fighting holes and returning fire now. Another slat shattered and the roof of the latrine sagged. Hank watched the roof slowly sag into the latrine as the walls holding it up were shot away.

Suddenly the roof collapsed and Stout burst out of the latrine bear-assed naked except for his boots and crossed the open ground to the bunker with machine gun rounds hitting right in his tracks.

He made it underground just as the 4.2-inch mortar got into play and started dropping big rounds on the machine gun. That put an end to the machine gun or at least stopped it firing.

Stout emerged from the bunker still bear-assed naked, but now he had his boots and his green beret on. He was pissed out of his mind. He just stood there facing the direction of the machine gun incoming and giving the NVA an Italian bent arm salute. Even the CIDG cackled at Stout's antics. Hank just shook his head. You had to give it to him. Stout had style. That was the end of the humor though. The NVA weren't through. Mortar incoming started next.

Fifteen rounds of NVA 82mm mortar hit the camp in the next thirty minutes. Two CIDG hooches were hit, but no one was injured largely due to fortifications made possible by the Seabees and their equipment. Every fighting position on the perimeter was connected by trenches and had overhead protection. The command bunker was buried under so much rock, dirt, sand, steel, and brass, it could take direct hits from mortars all day long. There was one casualty though that really pissed Hank off.

Stout moved the Seabees out of their fighting holes and into bunkers on the inner perimeter in case the mortar barrage signaled a ground attack. That move turned out to be a good move when Hank's fighting hole took a direct hit.

Hank was watching the outer wire closely. That's where trouble would start if a ground attack was going to happen at all. Stout stayed with the Seabees on the perimeter to give them some direction and support if things got hairy on the ground. He was staring hard at the outer perimeter when snow started falling around the bunker and in the open area between the fences.

"What the fuck now?" he asked of no one in particular.

A Seabee replied with a bit of awe in his voice, "It's snowing."

Everyone on that side of the perimeter was looking around at the white stuff falling and some even stood to get a better look.

"Get your asses down!" Stout screamed.

Hank caught a snowflake in his hand. He stared at it for a moment uncomprehending until awareness of what he was holding broke through.

"It's popcorn," he yelled. "It's my fucking popcorn. Those sons a bitches blew up my popcorn."

"How much of that shit did you have in there?"

"A thousand packs," Tubby shouted. "Those rotten sons a bitches."

Hank and Stout turned to look back at his fighting hole just as a gust of wind caught up a huge cloud of popcorn and blew it toward them. It looked like a giant white wave about to break on the perimeter. The popped corn was welling up out of Hank's hole and forming a huge white mound made up of a couple thousand gallons of popped popcorn. The white cloud descended on the perimeter and continued on like a breaking wave right across the inner perimeter and across the open killing ground between the fences.

Suddenly what looked like a platoon of NVA jumped up and started running down the hill and back into the jungle.

"Open fire, damn it!" Stout yelled and cut loose with his RPD. An instant later the whole perimeter opened up. Three of the enemy fell at the edge of the jungle, but the rest made it to cover. Stout called the command bunker and told Hank to continue watch on their piece of the perimeter. He took off running back to the bunker.

After the four-deuce mortar dropped six rounds outside the outer wire everything got quiet. Stout returned to the Seabee bunker. Soon CIDG began forming and moving out through the safe zones in the wire.

"I hope at least one of them survived," Stout said. "We need some intelligence."

It turned out one of the Sappers did survive and the CIDG brought him inside the wire. While the SF took the prisoner inside the command bunker, Hank organized his crew and got the teams working on repairs. He was thinking the timing for wrapping up the work at Bu Duc was cutting it close. It was time to get his crew the hell out of harm's way.

Later, Stout found Hank.

"Tucker, you have achieved a status few human beings have ever reached."

"The only status I want is project completed, ready for reassignment. What are you talking about?"

"You have become our new secret weapon. Those VC didn't know what to make of your popcorn. They weren't sure if they were being gassed or bombed. They didn't hang around to find out though."

The crew was still shook-up from the firefight but had a laugh over what the surviving VC were probably telling their commanders about the American secret weapon. They checked out what remained of Hank's fighting hole. The entire stash was ruined. There was a two-foot layer of popcorn forming a wide apron around the hole, but most of it had blown away.

"Smells like a barbecue," Stout said.

"Canned meat. Every damn thing I had in there is ruined or gone."

"Well, look at the bright side," Stout said.

"What bright side. Five-hundred-dollars-worth of gedunk is ruined."

"You won't have to carry all that crap back to Dong Ha. Look, get your crew in and under cover by 1100. The boss called in an artillery H&I around the camp."

"H&I?"

"Harassment and interdiction. Our artillery support base is preregistered on important points around the camp. They'll start firing at 1100 and hit all the points. If any more of those little fuckers are observing us, we'll make it unhealthy for them. I want everyone under cover during the H&I. With artillery, you never know when something will go wrong."

"Don't worry. Those mortars made a believer out of me."

The H&I started right on time and it was big stuff. 155mm. The Seabees were all below ground but still got bounced. Most of the rounds hit within half a klick of the wire, some closer. One or two sounded like they hit further away toward the Khe village. The noise was uncomfortable and comforting at the same time. It was good to know that kind of power and destruction was just a radio call away.

As Tubby listened to round after round, memories of the attack on Dong Ha came back. He wondered what he and the crew would be going back to.

Chapter 20

The H&I finished up after forty-five minutes of bombardment. Hank gathered the Seabees and told them to move their personal gear into the command bunker. All of the A team was already moved in, but it was a big bunker with plenty of room available.

The rest of the day was spent fortifying the CIDG bunkers and building revetments for the equipment. The green berets were worried about the coming night. Since sappers had been messing with the outer perimeter in broad daylight, they must have been probing for weaknesses to use later, perhaps creating weaknesses for later use. The SF turned out and inspected the outer perimeter.

As expected, the wire was cut in several places while the mortars had diverted the attention of the defenders. The cuts had been carefully twisted back together and smeared with mud to hide the cuts. Repairs were made and extra ammunition was moved to the inner perimeter bunkers. Stout found Hank.

"I'm going to need your Seabees on the perimeter tonight, Hank. I want your people to man the section to the left of the gate. You and I will take the center bunker."

"Okay, not a problem. What time?"

"Have them in the bunkers by dark. Were your troops trained on the M79?"

"Sure. They aren't experts but they know how to shoot it."

"I'll issue one to every bunker with HE and shot rounds. Get them together around 1900 so we can go over what I expect of them."

"You got it."

It had been a long day with a lot of work and excitement. The dark came quickly with an overcast sky. The Seabees moved into the perimeter bunkers left of the gate and settled in for a long night.

Hank was having trouble keeping his eyes open. His mind just wanted to check out and rest for a while. All his life he had been the boss. Even as a kid he led the gang. It was just the way it had always been, but sometimes he got tired of being the boss. Others could slack-off, but he couldn't. He had almost fallen asleep during Stout's briefing at

1900.

Tubby was in the next fighting hole to the left of Hank and Stout and he was sulking. He was pissed that Stout was manning the center bunker with Hank. Hank was 6'4" tall and Tubby was 5'7" tall, but Tubby felt like he had to take care of Hank. Hank, with a big man's confidence, didn't even notice.

The first two hours after dark hadn't been too bad, but as the night went by without incident, Hank's eyes were drooping. Suddenly, Stout nudged him and spoke quietly.

"Hank, get on the horn and alert the perimeter, I do believe we have some company in the outer wire again."

Stout got on the radio and alerted the command bunker while Hank alerted the watch points on the field phone. The men on watch knew what to do. The dark was their friend right then and they wouldn't reveal their positions by firing at shadows or swirls in the fog or moving around unnecessarily. Stout had driven that point home during his briefing. The SF had trained the CIDG and the Seabees were happy to stay under cover and let the SF lead. Hank's section knew Stout was out there with them and would be standing a good watch.

"Where?" Hank asked.

Stout had his rifle resting on a sandbag and

sighting on the perimeter directly ahead. “Don’t worry about where. Watch your sector. Don’t fire on anything until I give the command. They don’t usually come alone.”

Hank peered into the dark and fog until his eyes started playing tricks on him. He flinched and tightened his hand on his rifle when a swirl of fog caught his attention out where the wire was. Moonlight made the fog look substantial when it swirled in the breeze. He looked slightly to the side of what he thought might be movement, but nothing moved. He began to relax again. It was just what Stout had drilled into them. Fog phantoms, he called them.

Hank hoped the rest of the crew were remembering their lessons. This was tense stuff for men who made their living hammering nails and operating heavy equipment no matter how many hours they had spent on the range or how many days in infantry training with the Marines at Pendleton and Lejeune.

The sky had cleared some with passing clouds and a bright moon peeking through. Then a gust of wind cleared the fog and Hank could see the wire, not clearly, but well enough to tell what it was. Then his eyes registered the small, dark shadow in the wire that shouldn’t be there. It was small at that distance, but in the moonlight without the fog, it was distinct. They had all stood enough perimeter watches staring intently at their sector to know exactly what normal looked like even in the dark, especially in the dark. That shadow didn't belong there and drew his eyes to it as surely as if it had a spotlight on it.

"Sergeant, look slightly to my right, in the wire. Something is there that shouldn't be."

Hearing his rank alerted Stout better than a shout. He and Hank had become buddies and never used rank.

"Alright, stay calm."

Stout moved behind and leaned over Hank's shoulder. "Put your sights on it."

Hank moved his rifle to point at the shadow. He couldn't see his sights, but he could point the whole rifle. "Right there, bottom of the wire. Shit! It moved."

"I see it. Good eyes. I'm calling for a flare."

Stout alerted the bunker that he had definite movement on the wire and requested one round of light. Hank cranked the field phone once and told the rest of the watch a flare was on the way and to get down low in their holes.

He heard the tubing sound from the 81mm mortar back by the Command bunker and a moment later the distinct pop of the flare igniting over them sounded. He began searching for the shadow again.

The light started as a wavering dim twilight and it was enough to see a man-shape run away from the wire toward he elephant grass. Stout's rifle barked and the moving shadow fell.

The flare reached its full brightness and night turned to day on the outer wire. "Keep your eyes on him," Stout said. "If anything moves you have permission to fire."

Stout notified the bunker of enemy contact and requested a squad of CIDG to reinforce the Seabees. Hank watched the place where the man fell, but he couldn't see him now. Light from the flare dimmed and finally disappeared completely. He couldn't see anything now. His night vision was gone.

"I can't see anything," he said.

"Just keep your rifle pointing where it was. Your night vision will come back soon. Stay alert. It was just a probe and I doubt anything else will happen. I'm going to check the watch and let them know a squad of CIDG will be coming in and doubling up with them."

"We know what we are doing too," Hank said.

"I don't doubt it, but I know what the defense group can do under fire. Your people haven't been in a serious firefight yet."

Stout left Hank alone in the bunker and the night got real tense. He still couldn't see the wire yet. He couldn't see more than a few feet beyond the bunker. He held his rifle right where he had it when he was covering the fallen intruder and waited for his vision to come back.

"Hank!" Tubby called. "Can you see anything?"

"Not yet. Keep quiet and don't give your position away."

Tubby was nervous, but he quieted down. Hank waited for his vision to return; It came back slowly. Soon he could make out the smudge in the dark that was the concertina outer perimeter, but the fog had moved back in and even the smudge disappeared. Now he had to contend with the fog phantoms again.

He was concentrating hard on the sector directly over his rifle when Stout returned silently and scared the hell out of him. "Damn, settle down, Hank. See anything else since I left?"

"No. I couldn't see anything until a few minute ago. Do you think he's still out there?"

"Hard to tell. If he was a sapper working alone, maybe. If not, his buddies will drag him away.

"What's a sapper?"

"Sort of like our Recon or Navy SEALs. Commando types. Don't see many of them. They seem to specialize in infiltration and getting through our perimeters. Pretty damn good soldiers. When it gets light, the engineers will inspect the wire to see what he was doing. Want to bet the wire has been cut again?"

"Hell, I don 't know enough about it to have an opinion. What do you think?"

"Yeah, I would bet it's cut. The only question in my mind is what else he was doing. Are you finishing up the towers tomorrow?"

"Yes. Not a whole lot left to do out here."

"Still want an RPD?"

"Hell yes.

"I figured out what I want in trade. Before you leave, can you rebuild our latrine and shower point in reinforced concrete? That would be worth an RPD to me."

"I don't see why not. I have one concrete man with me. The rest of us can pitch in. I'll need some rebar and ready-mix concrete flown in. We have enough scrap lumber to build the forms. It's not going to be big though. We can't mix that much concrete locally."

"How about just a two-hole shitter in concrete and use what's left of those big thick planks you sheathed the bunker in to enclose the showers? Those four-inch planks would stop a bullet and the concrete shitter would give us protection from mortar shrapnel if we get caught in there."

Hank thought about it for a moment. It sounded feasible.

"Yeah, I think we could do that. I don't have

any plans for that lumber."

"Sounds like a plan. Get it done and you are the proud new owner of a genuine SOG modified RPD."

"What the hell is a SOG?"

"You don't need to know, but they got the best armorers in Vietnam."

Chapter 21

Stout was wrong about nothing else happening that night. Near 3am one of the CIDG bunkers alerted the perimeter. They had definite probing on the outer perimeter. Two minutes later CIDGs on the other side of the camp alerted also. All the SF moved out to the CIDG bunkers and Stout made sure all the Seabees were awake.

The command bunker notified everyone the mortar would begin putting up light in one minute. A minute later the first flare round lit up the night on the other side of the camp. A moment later a round lit up the Seabee's side of the perimeter. Everyone concentrated on the outer wire looking for any sign of probing. Nothing. Not one damn thing out of normal.

Hank had helped construct the obstacles between the concertina fences so he wasn't seriously concerned about anyone getting through that killing field, but paid attention to the wire anyway. Stout was focusing on the outer wire and his shoulders were stiff and tight.

The flare dimmed out and disappeared. The dark returned again.

"Keep everyone in their holes and quiet," Stout said. "Keep your eyes on the tangle-foot and apron barrier. If they get inside, that's were trouble will start. I'll be right back. I want a starlight scope."

He was only gone for a few minutes and returned with his night optics. The starlight scope didn't have any magnification in size, but it amplified ambient light by about 10,000 times and gave the operator a green, twilight kind of picture of what was before him. Stout braced it on a sandbag and began examining every inch of the outer perimeter.

The mortars began ten minutes after Stout returned, but they weren't hitting the camp. The first incoming mortar round hit in the killing field between the inner and outer perimeters directly in front of Hank and Stout's bunker.

"Forget the mortars," Stout yelled. "Focus on the outer wire. Kill anything that moves out there." He got on the field phone and alerted the rest of the Seabees to do the same.

The 81mm by the command bunker put up

flares in the cardinal directions and the 81mm mortars in the CIDG area tried to get some counter battery on the NVA mortars as the SF advisors estimated their positions.

"Why are all the rounds falling short?" Hank yelled.

"They're right where the bastards want them. They're trying to open up a path through the obstacles to the inner perimeter. You can bet your ass a ground attack is coming. Get you asses ready."

Hank hardly heard the reply. Movement on the outer perimeter caught his attention and his breath caught in his throat. All along the wire, shadows were pulling the wire back. Those were real soldiers, not fog phantoms, and they were trying to get in. He knew now what the probes were for before the mortars started. Sappers had cut the wire into sections and it was now being pulled back like gates.

"Sarge! Sarge! They're pulling the concertina down!"

"Open fire, damn it!"

Stout got on the radio and notified the command bunker of the start of the ground attack.

Hank began emptying magazines into the outer wire. The rest of the Seabees followed his lead and opened up. The entire area between the two perimeters was lit up with outgoing red tracers that terminated in the outer concertina.

Other than the machine gun, this was his first real action and it was exciting and made his heart pound. He could hear Tubby laugh, but it was pure adrenalin, not humor. He tried to aim but he couldn't see his sights. Even the night firing exercises in training hadn't prepared him for this. With his excitement rising, he lost all fine muscle control and his finger jerked at the trigger. Then tracers started coming at him. Green ones. Suddenly incoming rounds hit all along the sandbags he was leaning against. He dropped to the bottom of the bunker, but Stout started yelling.

"Get up! Fire, damn it!

Hank eased up again and pushed his rifle over the sandbags and started pulling his trigger. The bolt locked back and he got confused. Why wasn't the damn thing firing? He kept pulling the trigger. Nothing happened. He started to panic.

"Change your magazine," Stout yelled and kept firing.

Hank stared at his rifle in confusion.

"The magazine. It's empty. Change the damn magazine!"

That got through the fog and he dropped the magazine and inserted a fresh one and released the bolt.

He squeezed his eyes shut. Settle down, he thought, and opened his eyes. He couldn't see the sights, but he could see the barrel. He started firing and watched his tracers. Okay, I've got it now, he thought. His blood was overloading with adrenalin.

More rounds hit the sandbags and one cracked next to his ear, but he stayed up this time and kept firing. His eyes were as wide as his lids would let them get. He was seeing with an acuity he had never experienced. Tubby let out a war cry and Hank yelled at the top of his lungs.

Stout was emptying magazines on automatic but stopped for a moment to look at Hank.

"Knock that shit off!"

Suddenly, the CIDG perimeter lit up with outgoing and the .50 caliber and M60 machineguns got in the act. The mortars had targets now and began dropping HE just outside the outer perimeter. Hank couldn't believe anything could survive that response.

"Use the grenade launcher," Stout commanded. "Drop HE right on them. Put it right in the wire."

Hank set his rifle down and broke open the M79 and dropped an HE round in the chamber and snapped it shut. He had fired M79s in training, but never in real battle. He used his left hand as a fulcrum to lever the piece up and down trying to estimate the angle. The sights were useless in the dark. Hell, with his lack of experience, trying to aim was useless anyway.

His first round was over. He raised the angle

to loop the round high in the air. That one was short and set off a mine.

"It's just a hundred yards, Hank. Aim a foot over their heads."

Hank loaded another HE and did as he was told. That one hit in the wire. While he was playing around with the range, Stout was on the field phone telling the other Seabee bunkers to use their M79s.

Soon, 40mm M79 rounds were dropping on top and on both sides of the wire. No shadows had made it inside the outer perimeter yet. Hank was so excited his hands were shaking and his breath was coming in gasps. Then the NVA mortars changed their elevation and the rounds began hitting along the inner perimeter. That got everybody's head down and the sappers didn't waste any time. Large explosions erupted at several points on the outer perimeter. When Hank looked up, large openings had been blown in the concertina.

"Fire into the openings," Stout yelled.

Then it got very busy for everyone. The enemy was still only shadows and muzzle flashes in the night a hundred yards away, but they were shooting now and the camp started taking casualties. Hank was pulled along with the craziness and lost track of what was going on around him. Fire. Break open the M79. Load a round. Elevate. Fire. Break open the M79. Load a round. The cycle seemed to go on endlessly. Then the M79 rounds were gone. He picked up his rifle.

A flare was up. He could see the wire dimly and the NVA even more dimly, several dead in the wire, but he had enough of an image to get a sight picture even though he didn't have the emotional stability to use it right then. This was his first battle and all he wanted to do was put rounds down range to keep them away. He wasn't firing blindly, but in his excitement pointing was the best he could do. Tracers helped when one came up.

He emptied a magazine on single fire and loaded another. Life was reduced to that simple sequence. Load, fire nineteen times. Load again. Stout slapped him on the back and broke the trance.

"Hank, we need ammunition. Go back to the command bunker and pick up as many bandoleers as you can carry. Grab some M79 too."

Just as he was about to crawl out of the bunker all incoming stopped. He looked out at the wire and all the shadows had disappeared.

"Go now and get back as fast as you can. This isn't over."

Hank had always enjoyed being the biggest guy in the room, but not now. He ran bent over but at 6'4" even bent over was a big target. Fortunately the NVA seemed to be taking a break.

The SF were using the command bunker as a rally and ammunition resupply point. Hank found a large pile of bandoleers filled with full 5.56mm magazines for the M16s and slid as many as he could over his arms and looked for some M79 40mm rounds. Two grenadier vests were next to the bandoleers. He grabbed both. He started back to the perimeter.

He was a hundred feet away when the mortars started again, but they were hitting between the perimeters again, setting off mines and destroying tangle-wire and apron fence. When they built those obstacles, he wondered how anything could ever get through it. Now he knew. The NVA were taking the killing field apart with mortars. How the hell many of them were out there?

Stout took several bandoleers and told Hank to distribute the rest among his team. He got back in time to watch a large section of apron fence in front of his bunker blown away and half a dozen buried mines exploded.

Chapter 22

The sappers had blown several holes in the outer perimeter wire with satchel charges and long pipe bombs similar to Bangalore torpedoes. Now their mortars, big ones, were taking apart the obstacles between the outer and inner perimeters. The ground troops were staying under cover and letting the mortars do their work.

The attack had been going on since the middle of the night and dawn was approaching. The SF prepared everyone for the first wave of ground attacks.

"How many are out there, Sarge?"

"A shit pot full," Stout said. "They didn't spend all this time softening us up for a company. They're NVA, not VC. Maybe a battalion, or more."

Some of the inner perimeter had holes in it

too. Most of the hooches were damaged again. A lot of shrapnel had blasted around the camp. The equipment would have to be checked out before it could be used again, especially the hydraulic hoses, that is, if the camp was still there when this was over. Stout listened to a call on the radio for a moment.

"Get on the horn and tell your people some big stuff is on the way in," Stout said.

Even though Hank was close to exhaustion from the pace of the battle and stress, Stout didn't seem overly concerned, not like he should be if a battalion of enemy were about to come through the wire.

"Artillery?"

"Yeah. They should be concentrated in waves by now. It's time to bust up their party before they can get off the dime."

A moment later the first of the 155mm artillery rounds from the fire support base hit not far outside the outer perimeter. Then it was hold on to your hat. The artillery circled the camp and then moved outward hitting and saturating preregistered boxes identified by the SF and considered good assembly points or avenues of approach. Next, rounds rained down on points that had been used for camps by the NVA, points discovered by the CIDG patrols.

The artillery was still coming in when the

sun came up, but it was more random then and getting further away. The enemy ground assault had not materialized and Hank understood why Stout had not been in panic mode. Artillery blasts had extended the cleared field of fire outside the outer perimeter by another hundred meters in some places. Where thick jungle had been, now was broken trees, craters, and red dirt. But the cleared space between the perimeters was a mess of exploded earth, tangled wire heaved up in jumbled piles, and expended shrapnel glinting in the sun.

"We're going to need your help putting the perimeter back together," Stout said.

"Do you think there's anything left alive out there?"

"You'd be surprised. That was good artillery coverage, but my money says most of the NVA are gone and made it back into Laos. They were testing our defenses. I don't think they're ready to pay the price they'd have to pay to overrun the camp, but you never know. We have to get the perimeter rebuilt today, Hank. They won't wait for dawn if they come back tonight. Drop everything else and put everybody and all the equipment on the perimeter. Make sure all your operators keep their flak jackets on. We may still have some snipers out there."

The SF sent out recon teams made up of two SF and

six CIDG to see what damage had been done and see if there was any sign of enemy remaining in the area. Hank met with his crew and quartered the perimeter into assigned areas for their efforts that day. The SF remaining in camp divided up the rest of the CIDG and all hands turned to on reconstructing the perimeter.

Stretching concertina to fill the gaps blown in the wire by the sappers was the easiest and safest job and went quickly. The outer wire was complete by 0800. Then the dangerous work began and Hank teamed his Seabees with SF counterparts to begin reconstructing the apron fence and tangle-wire. It was dangerous because most of that area was already mined and the NVA bombardment had not blown all the mines. Using their minefield maps, the SF had to figure out where it was safe to work and what to abandon to fate and future attacks.

Even with the risk of working in previously mined areas, the work went quickly. The Seabees had learned lessons from the initial construction and quickly put those lesson to work rebuilding. By 1500 the apron fence and tangle-foot was repaired and SF were planting new mines and installing pop flares and noise makers in the outer wire. Sections of the old pattern were marked with fence and red tie-on flags where it was just too dangerous to work and the new obstacles were built around them. New safe lanes were marked on the maps and the SF pulled everyone out of the killing field.

One of the recon patrols returned around 1530 and they seemed to be excited or panicked. Both of the SF from the team ran to the command bunker. A few minutes later LT Taylor, the team combat medic, and Stout came out of the bunker in full combat gear. Stout came directly to Hank.

"Get your flak jacket, helmet, and rifle," he said. "I want you to go with us. The recon team said the Khe village took some incoming. I need you to see what it's going to take to fix things up."

"I'll be right there. Tubby, bring plenty of ammunition and some grenades."

Tubby brightened immediately. He thought he was going to be left behind again.

Hank, Tubby, and the SF with a platoon of CIDG left the wire at 1545. Lieutenant Taylor had received reports from all his recon teams and didn't expect to run into any NVA. All signs pointed to a mass and fast exodus to Laos for the NVA, but a small ambush was always possible. The patrol moved quickly through the jungle with scouts out, but they moved cautiously.

They skirmished to the edge of the village and observed for a few minutes before moving in. It didn't look good. The large community hut was destroyed and craters pockmarked the ground throughout the village. Hank wondered why the

NVA had attacked an innocent and unarmed village.

Chapter 23

Hank stayed with the medic as they entered the village and Tubby stayed with Hank. He was in full commando mode and locked and loaded. Hank began smelling an odor he hadn't smelled before, like burnt hamburger only more repulsive. It wasn't long before he lost his breakfast. The first of the burnt storage huts contained a half dozen burnt and ripped apart bodies. The smell hit him full force and he just managed to get bent over before everything came up.

Staff Sergeant Benton looked once and turned away. He slapped Hank on the back and said, "Come on. It's going to get worse. By the size of those craters, it was our own artillery did this."

Hank was having trouble dealing with the shock of seeing all those bodies. His first thought, when he could think again, was about the little girl.

Where was Peanut?

They approached the wreckage of the community hut and could hear the flies from a hundred feet away. Bodies decomposed quickly in jungle heat. The smell started fifty feet away. It can't be compared to anything else. Nothing compares to the repulsive sweet smell of many decomposing human bodies in a small area. The whole structure was demolished. They would have to look through the wreckage for survivors. Benton wasn't hopeful.

The rest of the patrol came to the wreckage and LT Taylor divided the area up into search sectors and assigned teams to go through the rubble. He sent patrols into the surrounding jungle to see if any of the villagers made it to cover somewhere close by. Hank and Tubby were assigned to a patch near the center of the community hut. Fires were smoldering in different places and threatened to reignite at any moment.

The work was slow and had to be methodical. The men worked together lifting one piece of rubble at a time. Hank was pulling up a piece of thatching from the roof when he heard a whimper, just a terrified little cry. He started throwing thatch and rafter wood out of the way. Something was alive under the rubble. He got to one of the heavier roof beams and didn't even slow down. He squatted, wrapped his arms around the beam and straightened his legs letting out a loud groan. The beam came up and he walked it away from the opening. He turned quickly to see what was making the noise.

There was Peanut sitting on the ground between two adult bodies, but it wasn't the happy little Peanut he remembered. She was shattered.

That was the only word he could think of, shattered. Her body appeared whole and he couldn't see any bleeding, but she was shattered. Her little arms were held out waving around aimlessly, no pattern or control to it. She sat staring at him and twitching and trying to smile, but it was a horrified little smile that ripped his heart apart. The lips were formed, but the eyes were staring in silent horror that only an innocent, terrified baby could feel. She only managed quick little twitches of the mouth that turned quickly into silent screams. Her eyes were wide open in permanent panic and darted around looking for the next horror. Quite whimpers escaped her lips and small tears wet her eyes. Her body was intact, but her spirit was shattered.

"Oh God, no" Tubby said.

Hank's heart broke as he reached out for her. Her eyes and expression jumped between sanity that begged not to be hurt, and a panic that caused her to gasp air into her lungs at every loud sound.

He got her in his big hands and pulled her up into his arms and snuggled her into his chest and arms. She could only twitch and make mewing sounds. He couldn't even imagine what she had gone through. How many of the big artillery rounds had hit the village? How long had she lain there between the bodies of her parents? Each time she mewed, he felt like someone had kicked him in the gut. He held her tight and walked out of the wreckage hardly able to see for the tears in his eyes.

"Let me have her, Hank," Benton said. "I've got to check her out."

"I'll hold her. You check her. I'm not letting her go."

"Come on, Hank. I know what I'm doing. You've got to continue the search. There may be others alive in there."

Hank didn't want to release her. She was his Peanut. She had chosen him over all the SF and CIDG. But he knew Benton was right. SF combat medics are as close to being doctors as you can get without a medical degree, and there still might be others alive.

He tried to hand Peanut to Benton, but she had his neck now and wouldn't let go. She panicked when he tried to pry her loose and started mewing loudly. Her twitching got really bad. She was going to come completely apart. He pulled her back tight against his chest and held her.

"Do what you can," he said. "I can't let her go. I'm sorry. I can't let her go."

"Okay, buddy," Tubby said quietly. "Take it easy. You hold her but open your arms one at a time so the medic can examine her."

Hank started to snap at his friend, but when he looked, Tubby had tears in his eyes and they were dripping down his cheeks.

Benton managed to get her examined without sending her into total panic. Hank had become her safe place and she couldn't stand to be separated from him. Two other survivors were found and Benton moved off to check them out. Hank held Peanut tightly and rocked back and forth. He talked quietly to her hoping to break through her panic and bring her back to something resembling a normally frightened child. She was way beyond that. For her, there were only the horrible sounds in her head and Hank.

Later, he didn't know how long, Stout sat next to him.

"Some of the CIDG found a group of villagers that made it into the jungle and found some cover. They're bringing them in. Maybe some of her family is with them."

"I'm not letting her go. I'm all she has. She's shattered, Sarge."

"Hank, she's a baby. She belongs here. What would you do with her anyway?"

"She'll get better. We can find an orphanage

or something. I can't just leave her here. We did this to her."

"Easy, buddy. Shit like this happens in a war. It ain't right and it ain't pretty, but it happens. This is her home. We can't stay here much longer."

Stout looked around and then looked at the baby again. "Shit! We'll take them all back to camp and see what can be done for them."

"I'll carry her back."

"Okay. Let me have her while you put your flak jacket back on."

Hank managed to get her away from his neck and into Stout's arms. He held her with her little arms waving around and her eyes wide open and darting around. Hank couldn't tell if she was even seeing what was around her. He got his flak jacket on and his rifle slung. As soon as he took her back she clung to his neck. He loosened his flak jacket and pulled her against his chest.

A small group of children and adults were led into the wrecked village by the CIDG. They stood quietly and looked around. Everything they had ever known was gone, just wreckage and destruction were left. A woman saw Hank holding the baby and approached him and held out her arms.

He turned so Peanut could see the woman. He waited to see if the baby was able to comprehend what was in front of her.

She lifted her head off Hank's chest and

stared at the woman for a moment.

The twitching continued, but she leaned away from Hank and he handed her into the woman's arms. She was quickly cuddled into female arms and the mewing ceased.

He didn't understand why, but he felt an awful loss.

Chapter 24

The light was failing when the patrol with the surviving villagers approached the gate to the camp. The camp was on full alert and LT Taylor took them in carefully. A helicopter was on the landing pad, but everything else looked the same as before the attack. Hank and Benton took the survivors to the Khe section of the camp and put them in a reinforced bunker. Several of the Khe CIDG built a fire and began cooking a meal for the survivors.

The villagers were resilient if nothing else. The two women survivors immediately began helping with the meal, one with Peanut hanging on her neck. Hank watched for a moment and then walked back to the Seabee camp feeling empty and exhausted. War was no longer exciting or an adventure. It was a place where babies were shattered.

Clark, Thompson, Kaufman and two builders were in the bunker working out plans for erecting the towers. That was comforting in a way. No matter what else happened, the job still had to get done. At first Hank just wanted some private time for himself, time to figure it all out, but his team depended on him. He'd deal with his own feelings later. He got an update on the day's work and got involved in planning the next day's work. Stout stopped at the bunker to talk with Hank.

"Hank, we're on full alert again tonight. Everyone on the perimeter. Not sure what's going to happen. How are you doing?"

"I'm good. Sorry about how I acted at the village. I just . . . I don't know. I just couldn't leave that little girl."

Stout laid his hand on Hank's arm.

"Don't let it bother you. I've seen some bad situations working with the indigs, but I'll admit, that's about the worst I've ever seen. We've got a couple majors from Fifth Group here to investigate the incident, but hell, it's war, damn it. Somehow the no-fire zone got mixed up in the preregistered free-fire zones. When a thousand things are happening at the same time, and your life is on the line, shit happens. Wish it weren't that way, but it is. One more nightmare to add to the rest that will keep me awake in the future."

"How about tonight? What happens if we

need artillery again?"

"It will be there. Everything is being double checked, but they won't hesitate. Our lives depend on it. It might sound horrible to think about it like this, but there aren't any villages in our artillery fan now."

Hank wasn't really listening.

"I don't think I'll ever get over this." he said. "I keep seeing Peanut's eyes."

"Peanut?"

"Yeah, the little girl. That's what I named her. She's hardly bigger than a peanut. I still feel like somebody kicked me in the gut."

Stout looked out at the perimeter and was silent for a moment.

"Wish I could tell you it gets easier," he said finally. "That's not my experience. Seeing the enemy die is one thing, but when innocents are hurt, that's hard, especially when they are children."

Hank continued to stare out at the wire. He didn't want to look at Stout. He had a hard time keeping the tears back.

"Thanks for not trying to sugarcoat it," he said. "I don't think I could handle sympathy right now." He took a deep breath. There was work to get done so they could get out of this place of death. "Well, enough of this. We're going to start on the towers in the morning if we're still here."

Stout laughed. It was forced, but at least he

tried. "We'll be here. Make sure you bring plenty of ammunition to the bunker with you. I have a feeling it's only going to be probes on the wire tonight, but you can never tell. They'll want to know how well we recovered before they try a ground attack again. One thing is for sure. They know we have teeth now."

"All right, let me get this schedule done and make sure the materials are in place. Are we together again?"

"Yeah. Taylor wants me to stay with the Seabees."

Hank wrote a letter to his wife that evening and told her about the little girl. He shared all his feelings and anguish with her in the letter. He didn't know why he did that. He had vowed he would keep the unpleasant stuff to himself so she wouldn't worry, but he felt better after he did. He put the letter in the mail bag in the command bunker.

He worked for a while designing the concrete latrine for Stout. The rebar and concrete were in. He wasn't sure he had enough rebar to complete the job, but he'd leave that to Tubby. He was the rebar man. At 2100 Clark and Thompson came by to gab.

"How much longer are we going to be here,?" Thompson asked.

"Hell, I can't remember how long we've

been here. What's the date?"

"It's the fifteenth. We've been here a month already."

"I want to add another job to the schedule, but it's a one-day effort if we all turn-to. The SF want us to build them a reinforced concrete latrine. The material is in so it won't take long. If we don't get any more delays, I think we can wrap it up here in about a week."

"Well," Clark said, "I won't be sorry to see this place from the door of the bird taking us back to Dong Ha."

"Me too," Hank said. "You guys make sure everybody loads up on rifle and M79 ammunition. I don't want to make another ammo run while we're getting incoming."

"I hope we can get some damn sleep tonight," Clark said. "I've been fighting or working for twenty-four hours. I won't be in shape to operate equipment tomorrow without some sleep."

"Flip for first watch," Hank said. "You decide how you want to do it. Just make sure everybody gets some rest."

Stout took the first watch. Hank was beat both physically and emotionally. His fatigue was almost overwhelming and he would have been useless on the first watch. He was amazed at how quickly he was becoming accustomed to something as frightening as knowing people who wanted nothing more than to kill him were maybe just a hundred yards away. It had only been a few weeks since the most dangerous thing he faced was the California freeways.

He squirmed in the dirt at the bottom of the bunker trying to find a comfortable position. That was another thing. Sleeping in the dirt. It no longer seemed unusual. It took millions of years for humans to advance to innerspring mattresses, he thought. But it only takes weeks to sink back into the dirt again. For just a moment he thought he was experiencing something profound and wanted to take it further, figure it out, but it slipped away as fatigue took over and his brain shut down.

Later he struggled through mud, struggled to get away from something dark and dangerous coming through the wire. He couldn't see it or hear it, but it was there, and it was awful, coming forward and he couldn't run. His legs were stuck in deep mud, his boots were being sucked down, and he just couldn't make them move faster. He pulled with his arms, grunting, trying . . .

"Hank! Wake up."

The shock of sudden consciousness made his heart race. He looked around in panic.

"Get up, damn it. We've got company on the wire."

Hank felt around in the dark and found his rifle. He slid up the side of the bunker and looked out at the night through the firing port. His eyes were already adjusted to the dark from sleep and he could see all the way to the outer perimeter. It was lighter than the night before. Pale moonlight made the scene in front of him glow.

Stout was using the starlight scope and holding it steady on one point on the perimeter.

"Take the scope and keep your eye on that fucker. I'm going to take him out."

Stout held the scope steady and let Hank slip in behind it. He pressed his face into the gasket that kept the screen from illuminating his face. He knew he was looking for a man figure and found the target quickly.

"Got him," he said.

"Keep your eye on him. Once I fire, I won't be able to see."

Hank watched. The sapper was flat on the ground and pushing something under the wire. Stout fired without warning and his muzzle flash blanked the screen on the scope for a moment, but it cleared in just a few seconds. A dark, still shadow lay below the wire.

"I think you got him. He's not moving."

"I can just see the shadow," Stout said. "Keep your eye on him. I'm going to make sure."

Stout fired again and the screen washed out

and cleared again. The shadow was moving back away from the wire.

"He's moving. You missed."

"Bullshit. I don't miss a stationary target at a hundred meters. Keep your eye on him. If he's moving, somebody is moving him."

Sure enough, Hank saw a second shadow bent over the first. Stout's rifle fired again. When the screen cleared there were two shadows on the ground.

"Okay, you got the other one."

Suddenly it occurred to Hank he was talking about two human lives, not shadows. He pushed the thought away. It was easier to think about them as shadows.

"Stay down. I'm calling for a flare."

When the flare popped, the bodies could be seen without the scope. They were clearly human bodies. Hank watched them waiting for the guilt to come, but it didn't. Two points for our side, he thought.

Chapter 25

The rest of the night was quiet and Stout let Hank get some extra sleep. He also let most of the Seabees get extra sleep by keeping only one up with him and allowing them to work out how they wanted to share the watch. The probe near midnight was the only activity other than CIDG shooting at fog phantoms. Hank woke up stiff and hungry and ready to kill for some coffee, but all that had to wait.

It was 0400 and Stout was waking everyone and getting them alert. This was the witching hour, the hour when the NVA would attack if they planned to attack at all. Everyone in camp was on the perimeter and ready. He released the magazine in his rifle and made sure he had a full one. That was just nervous energy. He hadn't fired the weapon all night.

The SF weren't taking any chances after the aborted attack the previous day. Stout told everyone to stay low in their holes. The LT had called in a pattern of artillery to start the day.

"Here it comes," Stout shouted. "Stay down."

Damn it was close. The big 155mm rounds began hitting not far outside the outer perimeter and walked right around the camp. Hank felt every damn explosion. After the tenth one hit, Stout shouted, " That's it. Stay down. If anything is going to happen it's got to happen now."

They waited. And waited. No movement. No NVA. No incoming.

"All right," Stout said. "Turn your men loose to get some chow. Let's see if there's some coffee in the bunker."

It was absolutely crazy. Like getting off a night shift at some job. Work's done. Let's get some coffee. It was surreal. Hank got the crew moving and told Thompson he'd meet him at the site for the first tower in an hour. He and Stout went looking for coffee and C-Rats.

Coffee was on and it was brewed coffee. The SF lived well. Hank got a cup and a box of C-Rats and joined Stout and Tubby outside. The camp was coming to life and cooking fires were smoking in the CIDG camp.

From the corner of his eye he saw Benton running toward the CIDG camp with a CIDG soldier. He had his medical pack. Hank thought about Peanut.

"I'll be right back," he said and started running.

As Hank approached the CIDG camp, Sergeant Benton ran into the bunker where the village survivors were staying.

Oh no, he thought.

He spotted her as he came through the door. The baby was on a blanket. She wasn't moving, just staring at the ceiling through wide open eyes. She wasn't twitching. She wasn't mewing. She wasn't making a sound. Hank felt a horrible pain in his chest.

"Let me have her. Get out of the way. Let me have her."

He pushed his way past Benton and the woman and grabbed the baby up in his arms. He hugged her to his chest and spoke softly to her. He walked around the bunker holding her, speaking to her, but she didn't respond in any way.

"Hank," Benton said softly. "Hank, put her down. You can't help her now."

"She just needs to feel secure, that's all. She'll be alright when she feels safe again."

"Hank. It's too late. She's dead. Put her down."

Something snapped in Hank and he screamed at Benton.

"She's just scared, damn it! You're a medic. Your supposed to save people. Save her." But he knew better. There was no warmth in her skin. The anger subsided as fast as it came. The Khe woman pulled at his sleeve and Hank looked at her with tears in his eyes. She held her arms out and Hank gave her the baby. She laid her back on the blanket. Peanut still stared through unseeing eyes.

"How?" Hank asked.

"The woman says it was the noise from the artillery," Benton said. "She never recovered from yesterday. Probably cardiac arrest. You okay?"

"No," he said and just stared at the tiny body. The Khe woman tugged on his sleeve again and motioned for him to bend down. She put her hand softly on his cheek and left it there for a moment. Her eyes were brown and wide and understanding. Then she nodded at him and patted his hand.

Somehow that simple gesture of understanding eased the awful grief he was feeling. Except for a very few survivors, her entire village was gone, her entire life, but she had enough compassion and empathy to know what Hank was feeling and was able to share a moment with him. He reached out and pulled her into his big arms. It was like hugging a child, but he held her for a moment and then left the bunker.

Stout somehow already knew about the baby when Hank returned. Tubby just touched Hank's shoulder and handed him a cup of coffee. The cup was full of fresh coffee. Another simple gesture that eased the pain. Stout left him to work through his feelings with Tubby.

Working through feelings wasn't what Hank wanted. He had failed to save the baby. He needed work. He needed to push his big, powerful body to its limits. He'd had enough destruction. He needed to build something. He needed to do something and not fail.

Thompson had the rest of the crew already working on the tower. The design was simple, familiar, and repetitive. The crew had already cut the timbers from jigs and staged the materials at the site. The tower would go up like an erector set. It was what Hank needed. Mindless and mind-numbing labor.

He stripped to the waist and laid his shirt across his shoulder and squatted next to one end of a 6"x6"x12' timber. He lifted and walked it up in the air until he could balance it on his shoulder. As the other end came off the ground and the full weight of the beam pressed down on his shoulder his knees buckled just a bit, but he groaned and straightened and walked the beam to the assembly point. He didn't say a word, but no instructions were needed. The rest of the crew sensed his distress and worked silently. That was the beginning of probably the fastest tower assembly ever performed by a four-man crew.

It was close to 1300 when Hank finished tightening the last big nut on the last big bolt to lock in the final beam on the top stage of the tower. The observation bunker at the top of the tower was thirty-six feet above the ground and Hank stood there looking out over the jungle. He was covered with sweat and dirt. His crew was resting from the awful, grief driven pace he had set. His shoulders and arms were raw with scrapes and digs from rough cut timbers rubbing bare skin and from sunburn, but his spirit was calm. Life has many problems that have no solutions. Sometimes we break things that can't be fixed. Hard work and building something new was Hank's way of moving on and dealing with things that can be fixed. He failed to fix peanut.

While half the crew started cutting and drilling timbers for the second tower, Hank and Tubby began constructing the forms for the new latrine from scrap wood. Hank was experiencing the emotional dissonance a lot of Seabees must go through in the mixed-up world of combat construction. Seabee casualty rates were lower than for most combat units. Except for the security platoons, Seabees didn't go out on patrol or seek out the enemy, but they often worked where the enemy sought out Americans and they did suffer casualties. They had to learn to deal with the dissonance of having to be combat troops occasionally and immediately revert to their role as builders. Destroy or build, the work had to get done.

Whether it was a rocket or mortar attack, ground attack, or just a sniper trying to shoot them off their equipment, they had to get their minds back on the job no matter what had just happened. Seabees weren't sent out on optional work. They were there because the work they were doing was necessary, absolutely necessary.

Still, the transition was difficult. Hank learned a lesson all combat troops have to learn. He learned there was a place in the back of his mind where he could move emotions and memories so he could focus on what needed to get done now. The problem with that was when he put those memories and emotions away, he put a small part of himself away with them. There was a price for that to be paid later, but that was later.

Chapter 26

Except for Stout, Benton, and LT Miller, Hank and his Seabees hadn't had much to do with the rest of the SF at Bu Duc. It wasn't that there was any animosity between them. They just didn't cross paths that much even in such a small camp. Most of the A Team worked directly with the CIDG and patrolled constantly. There were others connected to the camp the Seabees had no contact with at all.

The next day, as Hank was finishing up the forms for the latrine, an all-black Huey slick landed on the pad and shut down. Two men in what Hank thought of as Ramar of the jungle clothes, sans safari helmets, were greeted by LT Miller and led to the command bunker. A small Vietnamese man got off the helicopter and followed them. Four green berets appeared and started unloading boxes from the bird. Hank was focused on finishing up the forms and forgot about them.

Tubby was setting up and wiring the reinforcing rods. “Bet that’s the spooks,” he said.

“Might be. They don’t look like soldiers. Wonder who the Vietnamese guy is.”

“Maybe it’s Ho Chi Minh and he wants a concrete shitter too,” Tubby said and laughed.

Later over lunch Hank asked Stout about the visitors.

“Yeah, that’s the agency,” he said. “Forget about them. They are not bearers of glad tidings. Whenever they show up, shit is about to hit the fan. How’s the latrine coming?”

“The forms are done. As soon as the rebar is wired we can start mixing and pouring. You are going to have a Cadillac shitter my friend. You got my RPD?

“And two drum magazines. One fifty and one hundred-round drum compliments of the Team. We do appreciate your shitter expertise. I can give you four-hundred rounds of ammunition, but that’s it. You’ll have to find your own ammunition after you use it up.”

“What’s it take?”

“Same round as the AK47. Find a VC and take his ammunition.”

Hank grunted.

“Once I get the hell out of Bu Duc, I don’t

plan to get close to any VC."

Stout grinned and slapped Hank on the back.

"Good luck. They don't always give you a choice."

Hank was silent for a few moments, thinking.

"You know, that's true," he said. "Hadn't thought about it before, but that's true anywhere, isn't it? Here, back in civilian life, any place. If an enemy, any enemy, even a mugger or psychopath, chooses to attack you, no matter how much you want to remain peaceful, you don't get a choice. You can surrender or just accept fate, but you can't really opt out. It's fucked up, but only the attacker has a choice."

"Yep, unless you're armed better than him. Overwhelming firepower lets me sleep well at night. Well, I better go see what brilliant idea the fucking agency has come up with now."

Clark used the forklift to move a ready-mix pallet to the latrine site and returned to get the mixer. Thompson used the loader to tow the water buffalo to the site. Hank chose to do the labor himself, mixing and carrying buckets of concrete to the men on the forms who did the pour. He was still working strong feelings out of his system.

They mixed and poured the walls by 1700 and Hank was glistening with sweat and almost white from the Portland that escaped the mixer and coated his skin. His ears were ringing from standing next to the gas engine that powered the mixer. Sitting under the spigot, he used the water buffalo as his shower and managed to get the cement off his skin before it could burn him. He was starving and he was calm. Hard work always balanced him and concrete work is as hard as it gets.

The black helicopter wound up and the CIA men ran to the pad and loaded. It lifted off and disappeared to the west. Hank went to the bunker to get some C-Rats and was pleasantly surprised. The utilitymen had piped water to the bunker and a Vietnamese man was cooking a meal in a room that had become the kitchen.

The aromas made his mouth water. Food, real food. Garlic and spices. Lord it smelled good. Stout slapped him on the shoulder.

"Tell your men to wash up and get over here. Nguyen is cooking up enough to feed all of us."

"Damn, it smells good."

"Ribeye steaks, baked potatoes and some kind of Vietnamese salad. Hard to tell what will be in the salad. Sometimes he thinks bugs are food. And I almost forgot. Beer, real six-point-zero Bud. None of that 3.2 shit they serve in the clubs."

"How . . . Where . . .?"

"The agency did their good deed for the day.

Course they want something, but hell, they always want something. At least we're getting a good meal out of it. And Nguyen is here to stay. He's the Team cook and goes with us. We had to leave him behind until we had things pretty well livable. There will be eggs to order in the morning. Get your boys over here."

Hank ate two twelve-ounce stakes, two potatoes, and washed it all down with three cans of Bud. He decided to forgo the salad when he saw something in it he couldn't identify. Suddenly his world was sunny again and the future looked bright. Amazing what a belly full of steak and beer can do for your outlook.

While he was eating, Thompson had remarked they hadn't had a single round of incoming all day, not even small arms. Maybe the NVA decided this camp wasn't a nut they wanted to crack yet. He could hope.

"How much more have you got to do?" Stout asked.

"We'll pour the roof for the latrine in the morning and I'll do the woodwork. The crew will put the east tower up. We'll start disassembling the equipment for movement when the tower is up and Phu Bai can begin flying it out. We should be out of here in three days."

Stout reached behind him and lifted a

modified RPD to his lap.

"Take care of this like it's a baby, Hank. You leave it alone in Dong Ha for ten seconds and some jarhead will steal it. This baby was modified by SOG armorers. It's balanced and is probably the best submachine gun in the world. Want to take it down by the wire an try it out?"

"Damn right I do! I need a little OJT."

"Come on. Grab those drums. I'll show you how to clean it when we're done."

On the way to the wire Tubby spotted them.

"What are you going to do with that thing, Hank?"

"Want to fire my new machine gun? Come on."

"Hot damn. Bet your ass I do."

Hank was surprised at how light the gun was. It was heavier than the M16, but lighter than the M14. That is, without the 100-round drum attached.

He had loved well-made tools since he was a boy, and the RPD was a well-made tool. It just felt good in his hands, like a well-balanced, high-quality hammer. The one Stout gave him was significantly modified from the original though. The barrel was shortened to 17.5 inches and the stock was cut off behind the pistol grip, so it was short enough to be comfortable slung on his shoulder and the balance was perfect for firing on a sling from the hip. It didn't have sights and wasn't meant for long range accuracy. It was a firehose of fire power. The SF used it as an ambush buster.

"I'm not going to make you an expert," Stout said. "But I'll make you proficient enough to fire it safely. First of all some statistics you can remember if you want. The RPD is produced by the Russians and Chinese. This one is Russian. It fires the 7.62x39mm Warsaw round at six hundred fifty to seven-hundred-fifty rounds per minute adjustable with the three-position gas adjustment valve. The standard version with the full-sized barrel has a muzzle velocity of twenty-four-hundred feet per second. This one, because of the shortened barrel, has a muzzle velocity of about two-thousand feet per second. Don't worry about it. You'll never know the difference."

Stout demonstrated as he continued.

"It feeds ammunition from the left, right here, with a metallic, open-link, non-disintegrating belt usually holding one hundred rounds, but fifty round belts are available, or you can just snap one apart to make your own. The weapon fires fully automatic only. There is no single fire option. Once you are used to the trigger you will probably get where you can tap out singles and two round bursts though. The major flaw in the weapons system is the drum magazine. As you can see, it is just a medal belt holder and can become clogged with dirt in bad conditions if you're not careful."

Stout was in his classroom mode. He was the team's weapons man and must have stood before classes of green berets giving this same speech a hundred times or more. He obviously knew it by heart.

"The weapon is a gas operated, long-stroke piston, hammer fired machine gun that fires from an open bolt position. The chamber and bore are chrome-line making it easy to maintain and slow to jam or corrode. It has a two position manually operated safety lever. Okay enough of that. Let's load this baby up and shoot something. Lift the feed cover and slide the belt into the feed tray. The first thing you need to learn is trigger control. Try for four-round bursts. Just a quick tap of the trigger. The Russians make a tough barrel, but you can burn it up with long bursts. This thing has a permanent barrel. It's not like an M-sixty or M-two. You can't replace your barrel if you burn it out."

Hank burned through a hundred rounds a burst at a time, getting the feel of the trigger. Tubby was in his glory as he burned through another hundred-round belt. The gun was fun to fire and Hank would have liked to continue, but Stout was anxious to finish with the OJT and Hank had work to do.

Chapter 27

The final job was damming up the spring to create a pool of fresh water to support the camp's needs, running the filtered main feedpipe to the water point and making the connections to the latrine showers and the kitchen of the command bunker. This place was going to be a Special Forces home far from any American base and they planned to live as well as they could. Artillery might take the whole damn thing out at any time, but until then, they were going to have comforts Marines could only dream about.

Hank's utilityman had jury-rigged a gravity fed water connection to the kitchen, but now it was time to get everything connected to the pump. The backhoe was digging the ditches for the pipe and two men were constructing the pump bunker. Even though the area would never experience freezing temperatures, the pipes had to be buried three feet below ground. The problem wasn't freezing here. It was incoming artillery.

The pump system was needed because a water tower would be just too much of a temptation for the VC. Hank felt a pressurized system would probably last about a week, but it was what the SF wanted and they had the pump and the generators to run it.

The EO's and the CM were disconnecting the blade from the dozer and preparing it for movement. The crane and forklift were ready and in place to be lifted out. The backhoe would be prepped as soon as the ditches were covered. All the authorized work was complete as well as one unauthorized job, the latrine. That night was the Seabees last night in Bu Duc.

Five weeks on that hill had changed Hank. His gentle nature had calluses now, and he had memories he had to suppress to keep depression from setting in. Soldiers and Marines experienced much worse, but he wasn't a soldier or a Marine. He was a carpenter. He built things, things that made people happy, that protected them, homes and places to work. He decided getting close to natives, especially kids, was not a good idea. It just hurt too damn much.

Stout and LT Miller found him at the pump bunker.

"The bird to take your crew back to Dong Ha will be in tomorrow," Miller said. "Your guys did one hell of a job here, Tuck. I want you to know I sent a letter of commendation up through Fifth Group. When you wrap up the work, you guys cool it. Your time on the perimeter is over. We're having steak and beer again tonight. Enjoy it and get some rest."

Hank did a quick inspection of the equipment by the landing pad. There was a lot of shrapnel damage, but most of it was superficial. His CM had repaired damage to hydraulic systems and did what he could for the structural damage. Hank was glad he was turning the equipment back to the Army. If it was Seabee equipment it would have to pass a much tougher inspection before he could turn it back in. With only one previous inspection, the Army was taking it back no questions asked.

At the end of the day another pleasure awaited. The showers were working. His final shower at Bu Duc wouldn't be under the spigot of a water buffalo. He wondered how long that simple luxury would last. Even with buried pipes, the system couldn't last long if the camp continued to receive incoming like they had the night of the big attack, and that was just mortars. If the NVA decided to get serious and used the big 152mm artillery Dong Ha got, three feet of dirt wasn't going to protect the pipes. Well, it wasn't his problem. This wasn't civilian life and the system didn't come with a warranty against artillery.

Finally around 1800, the work was done. Hank and the crew enjoyed a beer together outside the command bunker and talked about the previous five weeks. They all felt like it had been much longer than that. Five weeks ago they had landed at the bottom of the hill and started moving equipment up a creek bed to a raw site covered with downed trees. Now that site held an underground command bunker that could withstand a direct hit from artillery, hardback hooches, boardwalks between all important points, two massive guard towers, and a perimeter that could resist a battalion. And they had running water from the pump and electricity from two bunkered diesel generators.

Knowing they would load on a bird in the morning and head back to new jobs at Dong Ha lightened the mood and the jokes started. The A Team joined them and it wasn't long before everyone was buzzed.

Stout and Miller got Hank aside to talk. Miller handed Hank a brass coin. It had a banner across the top with 5th Special Forces Group and a Special Forces shield in the center.

"What's this?"

"That's a Fifth Group challenge coin, Hank. Keep it with you for luck. If you're ever in a spot and need a friend and SF are around, hand one of them that coin. You will have an instant friend. We don't hand them out to everybody. Only people who have gone above and beyond the normal for us and have proved they can be depended on get them. Each of your troops are getting one too."

"Well, damn. Thanks. We didn't do anything special though. Hell, we're Seabees. We build things."

"You damn near got your asses shot off too," Stout said. "You boys hung in there on the perimeter and I appreciate it. That coin lets any SF troop you show it to know you've been in the shit with the SF. You don't have to explain. They know what it means."

"Well, thanks again. I'll keep it with me. You sure you don't need us standing watches tonight?"

"No need. We have to get the perimeter reorganized anyway. You won't be here tomorrow night."

Hank's Utilityman and the Mechanic flew out that evening on an Army bird leaving just the EOs and Builders at Bu Duc to fly out the next day. Those remaining turned in early in the bunker. Even with a full belly and a buzz on, sleeping in the bunker took some getting used to. It was comfortable and quiet and that was the problem. It was so quiet inside there was no way to tell what was going on outside.

After five weeks of perimeter duty on top of building the camp, always outside, the Seabees developed a kind of split brain. The work took most of their attention, but a part of their mind was always on the perimeter. Always being aware of the situation became a mental defense against the unknown. Bad things could happen in a moment and they didn't have much time to find cover when the enemy decided the camp had had enough peace.

Now, under six feet of earth, steel, wood, and brass, that need to know was frustrated and that made sleeping difficult. At 0300, Hank gave up. They would all have to be up at 0400 anyway for the witching hour. He decided to clean his RPD.

Stout came to the arms room as Hank was reassembling the machine gun.

"You're up early."

"Couldn't sleep. Too damn quiet in here."

"We all go through that in a new camp, especially if the opposition has already had a little fun. You get used to it and learn to trust your team. The com-room is in touch with all the bunkers and the towers. If anything is happening, you'll know about it soon enough. Time to get your men up. Double up with the Khe in the same bunkers you had before."

Hank pushed the final pin in on the RPD and

looked up.

"Do you think the NVA will try to overrun Bu Duc sometime?"

"Maybe, when it's more important to get rid of us than to keep the area quiet. It's a game for now. They don't like having this camp here, but if they try to get rid of it, then someone will wonder why getting rid of it is important enough to take the risk. I suspect they'll try to neutralize us by inhibiting our ability to patrol, or through harassment, or both. We're not really important enough to draw attention to the area. Not yet. A day will come though. That's the game. Getting ready for that day and being ready."

"Not today though, right?"

Stout grinned. "That's the game. Who knows? Get them up."

Chapter 28

It was a beautiful morning as most mornings in Vietnam are, except when it is raining. No rain that morning and the sky was clear. That was good news. The helicopter wouldn't have a problem getting in. Tools and personal possessions were packed and Hank and the Seabees were ready to go home. The camp was on 100% alert and 206 SF and CIDG, and six Seabees were on the perimeter. Miller and three men were in the command center.

The towers were sandbagged and M2 fifties were mounted on the observation decks. The four-deuce mortar was manned and ready. M79s and Laws were liberally distributed around the perimeter. The camp was about as ready for trouble as the SF could make it.

Hank prayed the morning would remain quiet and slid the hundred round drum on its tracks on the bottom of the RPD. He opened the feed-cover and used the cloth strap to pull the belt into the feed tray. He closed the feed-cover and sat back. Getting ready to fight at 0400 had become routine.

Trouble came, but not in the form they were expecting. The sound of rotors beating the air could be heard as the sun rose above the trees.

"That's strange," Stout said. "We're not expecting a bird this early."

He called the CP to find out what was going on and kept the transmission on the handset. When he was done he turned to Hank.

"Looks like you're getting a ride out of here early. I know this seems a bit sudden but get your guys together and get over to the landing pad. Soon as this bird is unloaded, Load your gear and get aboard."

"What's going on?"

"Some bullshit you don't need to get involved in unless you want to get stuck out here."

"No thanks. I'll get the team moving."

At the bunker Miller gave Hank more information.

"The bird will take you back to Phu Bai. You'll have further instructions from your command there. Sorry to rush you like this, Hank. Look, hang back until the bird is unloaded. Don't talk to anybody until you get to Phu Bai. Good luck. We appreciate all you did out here."

The twin rotor helicopter circled the camp for twenty minutes waiting to be cleared to land. Hank and crew got all their gear to the landing pad and then waited by the equipment away from the pad.

The bird landed and four men got off. Two of them were civilians with cameras hanging from straps around their necks. The other two were Army officers. Strange doings, Hank thought. As soon as the four men reached the command bunker, Hank and the Seabees loaded gear on the helicopter and got aboard. The bird lifted off immediately.

Phu Bai was a busier place than the last time Hank had been through there. He would have liked to look around to see what was going on, but he wasn't given the chance. A pickup truck was waiting at the landing pad for the Seabees. A Chief Builder met them as they came off the bird.

"Are you Tucker."

"That's me, Chief."

"Tell your crew to load their gear in the truck and get in."

"Where are you taking us?"

"A Marine helicopter is waiting for you on Marine-side."

"Man, I'm glad to hear that. I'm ready to get back to Dong Ha."

"Well, you can forget that. Detail Bravo at

Khe Sanh is being augmented and your crew is available. Chief Murphy asked me to be sure you made the Marine flight to get out there."

"Khe Sanh? I just spent five weeks in the boonies with the Special Forces."

"Khe Sanh Marine Combat Base. It's south of Dong Ha about forty miles. Shouldn't be bad duty. It's mostly runway work and a lot of hardback hooch building. They get some rocket and mortar incoming, but hell, who don't? Dong Ha has been getting a lot more than that. Murphy said the North has a hardon for Dong Ha."

"Shit, I was looking forward to getting back to the unit."

"Detail Bravo is a permanent detail and pretty big right now. It ought to be like home to you. They have people coming in from Da Nang and Dong Ha to boost it up to about eighty Seabees to finish the runway. It's probably going to be better duty than Dong Ha."

"Did Murphy say if this is a permanent assignment?"

"Not to me. He just said you were augmenting the Detail."

"Well, that something anyway. Maybe we won't be there long."

The Marine bird was filled with crates of C-Rats for the Marines at Khe Sanh, but they had room for six

Seabees and their gear. It lifted off ten minutes after Hank and his crew were loaded.

The landing at Khe Sanh was uneventful except for cat calls from the Marine cargo handlers. Hank walked off the ramp with his RPD on a sling over his shoulder and Tubby right behind him. The hundred-round drum was attached, but the belt wasn't loaded.

"Whoa, looka there. Hey John Wayne, where'd you get the gat?"

Hank walked right up to the cargo crew and looked them over. He was grinning, but it was a grin that said, I am taking no shit today.

"Are you the bell boys?" he asked. "How about getting our bags while I check in?"

They were just a bunch of kids having fun. Kids doing a man's job in a bad place. One of the Marines grabbed his balls and said, "I got your bags right here, squid."

Tubby shoved past Hank and right up to the Marine. He had to look up at him. "More like a big jarhead pussy," he said.

Hank grabbed Tubby and pulled him back just as the sergeant in charge of the detail saw his Marines screwing off.

"Unseat your asses and get the bird unloaded. What the fuck do you think this is, summer camp. Move!"

Hank spotted a Seabee he recognized on a

forklift moving pallets of AM2 runway matting and trotted over to the machine. The operator cut the engine.

"Hey, Hank. I thought you were on an Army job out in the mountains. What's happening, my man?"

"Got that job done. Murph sent me and the crew out here. Where's the office?"

"Right over there just off the apron. Welcome to Khe Sanh."

"Thanks, Kit. See you around".

It was good to be back around the guys he trained with in California and in some cases had trained. Many of the Seabees in CBMU 301 knew Hank from long before the Maintenance Unit was commissioned. After initial training when he entered the Navy, Hank was assigned to the permanent training staff first in Rhode Island and then in Gulfport for his first year of duty. He had trained many of the builders who later ended up in CBMU 301. After six months of his own initial training and a year on the training staff, he was assigned to the staff preparing to commission CBMU 301, and the Navy got their pound of flesh for making him a PO1—twelve months in Vietnam.

He took the crew to the office to check in.

Chapter 29

Khe Sanh combat base sat on a triangular plateau, each side of the triangle measuring about five to six kilometers, kind of rolling but still a relatively flat area sitting about 1500 feet above sea level. The northeast side of the plateau ended at the Rao Qung gorge; a 300-meter-deep gorge formed by a tributary of the Rao Qung river. The Annamite mountain range reaches 5000 feet north of Khe Sanh and 2000 feet to the west. Closer in, several hills reaching 3000 feet surrounded the base. Those hills were dangerous high-ground and were occupied by Marines since the hill fights the previous spring.

The base was laid out with the long axis running east to west. The runway began outside the wire on the east side of the base near the gorge and extended a little past the middle of the base. Detail

Bravo's camp was near the midpoint of the runway next to the parking and loading apron.

The area inside the wire was about a mile long, east to west, and a half mile wide north to south. The west end was designated red sector with a semi-circular perimeter. The north perimeter, parallel to the runway, was blue sector. The east end and southside perimeter was gray sector. Just outside gray sector wire on the west end was an Army Special Forces camp called Forward Operating Base 3 or FOB3. East of FOB3 and outside the gray sector wire was the garbage dump.

A dirt road ran on the north side of the runway along the blue sector wire from the east end to the red sector where it turned south and continued through a gate between gray and red sectors. Another dirt road, called main street, ran along the middle of the base south of the runway from the east end and joined the north road where it turned south. It had a branch near the center point of the base that turned south and provided access to the dump through Gray sector's wire. There were other, shorter roads off the main roads to service various storage areas, ammunition storage points, artillery points, sleeping hooches, mess halls, and shops. The graders and dozers maintained those roads. Almost all the construction and engineering except combat engineering was done by the Seabees and the Seabees often assisted Marine combat engineers with heavy equipment. The Marines had their own combat engineers for maintaining the perimeter, laying mine fields, etc.

At one point earlier in the year an entire regiment occupied the base and the hill outposts. Now only one battalion was present and two of its companies were in the hills. Currently one company of First Battalion, Twenty-sixth Marines (1/26) were on base supported by a command group, two artillery batteries, and some armor.

About nine miles south down route nine where it turned toward Laos, the Special Forces had a camp at Lang Vei with about 400 Civilian Irregular Defense Group soldiers made up of Bru Montagnards and a few special forces.

The Laos border was about nine miles away, putting Khe Sanh well within range of NVA artillery placed there. A place of special concern was called Co Rock mountain on the Laos side of the border. Full of caves, it made a good artillery base for the NVA and the combat base took occasional incoming from there, nothing major yet, but the Marines figured the few rounds received from there were ranging rounds and the NVA were observing the strikes to preregister their guns for something bigger coming later.

Before August, access to Khe Sanh had been via National Route 9, a single lane, mostly dirt road that ran from Dong Ha to Khe Sanh and south, eventually turning and extending into Laos. In early august, a convoy attempting to bring 175mm guns to Khe Sanh ran into a massive ambush and had to turn back. Route 9 was closed to convoy traffic after that and all resupply for Khe Sanh was by air only from then on. From that day on, the combat base was cut off except by air.

The whole base had been primitive and raw when Seabee Detail Bravo arrived in July. The Seabee's first job had been to establish their own hooches, shops, and storage yards and stockpile materials. Since the base was subject to occasional rocket and mortar incoming, underground bunkers were high on the priority list.

The Khe Sanh area didn't really have a dry season due to the interplay between the mountains and the moisture-laden air coming in off the China Sea, but it was dryer before the northeast monsoon season began. Wet misery started building up in August. The weather in July had been good, comparatively, with only a couple downpours each day that quickly ran off or soaked in and construction of Seabee shops and hooches proceeded quickly. But August brought transition to the northeast monsoon, still not as bad as the full monsoon would be, but enough to make working outside miserable. For the Seabees and Marines on the plateau, monsoon spelled misery, muddy misery.

Another feature of the area was a phenomenon known as crachin, a word from old-French Hank was told translated loosely as wet spit. Every morning the fog would set in and cover all the valleys in fog so think it looked like you could walk on it. Crachin was an area-wide phenomenon, but it was worse around the combat base. The plateau having been chewed up by machines and artillery along with the metal clad runway heated much sooner and faster than the surrounding jungle and pulled the cooler moisture laden air up from the valleys and gorges early in the morning. When the cooler air hit the heat on the plateau, it condensed and formed fog so thick everything it touched dripped with moisture and visibility was reduced to a few feet. There was seldom more than six hours of clear air and good visibility a day and that was usually topped with overcast and low ceilings.

The men of Bravo Detail had been working on the runway since before Hank departed Dong Ha for Bu Duc. Dong Ha combat base to the north continued receiving almost daily and nightly rocket, artillery, and mortar incoming that began a week before Bravo left for Khe Sanh. Hank was thinking the move to Khe Sanh instead of going back to Dong Ha right away might be a good deal since Khe Sanh was getting only occasional sniper fire and rare mortar and rocket attacks of just a couple rounds that did little or no damage. Khe Sanh was rather peaceful compared to Dong Ha and definitely more peaceful than Bu Duc.

When Bravo arrived in July, inspection of the runway revealed weaknesses in the bed that repair wouldn't fix and command made the decision to replace the first 1500 feet with a new rock bed and new aluminum matting. Soil density tests revealed the subsoil would not support new AM-2 aluminum matting and the large aircraft needed for resupply. A bed able to withstand 50,000 pounds per square inch had to be laid.

The Khe Sanh project became a major construction project and the runway had to be shut down for large aircraft once men and equipment were in place. First, all of the current, and old, pierced steel planking had to be removed and the sub-grade had to be shaped for drainage and prepped to take a new rock bed. A hill was discovered not far from the base that was made up of rock suitable for runway construction and a quarry was started. Enough rock had to be crushed to the right size and hauled a mile from the quarry to the construction site. An eight-inch rock bed had to be laid and sealed with asphalt. Drainage had to be improved and all the runway matting had to be replaced. Finally, all of the runway lighting had to be replaced.

Augmented equipment and men were airlifted with Marine and Army heavy-lift helicopters to Khe Sanh. Work on the runway began on August 28 while Hank and his crew were still clearing the SF camp at Bu Duc. Detail Bravo's permanent manpower of thirty-five increased to seventy-eight as CBMU 301 operations was able to free-up men and get them out to Khe Sanh. With the addition of Hank and his crew the detail now had 6 Mechanics, 20 steelworkers, 10 builders, 10 electricians, 30 equipment operators, and two temporary engineering aides. With increased size and capabilities came increased construction demands. Two chiefs were added to the detail. One served as the assistant OIC and the other became the Detail Chief. The Officer in charge was a Lieutenant (JG).

Since the biggest task the detail would have during their stay at Khe Sanh was rebuilding the runway and runway maintenance, the officer in charge chose an area close to and on the south side of the runway to locate the Seabee hooches, shops, and equipment yard. With foresight the Marines didn't seem to have or appreciate, the OIC started the crew working on massive underground bunkers to get the crew and office underground. His foresight would save a lot of Seabee lives later.

Chapter 30

Even though Phu Bai had been clear, clouds were hanging at 2000 feet over Khe Sanh and the morning rain had stopped, but that wouldn't last. Hank hefted his sea bag and started hiking over to the office in the Seabee compound. Thank goodness it was a short hike. He was still beat from an almost sleepless night and 0400 alert. When he reported to the office he didn't get the welcome of the prodigal son.

"Tucker, what the hell is that? You look like Al Capone with that thing on your shoulder."

"It's a Russian RPD machine gun, Chief. Got it from the SF."

"It's not authorized. Get rid of it. Where the hell have you been? You were supposed to report-in two days ago."

Chief Sharp wasn't a happy camper. The

workload was increasing and stressing everyone out and the Marine Command with the communications shop wasn't always good about keeping the Seabee office informed about what was going on outside of Khe Sanh. Hank tried to explain but was cut off.

"I didn't even know I was assigned out here until this morning on my way back to Dong Ha. We just finished up the Bu Duc job yesterday."

"Never mind. While you were fucking off in Bu Duc or bum fuck or whatever the fuck it is, the rain was washing out bunkers and every damn thing else at Khe Sanh. Drop your stuff in a hooch and find Crowder. You can work in his crew until we get the new additions sorted out. The Marines are raising hell about getting some shelter up for the grunts and every man we have is working on the runway."

Chief Sharp wasn't part of the permanent Detail and was waiting to rotate out but hadn't been released yet. He was pissed with the whole world. Hank had worked with him before and knew he had a tendency to get excited when things got hairy. He was a Chief and Hank was a PO1, so Hank got busy doing what he was told to do. It would have been nice to have a little time to figure out what was going on out there, but that would have to wait. Marines needed shelter.

He turned his crew over to Sharp for reassignment to Bravo crews.

"What are you going to do with the machine gun, Hank?" Thompson asked.

"Hell, keep it, I guess."

"Didn't Sharp tell you to lose it?"

"Yeah, but he's already forgotten about it. Besides, he'll be gone as soon as he can get out of here. What the hell business of his is it anyway?"

"Good luck with that. Well, same ole shit, new place. See you around."

The detail was still working on their primary bunker and were living in one fifteen-man bunker and a couple aboveground tents. Hank got a rack in the bunker and was surprised that most of the men preferred the tents. The bunker was dark and dank and smelled like mold even though it had lighting, but he preferred it to a tent after his experience at Bu Duc. When the NVA or VC around Khe Sanh decided to make things exciting for the combat base, racks in the bunker were going to be hard to come by. He dropped his sea bag on an empty rack and got to work.

A lot of jobs were working all over the base. From the top of the bunker he could see the concrete batch plant making a cloud of white dust and wondered how they were getting the water they needed. The main Seabee bunker was under construction and it was going to be underground and huge. It looked like a larger version of the bunker he had built for the SF at Bu Duc with the same massive timbers.

The asphalt plant was a jury rig, something put together by the Seabees to compensate for not having commercial equipment. That was the Seabee way. If you haven't got it and can't get it, make it. It amounted to a tilted rack made from pipe to lay 55-gallon drums of asphalt on so they would empty by gravity into a large holding tank. A rough terrain forklift was lifting drums onto the rack.

Concrete men were pouring a large pad for one of the artillery positions. Most of the crew was out on the runway doing hot, dirty work, the operative word being dirty.

Hank found out where Crowder, another Builder First Class, was working. The rain started again while he was hiking to the job and it was cold. It was just the end of September and ought to be hot, but this transition season was a wet one and was dropping temperatures into the low sixties. Hank shivered and dipped his head to see through a torrential downpour.

A lot of work had already been done by the Seabees at Khe Sanh by the time Hank and Tubby arrived. While enemy activity was light and scattered at Khe Sanh during the construction period, the weather was the real enemy of the Seabees. The transition to the Northeast monsoon began in late August and made life and work miserable throughout the construction period. The cyclone that had soaked Bu Duc dropped a total of 20 inches of rain on Khe Sanh in just twenty-four hours. Think of that. That's up to your knees in just one day. Everything not above ground washed away and had to be rebuilt.

While work on the runway was the major project, the miserable weather provided plenty of work for the builders and additional equipment operators. Marine bunkers washed out and had to be replaced and reinforced. New command bunkers had to be dug and rebuilt. Since underground construction was washing out, aboveground and partially sunken berthing hooches and working structures were constructed. Construction materials got scarce, cargo containers, pallets, boxes, and every form of material that could be reclaimed and repurposed was put to use. Marines escorted Seabees and combat engineers to the surrounding jungle to harvest logs for bunker reinforcement.

As the old PSP was removed from the runway, it was stacked and then reused to reinforce bunkers and trenches. Hank made sure he kept some for the fighting holes on the Seabee security line.

Chapter 31

Hank was a hands-on kind of supervisor and had to turn in a set of greens and a pair of boots after working on the runway in an all-hands effort to get AM2 laid on top of the asphalt-sealed bed. He was on the off-shift and trying to clean tar off his second pair of boots. You had to keep one pair back just for the runway work. Tubby was chowing down on a C-Rats pound cake covered with C-Rats canned peaches. One of the equipment operators entered the hooch.

"Hank, you've done some civic action work, haven't you?"

EO2 Chambers squatted next to Hank and lit a cigarette. He was an augmentee and operated an asphalt machine and seemed to be permanently covered in tar.

"I guess you could call it that," Hank said.

"It didn't turn out well."

"That's more experience than I have. Look, the boss said if I could get a replacement, I could skip the assistance visit to CAG (Combined Action Group) at Khe Sanh village tomorrow. Hell, a builder would be more help to them then an equipment operator anyway.

"What's in it for us?" Tubby asked. Typical of Tubby, he didn't wait to be asked.

"It will get you off runway work for the day."

Tubby looked thoughtful. "Well, that's worth something. What do you think, Hank?"

"I don't know, man. Like I said, it didn't turn out well the last time I got involved with villagers."

"The little girl?" Tubby asked.

"Yeah."

"Come on, man," Chambers said. "It's just one day and you'll be working with the CAG advisors, not villagers."

Hank thought about it for a moment. Maybe he could get the smell of asphalt out of his nose if he could get away from the base for a day. But the Marines were starting to make contact with the enemy on patrol and the village was three klicks from the base. Still, tomorrow would be another all-hands on the runway day. What the hell? A change in scenery would be welcome.

"Okay, but you owe me. Who do I see?

"Thanks, man. Some CAG guys are coming in from the village in the morning. Meet them at the chow hall at 0800."

"Got it. Make sure the office knows about the swap."

"I'll do it right now."

"Tubby is coming too."

"I don't know about that, man, That's your problem."

One of the steelworkers had used a cutting torch to cut a fifty-five-gallon drum in half lengthwise and welded legs on the halves to make a couple barbecue grills. Charcoal wasn't available but burning some pallet wood down to coals worked just as well. The detail had received a couple cases of frozen steaks that day and the OIC decided to have a cookout with beer for the Seabees. That made the Seabees happy but pissed off the recon marines manning the blue sector perimeter. The smell of cooking steaks drifted across their positions in the smoke. They didn't get many treats like steak dinners and cookouts from their command.

The perimeter was open on the east end where the runway extended through the wire. Guarding that gap was the responsibility of the Seabees and the Marine recon platoon stationed at

Khe Sanh. It was a scary big gap in the wire with no obstacles between those guarding the opening and anyone who wanted to get in. Night watch on blue sector was tense.

To assist in covering that obvious weakness in the base's defenses, the Marines usually moved a twin 40mm duster or a quad-fifty truck or both to cover the hole. The duster was a tank with twin automatic 40mm cannons with a devastating rate of fire and the quad-fifty was a weapons system made up of four ganged, heavy-barrel, fifty caliber machine guns mounted on a truck, also with a devastating rate of fire. Both were anti-aircraft weapons, but also made powerful anti-personnel weapons. Standing night watch with them out there was a lot less stressful than without them.

Hank watched a duster clanking across the dirt to its revetment near the perimeter as he finished up his steak and tossed off the rest of his beer. The beer was always a disappointment. The taste was ruined with preservatives and the alcohol content was just 3.2 percent. It tasted like beer, but your brain kept wondering where the alcohol was. He mourned the loss of his stash. A shot of moonshine mixed in would have made the beer a lot better, but Bu Duc had finished that. He was dumping the remains of his meal in the shit-can when Tubby nudged him and pointed.

There came Toby with his sea bag over his

shoulder and a grin on his face. Hank ran to him and lifted him off his feet with a bear hug.

"Put me the hell down!"

"Where did you come from?"

"Just got off the bird. My Chief finally got tired of me bugging him when the call for EOs to augment Detail Bravo came in. Murph told me you and Tubby were sent out here when you didn't return to Dong Ha when you were supposed to, so I've been bugging Alpha Company Chief ever since. What the hell is this? A barbecue? Steaks? You got to be shitting me."

"Get your ass over there and grab a steak before they close up. Tubby's over there. I need to check on something. I think I might have company."

A Green Beret was talking to the detail Chief. The Chief looked around and spotted Hank. He pointed and the Green Beret came over and held out his hand.

"Tucker?" he asked.

"Yeah, Sarge."

"Willie Stout out at Bu Duc said I should look you up and buy you a drink."

Hank grinned. "Willie?" he asked. "I didn't know his first name. Somehow Stout doesn't come across as a Willie."

"I've had that thought myself," the sergeant said with a grin. "I'm Zahnopolis. First name is

Anatole, but just call me Zahn.

Tubby walked up with Toby.

"I'm Hank. This is Tubby and this here is another Tucker, my little brother, Toby. I'm all for you buying us a drink but all we have is 3.2 beer and I've had enough of that crap."

"Come on. I've got a Jeep. It's happy hour at the FOB."

Hank was happy to comply. Toby dropped his sea bag in the bunker and climbed in the back with Tubby. The SF usually had good booze and fantastic food. They could get things regular Army troops could only dream of. Hank grabbed his RPD and got in the Jeep. Zanh raised his eyebrows when he saw the RPD, but he didn't say anything.

FOB 3 was collocated with the combat base just behind the gray sector but not part of the base. The Marines, especially their colonel, had a serious phobia when it came to indigenous people. He wasn't a lot more trusting of the Army Special Forces. He called the FOB an Army county club where the green berets lounged around sipping their favorite tasty beverages. The relationship between the Army at Khe Sanh and the Marines had never been very friendly.

Zahn had to take the Seabees out the gate on the dump road and swing around outside the wire to get to the FOB gate. The combat base had a perimeter between the base and the FOB. The FOB was guarded by and housed a lot of CIDG and Yard MACV-SOG personnel, and the Marines didn't trust them. It was all kind of strange to Hank, but he wasn't in the infantry and let the Marines worry about those kind of things.

The FOB had their own helicopter landing pad and a fortified bunker for the SF. These guys weren't a regular A team and there were a lot of them. As he found out later, they were more concerned with small-team cross-border recon than training and leading CIDG companies and battalions. Zanh took Hank inside and introduced him around. His RPD caught a few more glances.

Finally, after they all had a glass of Jack or a can of real beer in their hands, Zanh asked about the RPD.

"Stout and I worked out a trade," Hank said. "LT Miller was okay with it. I didn't steal it."

"Didn't figure you did," Zanh said. "If you don't mind me asking, was it the shitter that got you that?"

"Please, I prefer the term concrete comfort station," Hank said with a grin. "Stout almost got his ass shot off using the wood latrine we built." Hank told them the story of Stout hot footing it across the camp bare-assed naked with a machine gun shooting up his tracks. The SF had a good laugh over that.

"That sounds like Stout," Zanh said. "I'd say that was a fair trade. Do you think you could work out something like that for our boys down in Lang Vei? The camp is supposed to be finished and they can't get an official work order so it has to be on the sly. Even we can't get work orders for concrete shitters. We could probably find something to trade."

Ah ha, Hank thought. So this isn't just a friendly visit to take care of Stout's buddy. He thought for a moment.

"A little sipping whiskey and a few cases of real beer would go a long way toward convincing me of the need for interservice cooperation. The NVA blew away my whole stash at Bu Duc. I can take care of getting the resources from the combat base, but I'll need a way to get the people, materials, and equipment down there. Ain't no way I'm convoying down that road."

"That's not a problem. Tell me what you need and we'll find a way to get it there. Drink up. There's plenty more where that came from. One thing though, I have to get you back before dark. The fucking Marines won't let us on your base after dark."

Chapter 32

Hank's visit to Khe Sanh Village the next morning was made with shaking hands and a killer headache. The SF delivered him back to the Seabee bunker shitfaced. Fortunately, he didn't have to stand perimeter watch that night, but he was desperate for coffee in the morning.

Tubby had almost mutinied. The Chief couldn't spare any steel workers from runway work. Hank got him settled down, but it was a close thing.

Khe Sanh Village was 3.5 klicks, about a mile and a half, south of the combat base. The South Vietnamese Huong Hoa district headquarters was there protected by a Combined Action Group consisting of two platoons of the 915th Regional Force Company, called Ruff puffs, and two platoons of Company O, 3rd Combined Action Group. The whole defense force totaled less than

200 men. Included in that number were five U.S. Army Advisors and 20 U.S. Marine advisors.

Hank got to know a CAG Marine sergeant from the Bronx on the way out to the village.

"Where'd you get the machine gun, Tuck?"

"Traded the SF for it."

"I could use a Green Beanie friend. Those guys can get anything they want. The crotch has to beg for everything. Want to sell it?"

"No. I like it pretty good. Do all you guys still use the M14?"

Sergeant Adkins was armed with an M14. Hank hadn't seen many of them at Khe Sanh. There were a few, but most of the Marines had the M16 by then. The M14 was powerful as hell, and the Marines liked it better than the M16, but it wasn't the best wet-weather weapon around. The wooden stocks warped and screwed up the accuracy.

"We have a few," Adkins said. "They're all select fire and give us some 7.62 automatic weapons capability. They ought to be M60s, but like I said, the crotch has to beg for everything, even the shit we need. The fucking Army has warehouses full of shit they don't even use. The CAG is even worse. We're the redheaded stepchildren of the crotch. I could make you a good deal on your RPG."

"No thanks. What do you guys need from the Seabees?"

Adkins eyed the RPD longingly for a moment and then gave up.

"A couple things," he said. "We could use some heavy equipment help to improve the fortifications around the headquarters compound for one thing. That's our fallback point if things get really bad. We'd also like to build a school house for the village. I'll show you around so you can see what everything looks like now, and then we can talk."

Hank was given the grand tour of the headquarters compound and its fortifications. He wasn't impressed. He was glad he wasn't part of the CAG. The regional Force soldiers they supported were about as irregular as they come and the District Headquarters didn't look like it would be a tough nut to crack if the NVA took a serious interest in it. Living out there probably wasn't bad duty most of the time, but if they ever had to defend the place against a determined attack, Hank didn't like the odds. He remembered the way the NVA had devastated Bu Duc's perimeter and the CAG's perimeter couldn't even compare.

"You can see where we need to reinforce the bunkers at the entrance. They need overhead cover and we need timbers to do that. The rest of the perimeter is about the same."

"Where do you normally get your

materials?"

"The Vietnamese. As I said, we're step children. This is the district headquarters and they're supposed to provide material support, but that's a joke. Any money they get goes into somebody's pocket. Do you think the combat base can provide some materials?"

"I can ask. Let me make a list. If we can't get the timbers from the materials yard, maybe we can cut some timber."

"Nice thought, but that takes tools, especially chain saws."

"Well, those we can get for sure. Give me a few minutes to make a materials list and then show me where you want the school house. I can't promise anything, but I can make the need known to the boss."

He went back around the perimeter and made his wish list, knowing they would be lucky to get half of what he asked for. Men, materials, and time were already stretched thin at the base. But this visit was the boss's idea, or at least he approved it, so Hank would ask for what was needed and let him worry about priorities. That's why the boss wore bars instead of stripes.

The more he saw, the more he wondered about the people running things out there. There was nothing even close to what the SF did at Bu

Duc. What the hell were these guy's bosses thinking? They put a handful of Marines out here with a bunch of indigs and no support. About the only advantage that duty had, as far as he could tell, was they were probably the only Marines in a hundred miles getting laid. But when he looked at the available action, he shivered. Maybe even those skinny, child sized women started looking good after a few months in the sticks, but he doubted it. Well, they are only three klicks from the base and had artillery support at least.

"I'll see what I can do. But don't hold your breath," he said. "I'm just here for the day. Somebody else will be assigned to do the work."

"Do what you can. Any improvement will be a help. I'll be sure the district chief makes the request official through channels. Come on. We'll look at the site for the school and I'll get you back to the base."

When Hank got back to the combat base and turned in his report, the Chief stopped him before he could get out of the office.

"Tucker, what the hell have you got going on with the Special Forces?"

"Not sure what you mean, Chief. What's up?"

"A green beret captain dropped in on the boss and requested you for a job down at Lang Vei.

You know we're stretched thin already. We don't need you out there drumming up more work."

"Oh. Yeah, a sergeant over at FOB3 I know asked if I could build a reinforced concrete shitter for them. They get sniper fire when they use the head."

"Why you?"

"I built one for them out at Bu Duc and they heard about it, I guess. I told them they'd have to go through the boss. It isn't a big job. One day to build the forms and put in the rebar. Another day to pour the walls and roof. We can use scrap for the forms. It's just a shitter. It don't have to be pretty. They said they could provide transportation for the men and materials."

"How many men?"

"I can build the forms and Tubby can do the rebar work. I figure me and a BUR (concrete builder) to do the pour. Three days total."

"You going to mix it on site? It's going to take more men and a couple mixers if you are."

"They say they can get whatever I want. We can use a two-yard bucket and helicopter. Pick up wet mix at the batch plant and fly it to Lang Vei. It's only a few miles."

The Chief watched Hank's face for a few moments. "Figured it all out, have you? Okay, level with me. What are you getting out of it? Let me rephrase that. What is the Detail getting out of it?"

Crap! Hank thought. *There goes my trading stash.*

"I'd say the SF will be very appreciative of our labor. What's the boss drink?"

"Scotch. Good stuff. Your leading Chief is partial to Jack Daniels. An assortment of whiskey, gin, and vodka would help fill out the club's inventory too."

"I believe that can be arranged."

"Put together your plan. I can give you one BUR for two days work and one steel worker for a day. You arrange for the concrete and bucket with the batch plant. You better get some chow and a couple hours sleep. You're petty-office-in-charge on the security line tonight."

Chapter 33

Two days later Hank took off in a black helicopter from FOB3 and landed at Lang Vei. He wanted to bring Howard, a BUR3, along to help lay it out and calculate the concrete, but he was tied up pouring concrete pads for the 155mm artillery pieces on the combat base. He wouldn't be needed until day two anyway so Hank and Tubby began getting the forms and reinforcing rods placed. Toby was running the forklift on the runway moving AM2 matting and couldn't come. Still, it was good having the Tucker boys back together again at Khe Sanh with Tubby there too. He wanted to feel good about that, but Hank didn't get a lot of feel-good moments since Bu Duc.

After meeting the SF Captain and some of the SF at Lang Vei, Hank had them show him where they wanted the latrine built. He got their idea of the size and then sat down to calculate materials. He didn't really need a BUR yet. He'd poured and finished enough steps, pads, driveways, and basement floors in his time. That seemed to be all he did when he was a helper. Hauling wet concrete in a wheelbarrow across the mud on long planks from the truck to the job had toughened him up as a teenager.

When he had the dimensions the SF wanted, he staked out the job site. Their wood latrine was twenty feet long and was meeting their needs for space. They wanted one fully enclosed in concrete except for the doorways at each end. That was enough information to get a rough estimate. All right, he'd keep it nice and symmetric and simple. He'd have to frame in the floor to leave the gap over the shitter drums. But, roughly, he needed a floor 20' long x 7' wide x 4" or .35 feet thick. 20x7x.35=49 gives you cubic feet, divided by 27 (the number of feet in a cubic yard) = 1.8 yards in the floor. Keeping it symmetric, front and back walls are the same and so is the roof. Keep it simple. It's just a shitter.

He calculated he'd need roughly 8 yards overall. The helicopter would have to make four trips with a two-yard bucket. So tell the SF he would need the bird for five trips. That would give him a little wiggle room. Better to have it and not need it than to need it and not have it. He'd let his concrete man work out the slumps he wanted, but they would have to work with whatever flow they got once it was in the bucket. As with every place in the area, the water source was limited. With what was falling out of the sky you'd think water would be the least concern, but with concrete you needed it where the job was and you had to be able to control it.

He stretched and walked over to the bunker. Stout had been right. The SF at Lang Vei had the Cadillac of bunkers. Hank stood in the entrance and enjoyed a moment of pride. Seabees built this, he thought. I'll tell my kids about this someday. LT Lacy, one of the SF officers spotted him and waved him in.

"Done for today? The bird can't get back here for another hour. Want a beer?"

"Hell yes," Hank said.

After they each had a beer in their hands, Lacy asked him a question.

"Tell me something. What's with the Marines at Khe Sanh?"

"How so?"

"I was up there the other day. It's beginning to look like a tent city. Everything is above ground. We keep giving them intel about enemy movement in the area but they just seem to ignore it. We tell them about artillery moving into Co Rock mountain and they still build stuff above ground. Do they have any idea how many NVA are camped within twelve miles of the combat base?"

"Hell, I'm just a builder. They don't tell me anything."

"Want some advice?"

"Sure."

"Dig deep and make your bunkers strong, like you all built this one. The NVA have left the combat base pretty much alone since the hill fights, but that's not going to last. I'll tell you what we've been telling the Marine S2. Our sniffer flights are detecting large concentrations of men and equipment just over the border. There's only one thing around here the NVA would mass troops for instead of sending them on south. That's Khe Sanh."

"What's a sniffer flight?"

"We have aircraft equipped with sensors that measure CO2, methane, diesel and gas exhaust, all the gasses that accompany military units. We can estimate the size of a unit just by measuring the concentration of those gasses. There is a large force staging just across the border in Laos. Brigade strength at least, but we're betting much bigger. Make sure you have a safe hole to get in. The pride of the North Vietnamese is their artillery. It's what they beat the French with. Bet your ass they are going to be using it soon."

Hank just shook his head and stared at Lacy.

"Damn, I was feeling pretty good until now. Are they going to attack the base?"

"I don't figure they're down here for training."

"Is it going to be safe coming out here?"

"Yeah. They're not ready to pull the trigger yet. It's coming though. We keep trying to tell the Marines that, but I don't think they're listening."

"I thank you for the advice. I'll pass it on to my boss."

When the helicopter returned him to the combat base he stood near the site of the new Seabee bunker and looked around. He hadn't even thought about it before, but Lacy was right. Marines were living above ground in tents and hardback hooches, mostly built by the Seabees. Most of their offices, mess, and working spaces were also above ground. Even the medical facility was above ground.

The Seabee compound wasn't much better. The office and shops were above ground, but there wasn't much they could do about the shops. The equipment yard was just a place to park the equipment and didn't provide any protection for it. At least the OIC was working toward getting important spaces protected. The new bunker was huge and built with massive timbers. When it was done, it would be covered by eight feet of earth, steel, wood, and stone.

Lacy was right about the Marines. They didn't seem to be anxious to get below ground. It was more than a lack of motivation though. Hank had talked with a lot of Marines at Khe Sanh and was familiar with the perverse sense of pride that led to a reluctance to dig in. They weren't bashful about it and would tell you right out that Marines were assault troops. They weren't trained to hide in holes under the ground. That was for the Army.

Thinking back on what happened at Dong Ha and Bu Duc he had a feeling everyone on this trashy looking base was going to wish they had listened to the Army. He was glad he had a place to sleep with several feet of dirt between him and incoming.

For the next three days Hank and his small crew poured and finished the latrine for the SF at Lang Vei. Having a helicopter hovering over you while you worked the concrete was a new experience for him, sort of like working in a hurricane. He finished up on the fourth day alone, tying in all the woodwork, and left the sandbagging for the SF to take care of. Crafting the seats took extra care. No matter how tough you are, the seat you sat your naked butt on better be smooth with no splinters.

The SF were good hosts. He liked working for the SF better than the Marines. It was their attitude. A Marine tackled a problem like it was a wall to be knocked down. The SF's attitude was screw it, there's always a way around, over, or under the wall. Except for a small insanity that made them like jumping out of airplanes, they'd make good Seabees.

He was glad to get that off-sight job done. He seemed to be the one picked for off-site work all the time and he didn't want that to continue. He was an augmentee, though, and the permanent Detail had their own crews that would remain at Khe Sanh and had to remain tight. Khe Sanh Village CAG would probably end up on his plate too, but Hank hoped that would be the last job away from the combat base. The SF had put a scare into him. Something nasty was out there.

Chapter 34

The rock crushing operation had begun on September 2 while Hank and his crew were still at Bu Duc and the job of staging crushed rock for the new runway bed was begun. Work on the original 1500 feet of runway was well underway when Hank arrived during the last week of September. The target completion date was October 24th and the Seabees were on schedule.

A couple things happened in mid-October that threatened the schedule. First, the Air Force crashed a C130 while landing and destroyed a couple hundred barrels of asphalt and damaged the subgrade in the process shifting the work from construction to repair, to say nothing of destroying a three-million-dollar airplane. Second, the enemy began to take a more active interest in the combat base and especially in the equipment operating on the runway. Snipers began harassing the operators and steel workers. Hank was worried about Toby. He was out there on a forklift or frontend loader every day or night with no cover.

Suddenly, the weather, heat, and physical fatigue were no longer the only limits on progress. Sniper activity wasn't constant or even a regular part of the day, but it was constantly on the minds of the workers. Sitting high up on a bulldozer or forklift, or working in the open on the runway, Seabees made wonderful targets for the occasional sneak attack. It didn't have to happen often or take many rounds. After the first time a sniper zinged a round off the steel next to them, he definitely had the operator's attention. Fortunately, the enemy didn't seem to be putting their first string in the game yet and the sniper activity wasn't producing any casualties. Believe me, the fact that no one had been shot *yet* did not comfort the runway crew. As the old saying goes, even a blind pig finds an acorn occasionally. Regardless, the work had to go on.

The work was progressing twenty-four hours a day and as fast as the crews could operate. One shift completed 400 feet of runway in one twelve-hour shift. That was a side of Seabee construction a man who learned his trade in civilian life had to adjust to.

During your apprenticeship you learned to pace yourself. Pace has two sides to it. One, you have to produce at an acceptable level, a level expected of a journeyman, or if you worked for yourself, a level that allowed you to make a living. Two, you had to make your energy last all day to produce for the whole shift.

You learned to set up your job and place your tools and materials so you could get them with minimum movement when you needed them. Every extra step to get a tool, very trip up and down a ladder, is energy spent and time lost. The other side of that measure is the too-much side. If you do too much too fast, first you won't make it through the day, and second, some mechanic working above you will drop a hammer on your head. It might be a near miss the first time, but if you don't get the message, expect a clearer message. Everybody on the job had to make it through the day. Hot shots are as bad as slackers, and that's true for both union and non-union jobs.

The Seabees didn't always have the luxury of pacing. The 24h deadline was looming and over a thousand men depended on it being finished on time to get the supplies they needed to survive, so when the unexpected and unavoidable happened, the Seabees just had to suck it up and dig deeper into their energy reserves.

Somehow the detail stayed on schedule and the initial 1500 feet was complete on October 24th. That wasn't a reason to celebrate or let down though. Before the Detail could begin planning the return of augmented Seabees and equipment to Dong Ha and Da Nang, the crews got some bad news. About thirty Seabees looking forward to returning to their permanent assignments, including Hank, Toby, and Tubby were set for a major disappointment.

One day at morning quarters the Detail Chief held the crews back for a briefing.

"All augmented personnel have been extended at Khe Sanh for up to two months. You've already heard the rumors. Well, they're true. The Marines want the runway extended to twenty-nine-hundred feet and we got the job. Scheduled completion is December Second. We'll be able to release some of you in late November if we stay on schedule, but figure on being here until at least then. Materials staging begins immediately.

"For the next three days everyone is working on materials staging. We have fifteen hundred sheets of AM-2 aluminum runway matting coming in. It has to be recovered, moved, and staged along the job site. One thousand barrels of asphalt will also be delivered. Same drill. It has to be recovered, moved, and staged. On top of those deliveries, Army and Marine heavy-lift helicopters will be delivering equipment and materials. This is an all-hands, all-equipment effort. Jones has the crew assignments. Give them the details, Jonesy."

EO1 Jones stepped up and put his notes on the table.

"Here's the deal. C-one-thirty aircraft will deliver fifteen-hundred sheets of AM-2 runway matting via LAPES drops. For those of you who weren't here for the initial deliveries, here's what happens. LAPES stands for Low Altitude Parachute-Extraction System. The cargo is palletized and loaded on a C-one-thirty. The pilot approaches the runway extraction zone like he is landing and opens the rear ramp. He brings the plane in just a couple yards above the runway. As he gets close to the extraction zone, a drogue chute is released. At the right time the drogue pulls the big chutes out and they drag the pallets out of the plane to skid down the runway to a stop. The plane goes on and picks up another load at Da Nang. We don't have a lot of time to get the equipment out there, break down the pallets if necessary, load and move the material to its staging area. Getting fifteen-hundred AM-2 sheets in here is going to take some time."

After some discussion, Jones continued.

"Another thousand barrels of asphalt will be delivered by conventional parachute drops. That can get hairy. We know where the LAPES drops are going to land, but a lot can happen to a higher altitude drop. The target drop zone is between Red

Sector and the rock quarry, but crews have to be prepared to recover the drums anywhere on the plateau. The pallets are dropped from about 500 feet and the parachutes open at about a hundred feet above the ground so they usually hit the drop zone. But be prepared for some weird shit to happen. The wind can do some strange things. The Marines are providing working parties to assist.

"Finally, heavy lift helicopters will be delivering equipment and building supplies in constant round-robin runs from Dong Ha while everything else is going on. Again, it's important to get them unloaded fast so they can return for another load. The time we have them is limited. Three days, people. That's all we have and the weather is going to screw up every plan we have, so stay flexible. This is an all-hands effort until the deliveries are complete. I want to see the lead petty officers to work out the crews. The rest of you finish up what you can today and get ready to move material for the next three days."

Chapter 35

With the deliveries complete and everything in place, work routines returned to normal. Hank got up for the night shift cold, damp, and stiff. It was raining when he went to bed and it was still raining. It would be foggy and at least that was a blessing. The damn snipers were becoming a bigger problem. The crew was taking a few rounds every shift now. Knock on wood. No casualties yet, at least no casualties from sniper incoming, but twenty-four hour a day heavy construction in foul weather produces its own casualties and the Detail had a couple men recovering from injuries at Charlie Med and more on light duty recovering in the hooches.

At least he didn't have to stand perimeter watch tonight. Coming off shift wet, tired, and cold and sitting on the perimeter in wet, muddy holes and bunkers was the pits and came out of rest time.

"Tubby, let's go. We're pulling the last of the PSP tonight."

"Damn, Hank. I just got to sleep."

"You've been crapped out for six hours. Get up so you'll have time to eat."

"Yeah, yeah. I'm coming. You going to shave?"

"Why? It's cold, windy, and wet out there. If you shave you'll just be raw in the morning. Who the hell is going to notice anyway?"

"We have to muster."

"The chief is counting bodies, not shaves. It's really nasty out tonight so maybe the snipers will take the night off. Wish the damn Marines would get off their asses and do something about them."

"What are you worried about? I'm the one holding the cutting torch lighting me up like a damn star in the night."

Hank grinned.

"That's very poetic, Tubbs. Like a star in the night. Maybe you could put that on your helmet."

"Fuck you, Tucker. Let's get some chow."

Hank and Tubby with another steelworker were working as a team to remove some old PSP matting from the new section. It was dark as hell but that was more comforting than not. Tubby's torch lit them up more than they wanted anyway. The fog helped to conceal them, but not completely, and the fog was a two-sided sword. It also concealed the enemy snipers and let them get in really close to the runway.

Hank and his crew were lifting out several sheets of planking carefully and stacking them for the forklift to move back to the surplus yard. He wanted them intact and nice and flat to use on the Seabee bunkers on the perimeter and they were being careful with them. All the anchor bolts but one had been cut and the heavy sheet of pierced steel was lifted and braced at one corner so Tubby could get to the last bolt with his cutting torch. A stack of seven planks were right behind the plank Tubby was working on, and in the dark, and unknown to him, was not stacked evenly and was unstable. He was sitting at the edge of one sheet with his legs under the sheet they were removing to get the angle he wanted for his flame.

Everything was going good until Tubby's torch did what he feared most at night—became a beacon. A sniper round hit the steel and ricocheted off toward the camp causing the other steelworker to dive for cover. His boot caught the piece of stud they were using for a brace and knocked it loose. The sheet came down hard on Tubby's legs.

Tubby grunted. The plank weighed about seventy pounds. But then the stack they were saving gave way and slid onto the plank on Tubby's legs.

He screamed. Seventy pounds suddenly became over five hundred pounds.

Normally they would use a forklift to move the PSP, or lift them one at a time, but a forklift hadn't arrived yet and Tubby was screaming.

Hank heard his friend scream, sized up the situation in a second, and squatted like a weight lifter doing a deadlift and locked his hands on the edge of the steel. As he straightened and took the weight of the steel on his legs and arms his groan could be heard above the machinery. The other steelworker saw what was happening and understood what Hank was doing. He grabbed Tubby's shoulders and watched the steel.

Hank's face got red. The steel didn't move. He powered with his legs, harder and harder. His face got red and blood dribbled from his nose. He gave it more and his eyes looked like they were going to pop out of his head.

'It's moving," the steel worker yelled. "A little more."

Every vein on Hank's head was standing out and his face and ears were beet red. Tubby screamed again and Hank gave one last massive pull, everything he had. The steel moved up an inch.

"Hold it," Roberts yelled and jerked Tubby from under the PSP. "Got him!"

Hank dropped the steel and swayed for a moment. Blood was dripping from his nostrils and running across his lips. He didn't notice. He didn't notice anything for a few moments while his blood pressure returned to normal. Then he wiped his arm across his eyes and lips and turned to see how Tubby was doing.

Tubby was laying back with his eyes closed trying not to scream. His skinny legs looked dented. Other men seeing what was happening and knowing the result wasn't going to be good called for a corpsman. The corpsman brought a stretcher and he and a Seabee loaded Tubby and took him to Charlie Med.

Hank wanted to go with him, but the PSP had to be removed. He and Roberts finished the anchor bolt and then called Toby with his forklift to move the sheets to the salvage yard. He kept looking over his shoulder at Charlie Med, wanting to be there to check on Tubby, but the work had to get done.

Finally, at the end of the shift, he hiked over to the Med tent. His ass was dragging. Just lifting that steel had trashed his legs and arms, but he put another four hours of hard labor in after the incident.

"They're sending me back to Delta Med at Dong Ha," Tubby said as Hank walked up to his bunk. "Talk to the OIC, Tuck. See if you can stop them."

Before Hank could answer a doctor stopped

next to Tubby.

"No one is going to stop the transfer, sailor. You've got hairline fractures in both legs. You are going to be off your feet for six weeks. You'd just be a burden on your friends out here. Is that what you want?"

Tubby didn't have an answer for that. Hank could see the torment on his face.

"Go back and get fixed up," he said. "Murph will send you back when medical clears you."

"Who is going to look out for you? Without me here, you're going to get your ass in big time trouble sure as shit."

Hank grinned. Tubby, as usual, ignored that fact that it was Hank that was bailing his ass out. Didn't matter. Tubby was his friend.

"I believe I can get by for six weeks with Toby here."

Tubby groaned and tried to sit up and grab his thighs.

"He's bruised all the way to the bone," the doctor said. "I believe we can give you something for that. Visiting hours are over."

Hank took Tubby's hand and squeezed. "Get your skinny ass back here in six weeks. You hear me?"

Tubby tried to smile, but he was hurting. Hank waved and hiked over to the office.

The Chief gave Hank a good ass-chewing. Hank was a First-Class Petty Officer. He should have been supervising that job. It was his responsibility to see that his crew was working safely. After he was done chewing Hank out, he sat down and used some math to calculate the amount of weight Hank had lifted.

"Hank, how the hell did you do that? Considering the vector, the best I can figure, you lifted close to five hundred pounds of steel. Do you think you're a crane?"

"I didn't think about it at all, Chief. Tubby was hurting and I had to help him."

"And broke blood vessels in your face doing it. I expected more of you. Not the lifting but avoiding the need for it. Use your head out there, Hank. That's why you have the stripes."

"Yes, sir. It won't happen again."

And Hank vowed it wouldn't happen again. Seeing his friend hurt had really hit him hard. First he couldn't help Peanut and now he had let his best friend get hurt.

Chapter 36

As the Seabees labored into late fall to overcome new problems with saturated soil, cave-ins, undependable deliveries, and fatigue, new and scary working conditions began to complicate their lives. NVA interest in Khe Sanh ticked up another notch.

Hank and Toby were on security line duty one night in November. The bunker was wet and the night was cold with light rain blowing into the bunker and soaking everything, mostly them.

"Look at that," Toby said and pointed.

A frontend loader was moving a bucket of stone out to the runway.

"Looks like it is operating itself," he said.

Hank laughed. "Yeah, it does. The operator is crouched down so low on the floorboards you can't even see him."

"Only damn way I'll operate one on the runway," Toby said. "Two sniper rounds hit my machine today. One of these days the NVA are going to get some new glasses and that sucker out there is going to start getting some hits."

Hank just shook his head. Enemy action seemed to be heating up all over.

"A Marine patrol got ambushed today out near the quarry. They brought one guy back using a poncho for a stretcher. Man, that's too close for comfort."

"The Chief said the company out on hill eight eighty-one south got into a major firefight just a couple hundred meters from their base," Toby said. "What do you think? Are they going to make a try for the combat base?"

Hank wiped rain from his face and blew on his hands.

"The SF seem to think so, but the Marines don't seem too concerned about it. Who the hell knows? They seem to be getting closer, that's for damn sure."

"I hope we can get the hell out of here before they make up their minds. Look around. This base is a lot of territory for a company of Marines to defend. We must have three miles of perimeter all together."

"Yeah, that's stretching a company pretty thin. Well. We better get our minds back on our piece of it. Why don't you get a couple hours of sleep? I'll wake you up at 0200."

The work had to be completed regardless of snipers and mortars and the Seabees pushed on to complete the second phase of runway work. Sub-grade shaping was followed by laying an eight-inch rock bed. Drainage was improved. The rock bed was sealed with asphalt and new AM-2 matting was laid and secured.

As the runway work neared completion at the end of November, the augment personnel from public works in Da Nang were released to return to Danang and supplemental men and equipment from Dong Ha were gradually released and airlifted back to Dong Ha. Detail Bravo gradually reduced back to its thirty-five permanent party and the work changed to runway and base maintenance. Although the Detail hadn't had any casualties from enemy action yet, the work itself was dangerous and accidents were inevitable and replacements were needed.

At morning quarters on the first of December, Hank and Toby were held back when the crews were released to start the day shift.

"You two keep your bunks in the bunker."

"What's up, Chief?" Hank asked.

"I've got two men at Delta Med and they won't be released for two months. Expect to remain here at Khe Sanh until February."

"We're on the morning round robin back to Dong Ha," Toby said."

"Yeah, well, I'm sorry about that. The detail only has thirty-five men and we're down two. Murph agreed to leave you here until we get our guys back. Look, I really am sorry to stick you like this, but we need you."

Toby and Hank looked at each other and shrugged.

"Here is a good as there," Hank said. "Are you sure it's just for two more months?"

"As far as I can tell. Murph wasn't happy. He's got more work than he has people and he wanted you back right now. I suspect he won't be so accommodating in February."

Chapter 37

The Marines were finally becoming convinced Khe Sanh was in the crosshairs of a large enemy force. Contact with NVA units was becoming more frequent. Probes on the perimeter were happening almost nightly. On December 10th Gray sector Marines discovered places in the wire where the wire had been cut and carefully placed back together. Hank knew what that meant. When the sections that were cut were removed, neat tunnels through the perimeter appeared.

The following morning Marines all around the perimeter found their claymore mines turned around and pointing back at them. An immediate effort to strengthen the perimeter was started and the Seabees were called upon to help Marine Combat engineers construct a stronger perimeter with larger minefields and double apron barriers, and Seabees got additional military training with Marine advisors.

They had just received word another Battalion was being moved to Khe Sanh. 3/26 had been there in the spring and was on its way back. Looking around the base now, it was hard to remember the barren compound it used to be. Seabee builders and Marine combat engineers had changed the landscape. Offices, a large mess hall, a Navy exchange (PX), actually just a Conex box, bunkers and multiple hooches covered what used to be bare dirt. Charlie Med was bigger and reinforced with sandbags. The post office was in another Conex box and the Marine command bunker in what used to be an old French concrete bunker had staff hooches and tents surrounding it. Towering over all that was the concrete batch plant and the water tower. The whole thing managed to look like a construction site in a bad part of town.

The buildings were crude, without pretense at architecture, just rough framed and sheathed in plywood with tin roofs, a place to get out of the weather. Reinforced bunkers for munitions formed three ASPs. Revetments protected artillery and armor and where some green used to cover the ground, nothing was left but bare red dirt, actually mud most of the time. Some aboveground hooches damaged in the heavy rain and wind in September were rebuilt partially underground with floors at least five feet below the ground with tent roofs, but most were completely above ground on hardback frames. The batch plant and water tower worried Hank. Man, they made wonderful aiming points.

The days seemed to blur into one another. The main Seabee underground bunker big enough to hold the entire detail, was built as massive as the command bunker at Bu Duc and even bigger. Hank slept in a second underground bunker next to the runway with fourteen other Seabees. It was built and fortified just as massively. The Seabees had the skills, equipment, and materials and a strong desire to get underground and built the best bunkers on the combat base.

The Marines with the greatest need for protection, didn‘t seem to be in a hurry to fortify and get below ground. Their trenches were relatively shallow, sometime only waist deep. They didn't like digging. Actually, they didn't like acting like the Army sitting in one place and defending a piece of land. They were assault troops and wanted to be taking a piece of land, not holding it. The Seabees assisted when the Marines asked for help, but it was mostly replacing excavations that were washed out. Well, it wasn't his job to worry about Marines. They were supposed to be the fighting experts.

After ten hours of backbreaking work

clearing, reclaiming lumber, and reconstructing bunkers for the Marines that had washed out, Hank ate C-Rats and collapsed in his bunk hoping to get a few hours of sleep before he had to go on watch on the security line for the 12am to 4am watch. He was POIC, Petty-Officer-in-Charge, of the watch again on the security line.

He was so sick of mud, rain, and cold, he wanted to scream, or in his case, roar. The monsoon was miserable that year and it seemed like his whole life had become nothing but the drudge of digging and rebuilding. Every damn day was weather that would have shut the job down in civilian life. He was muddy. His tools were muddy. The materials were muddy. Every damn thing was muddy. Even his damn food and the water he drank were muddy. His skin was dyed red from the damn mud. Trenches washed out. Fighting holes washed out. Bunkers washed out. The runway bed washed out. Every damn thing washed out. The only good thing about the weather was the enemy was getting just as washed-out as the combat base. The bad part was the Marines wanted too many structures rebuilt above ground, and he couldn't blame them. Having water up to your knees in your living quarters made life harder than it already was. But Hank also remembered LT Lacy's words at Lang Vei. It's not a great idea to build above ground when artillery is your enemy's pride.

He woke at 2300 and ate another C-Rats meal and took the time to heat some water for coffee. He could have walked over to the office and got a cup of brewed coffee from the big pot, but it was raining hard and the wind was whipping around. He wanted to stay just damp for as long as he could. He would be soaked to the skin within an hour of beginning his watch on the perimeter. Staff Sergeant Rawlins, the military advisor, flipped the door flap open and stepped inside the bunker. He shook his poncho off.

"You got the center bunker with me tonight," he said.

That was bad news. While having a military advisor with you out there at night was kind of comforting in one way, it also meant Hank and Toby would probably be awake the whole watch. Rawlins saw the night watches he stood with the Seabees as learning opportunities for them.

Hank covered his disappointment. "Anything going on?"

"Just the usual. "Gray sector had a probe on the wire about twenty-hundred or thought they did. Red sector reported movement near the wire, but it wasn't confirmed. We need to stay alert tonight. I'll tell you something, Tucker. Things are heating up."

Before CBMU 301 left California for Vietnam the entire unit participated in tactical training exercises at a place called Conejo Grade a few miles south of Port Hueneme. The unit was marched to a hill they had to take and hold overnight with their sister unit, CBMU 302 acting as aggressor. It was good familiarization training but didn't really prepare anyone for the reality of guard duty on the perimeter in Vietnam—all alone—in the dark. Bu Duc had provided some experience to help steady his nerves though, and night watch wasn't nearly as scary as those first watches with the Special Forces, especially with a quad-fifty or a duster for back-up.

With the arrival of another battalion of Marines imminent, Hank was looking forward to the Marines taking over the entire perimeter so the Seabees could focus on building and runway maintenance and hopefully get a little more sleep occasionally. Not knowing the reason why the Marines thought they needed another battalion at Khe Sanh at just that particular time was a little troubling though.

Hank was leaning against the sandbags at the firing port when he thought he saw something move out near the runway.

"Toby, I think something is messing with the wire out there."

"Slide over," Rawlins said. He slid in next to Hank. Toby sat up and checked his rifle.

"Where?" Rawlins asked.

Hank pointed. "Right there close to the end of the fence."

Rawlins watched for a while but neither of them saw anything moving.

"Hold on. Let me give the COC a heads-up."

He gave the COC a call and requested permission to do a recon by fire and received permission.

"Okay, give that area a squirt with your RPD and see if we get a response."

Rawlins had been eyeing the RPD ever since he began advising the Detail. He had already tried to get Hank to trade it for various items Hank didn't need.

Hank checked the loading tray to be sure the belt was seated and flipped the safety to fire. He aimed the best he could and slapped the trigger twice for two bursts. He was nervous and the bursts were longer than he intended. Green tracers lit up the wire. The trouble with tracers at night is, from an angle outgoing doesn't look a lot different than incoming, especially when they are green. You see what you expect to see.

Suddenly the quad-fifty cut lose on the same area. Red fifty-caliber tracers from two of his guns lit up the night and a dust cloud formed in the wire right where Hank's tracers had ended. The PRC25 started squawking.

"Blue one, Blue one, are you receiving

automatic incoming? Over."

Rawlins laughed out loud. "I forgot all about you having Chicom ammunition," he said.

He grabbed the handset.

"Kilo Six this is Blue one. Incoming suppressed. Over"

"Blue one standby for light."

Hank heard the tubing sound from the mortar and a moment later heard the pop as the flare ignited.

"Tucker, you better let me take that thing off your hands. If they find out that was you, you're going to be in deep shit."

Hank though about it for a moment. Rawlins was right. Those green tracers might end up drawing friendly fire. That damn quad-fifty hadn't even hesitated. Besides, worrying about and maintaining the RPD was a lot less fun than he thought it would be.

"I need something in trade. What can you give me? And don 't just repeat all the stuff I already told you I don't need."

"You got a sidearm?"

"I can draw a forty-five when I need one."

"How about something personal, just for you? Something you can keep with you all the time, just in case. I got a Ruger three-fifty-seven magnum revolver I traded some squid for in Da Nang. I could give you a couple boxes of ammunition too."

A revolver? That would be cool, Hank thought. “Does it have a holster?”

“Sure, you can have that too.”

“Okay. I need to see it, but that sounds like a good trade.”

Chapter 38

Third Battalion, 26th Marines moved back to Khe Sanh and the base began to get crowded. For most of the time since the hill fights the previous spring when the important high ground around Khe Sanh was taken, the combat base was occupied by a company of infantry and a Headquarters and Services (H&S) company along with two artillery batteries and some armor. With the addition of 3/26, all the facilities were strained, especially the water supply.

Having another battalion on base was enough to make living and working conditions deteriorate, but on top of that the OIC said the commander of the 26th Marines was expecting an attack on the base or one of the outposts within two weeks and was discussing having 2/26 moved back to Khe Sanh also. How the base commander knew that or where he got the information wasn't shared with Seabees.

A lot was going on and it was hard to get any reliable information about what. All Hank and the rest of the Seabees knew was something unpleasant was brewing and it was unpleasant enough to make the Marines think they needed a full regiment at Khe Sanh. Khe Sanh was so far out in the boonies everybody there was just stuck. They couldn't convoy out and they couldn't walk out.

The immediate implication of a whole lot more Marines on the base and possibly new outposts, was a sudden need for a lot more hooches, shops, offices, bunkers, and hence a lot more building materials. Resources were already scarce and everything was used. Seabees had to be taken off construction projects to guard the materials yard because the Marines would steal anything they could get their hands on, often with the approval of their commanders, maybe just a wink and a nod, but approval none the less.

The base was changing quickly. Besides First and Third Battalions, new Marines were coming in on helicopters every day. Hank couldn't keep up with the new additions. Recon detachments, searchlight detachments, radio detachments, shore party detachments, headquarters detachments, and detachments of things he had never heard of and all had to find space and shelter.

Finally, the base itself was being fortified. The Marines had suddenly become aware of the vulnerability of all the buildings above ground. Ammunition was coming in everyday and being stockpiled in expectation of attacks and the ASPs were full to overflowing. Ammunition on pallets was stored outside the ammo bunkers. After his experience at Dong Ha, seeing all that ordnance stacked outside gave Toby the willies and he told Hank so. The main ASP was only a hop, skip, and a jump from the Seabee compound. Those pallets of green artillery shells had an ominous look, like living things just waiting for a chance to blow you up.

The Seabee detail was stretched to the limit keeping the runway open and putting up structures for the Marines. All of the heavy equipment was in constant use with very little time for maintenance. The monsoon was wet and cold, and accidents and normal wear and tear kept maintenance crews working two twelve-hour shifts. It was so muddy, equipment got stuck on level ground.

There was very little time or energy to worry about what was happening outside the wire or worry about the future. Just trying to make your energy last for the whole shift was challenge enough. The only good news was the water supply was holding and they had plenty of food, so far. The uncertainty was, the water supply was located outside the wire and food had to compete with ammunition and building supplies for space on supply flights. Hank was going through three C-Rats meals every shift and still losing weight. He was down to 240 and as lean as he had ever been in his life.

One thing was noticeable though. Enemy activity was picking up and the Marines were getting stressed. The wire was being probed every night. Hit and run rockets and mortars were more frequent making the nights more tense.

Marines rigged truck and jeep horns with batteries on poles in place of sirens for rocket warning signals. Often the hill outposts could see the launches and were able to radio a few seconds of warning. There wasn't much warning for mortars though unless someone heard the tubing sounds.

Recon patrols were reporting signs of massed enemy units in the AO and regular Marine patrols were running into ambushes and finding fortifications and trenches under construction near the base.

Even though life had become twenty-four-hour stress and work, Hank benefitted. He didn't have time or energy to brood over Bu Duc and dead babies. The memories were pushed deeper and he began resembling his old self.

On December 21, the Marines confirmed the

presence of NVA in division strength in the AO with more moving in from Laos. By January 2, the Marine G2 at Da Nang confirmed the presence of at least two divisions of NVA in the Khe Sanh Operating Area. On January 16, Second Battalion, Twenty-sixth Marines was diverted from another operation to Khe Sanh and the full battalion arrived on the 17th of January.

Hank and Toby were taking a break for coffee with Rawlins outside the main bunker on January 17th.

"Did you ever see so many jarheads in one place in your life?" Hank asked of no one in particular.

2/26 was forming up as the helicopters brought them in. They were preparing to go somewhere.

"Maybe during weapons and small unit training," Toby said. "What are they doing, Staff Sergeant?"

"That's our second Battalion."

"Damn! That's a lot of excavation and building coming up."

"Not here," Rawlins said. "The word I got is they're moving out to hill 558 to establish a strong point. The whole regiment is together at Khe Sanh now."

"Where'd they all go?" Hank asked. "We're a little more crowded, but nothing like a regiment."

"Well, let's see. Hill Eight-eighty-one south has India Company plus two platoons. That's about four hundred Marines. Hill Eight-sixty-one has Kilo Company plus two platoons from Alpha Company, first Battalion. That's about three hundred Marines. Those guys there, Second Battalion, are going out to hill five-fifty-eight, about a thousand Marines. We also have a platoon from first Battalion out on hill nine-fifty, about fifty Marines. The rest of the regiment is here on the combat base, plus our supporting elements."

"Damn," Toby said. "That's a lot of Marines."

"Yeah," Rawlins said, "but the NVA have a lot more."

The supporting elements included six Marine tanks with 90mm guns, ten Ontos each carrying six 106mm recoilless rifles, two quad-fifty trucks capable of almost 2000 rounds a minute each, two 40mm duster tanks with twin 40mm automatic cannons, 105mm and 155mm artillery batteries, and two 4.2-inch mortars. In addition, the weapons-platoons in the headquarters companies had 81mm mortars and the companies has 60mm mortars. And, of course, a battalion of infantry with personal and automatic weapons on the perimeter.

Rawlins meant to reassure the Seabees and he did. Khe Sanh might be isolated, but it was a hairy beast. Privately, though, a regiment of Marines didn't reassure him. The NVA were said to have two divisions in the area and the base was cut off.

Chapter 39

The first few hours after dark were noisy as tanks, Ontos, and quad fifties left their revetments and took up defensive positions around the perimeter. They moved around each night to keep the enemy from getting a firm grasp of the Marine's order of battle.

Incoming mortars and rockets were getting more frequent and most work was done before 1400 using the fog as cover. Runway damage, though, had to be fixed when it happened. Sniper activity had increased to the point where operators and steelworkers risked their lives just leaving the equipment yard. Only enough men to complete the fix were sent out.

On busy days when all the equipment was committed, Marine tankers assisted the Seabees using their tanks like bulldozers. Sometimes a tank would assist because it was just too damn dangerous to be on top of a bulldozer and the work had to get done.

A large NVA force attacked the outpost on hill 861 during the night of January 20. The sounds of distant battle were clear and ominous. This was not a probe or hit-and-run attack. Hank and Toby sat outside the hooch and looked for the light show.

"You know what?" Toby asked quietly.

"What?"

"That shit is coming here."

"You mean tonight?"

"Soon," Toby said.

"The Marines seem to think so," Hank said. "The boss was smart to make our own underground bunker the first priority. Have you looked at the ammo dump behind us lately?"

"Yeah. Scary, isn't it?" Toby said. "There must be ten or fifteen tons of artillery shells stored outside. Lord knows what else. What the hell are they thinking? I was at Dong Ha when our dump got hit. It was like the whole world blew up. And they weren't storing stuff right out in the open."

Hank grunted and wiped his hand through his hair.

"Rawlins said they are trying to build up a thirty-day supply of ammo in case the weather or NVA shut down the runway," he said. "The word I got is the NVA has two divisions around here. We have one regiment. That's a lot of damn enemy soldiers for a regiment to fight."

Toby leaned back against the sandbags.

"I'm glad we have more Marines on blue sector now. I don't want to be sitting out there alone in a hole at night now."

"Me neither. It's a lot better perimeter now though."

They sat quietly for several minutes watching for light flashes in the hills.

"We should be getting out of here in a couple of weeks," Toby said. "Didn't they say our extension was till February?"

"That's what the Chief said, but the first job was supposed to last only till December second. It wouldn't surprise me if we get extended again. I don't see any let up in the work."

A large explosion in the hills lit up the distant sky. That battle was heating up.

"I guess I wouldn't mind too much," Toby said. "I'd hate to leave the detail shorthanded just to get out of here."

And I'm going to make damn sure that doesn't happen for you, Hank thought. Your ass is going to be out of here as soon as I can work out way to make it happen.

"Well, I'm going back to bed," Hank said. "I've got to go out with the combat engineers tomorrow and see if we can lumber some logs to use as bunker reinforcement. All the beams are gone and who knows when we'll get any more. All the flights are bringing in ordnance, food, and medical supplies. The day is coming when they are going to wish they spared some room for some damn building materials."

"You can't eat wood," Toby said. "You know the drill. If you don't have it and can't get it, make it."

"Yeah, well I'm not looking forward to going outside the wire. I probably should have kept my machine gun."

Chapter 40

The base was a beehive of activity on the morning of the 20th long before first light. With a sense of urgency, newly arrived Marines were trying to dig-in and provide themselves some cover but were mostly still above ground and exposed to the weather, to say nothing of being exposed to the enemy. The Marines were digging in and Seabee equipment operators worked all night using backhoes and front-end loaders to help the Marines get at least partially underground.

The predicted attack on an outpost had happened and now the Marines were predicting a ground attack on the combat base. Suddenly, predictions by the Marine S2 gained a lot of credibility.

A rocket hit the center of the runway during the night and Seabee crews were taking up damaged runway matting and laying down new in the dark and fog. The perimeter trench-line was still being extended, deepened, and widened to completely encircle the base so the Marines could move around without having to move above ground. Sandbag blast walls were being built in the trench every fifty feet to contain the blast of any direct hit in the trench. The work had continued all night.

All sorts of materials were scavenged to use in roofs and bunker walls. Thousands of sandbags were being filled and distributed for reinforcement and cover and helicopters were warming up in revetments by the runway to ferry wounded from the hills to Charlie Med not far from the Seabee camp as soon as the fog cleared. Excavations were underway to get Charlie Med underground. Suddenly, somebody's lack of planning had become the Seabee's emergency.

Lima company from third Battalion was on the red sector. Charlie company from First Battalion was on the north blue sector. Bravo Company from First Battalion was on the south and east gray sector. Bravo Recon and the Seabees guarded the runway opening in the perimeter. Delta Company was in reserve and dug in near the center of the base.

It was noisy as hell too. Khe Sanh's artillery batteries were firing missions in support of the outposts and moving ammunition to their battery caches and breaking out rounds for firing missions. Diesel engines were roaring on heavy equipment, generators, and armor. Khe Sanh was a dangerous place for moving around. The whole nature of the place had changed. Suddenly Hank understood the meaning of combat base. For reasons Hank didn't know, the Marines were getting ready for all-out war.

He could sense the urgency from the activity around him, but like most of the Seabees around him, he didn't know what was driving it. He and Toby talked with everyone they knew to find out why the sudden urgency. They were in a dangerous place and suddenly it had become more dangerous. The problem was the danger was just a dark thing out there in the night. They weren't getting a lot of information about what was going on.

For the past week, Seabees had worked extra hours building heavier revetments for the equipment with fifty-five-gallon drums filled with dirt stacked three high. Crews were increasing the sandbag walls around shops and generators. The urgency around them was contagious. Something big and bad was approaching in the night and it had already taken a bite out of an outpost.

Fearing an attack and unable to sleep, he spent the night in the small bunker. Toby was out on the runway prepositioning matting along the runway.

Hank had his Ruger on his hip and an M16 next to him. Rumors were flying.

Some serious battles took place in the hills while Hank slept that night and although he had no way of knowing it, some unsettling intelligence had been obtained. The Marines were expecting an attack on the base and the base was not ready. Too much of everything was still above ground including tons of ammunition and explosives and newly arrived infantry. The Seabees didn't know what to expect but knew it was serious by all the activity on the perimeter. The Marines were turning-to and getting ready to fight.

A few rounds of mortar incoming hit the base during the night, mostly near the artillery batteries. It seemed a bit busier than normal but not enough to panic over. Hank woke up when they hit but went back to sleep. He felt secure in the bunker. Seabees built it.

He was up and dressed at 0430. The SF had conditioned him to be ready for the witching hour. There was no way to sleep with all the noise and activity anyway. Morning quarters was scheduled for 0530 that day and it was for all hands to be briefed by the OIC on the revised construction schedule due to the addition of another battalion on and near the base—and hopefully some intelligence about what the hell was going on.

The red sector at the west-end seemed to be

firing a lot of small arms during the night. Since the big mess hall was in that direction, Hank decided to skip the mess hall and grab a box of C-Rats and a cup of coffee in the big underground bunker. As he walked to the bunker, he could hear the sound of battle from the direction of hill 861. Something was still going on out there.

The OIC and the office staff were already in the bunker with what looked like all the office equipment. The bunker was big, well lit, and well-fortified. Toby was getting a cup of coffee.

"What's up?" Hank asked.

"The base is on one-hundred percent alert. We better get whatever we need from the hooch and get it in here. I think some serious shit is about to start, Hank."

"I think we're good in our bunker. Everybody and his brother will be in here."

"Then why ain't we, brother?" Toby said with a grin.

Next order of business was coffee. This was obviously going to be a busy day.

"Do you figure the engineers will be doing any lumbering today?" he asked.

"They won't be doing anything but getting everything they can underground. A Marine major briefed the OIC and said if we get a ground attack to expect the runway to be a major target first. That will be our total focus until whatever is happening is over."

That wasn't good news. Hank hated runway work. No matter what job you had, except maybe siting high on a forklift, you were going to be covered in tar by the end of the day, boots, trousers, shirt, hat, and skin. It was filthy, back breaking work, but it was the priority and an all-hands operation.

Over the next hour the base received some harassment incoming but it was scattered, mostly small arms, and didn't damage anything important. The night crew came in early for the all-hands quarters and the day crew was up early. Everyone was at the bunker and the Lieutenant was getting antsy. He told the Detail to fall-in for Quarters at 0520.

He took reports from the Leading Petty Officers and flipped his clipboard to the new schedule and then stopped.

Everyone heard what he was hearing.

They all turned their heads toward the hills and listened. The rumble of artillery in the distance was louder than usual and there was a whole lot more of it than anyone had heard before. The deep rumble of big guns grew in a crescendo that seemed to circle the base.

Suddenly Marines on the perimeter began screaming, "Incoming!"

Watching the Marines running and diving into holes, his shock slowly turned to comprehension. The boss screamed, "Dismissed! Take cover!"

Seabees scattered. Most ran to the big bunker and crowded down into the entrance ramp and pushed inside. Hank was closer to a fighting hole and ran to it. Rawlins was on his heels. Hank jumped in the hole and crawled into the covered and fortified portion. Rawlins landed right behind him. Hank turned to look out over the lip of the hole and Rawlins pulled him down. Suddenly they both knew they had made a big mistake by not running for the bunker. It was too late now.

"Get down. Curl up. Big shit is coming."

Rawlins knew the sound of artillery and he knew the NVA were unleashing their big 152mm guns on Khe Sanh, every round with eighty pounds of explosives. Everyone had been expecting it to happen sometime, but no one anticipated what was happening. The sound of artillery firing was coming from every direction. Other launch and firing sounds just as ominous were there also but were lost in the rumble of big guns. Rockets and mortars were also going to be part of the show.

As the minute hand crossed the 0530 mark like it was a trigger, the base began blowing up. Mortars, 122mm rockets, and artillery shells rained down on the plateau in a well planned and executed time on target attack. Multiple NVA artillery teams timed their firing and launches so that the combined incoming of the salvo hit the base almost at one time. No area inside the wire was spared. The attack was so violent with simultaneous concussive shocks, everyone on the base was stunned into confusion—and worse.

To Hank, it seemed like the world was blowing up and his life was coming to an end. It had been bad at Bu Doc, but nothing like this. This was hundreds of rounds hitting and blowing up almost simultaneously. He was bounced in the hole and slammed back down. His skull was compressed by concussion and his limbs were jerked around out of his control. The noise was so loud it ceased to be sound and became physical force and pain. He couldn't think or function. With all his experience, Rawlins was in no better shape. They were caught in a tempest and the hole gave them only partial protection. Unless something fell right in the hole, they were protected from shrapnel, but concussion got in. And it wouldn't stop. The NVA artillery kept firing.

Seabees inside the underground bunker couldn't leave and Seabees above ground dove into any hole they could find. Marines hunkered down deep in their fighting holes and bunkers. Equipment was left where it stopped and operators sought cover. All activity on the base ceased as the ground rumbled with the shock of uncounted artillery and rocket strikes. The runway began coming apart as delayed fuse artillery rounds punched through the aluminum matting and blew holes in the bed four feet deep.

The water bladder reservoir was punctured almost immediately and the water tower began spewing water through shrapnel holes in its side a few minutes later. Shrapnel blasted through the equipment yard and severed hydraulic hoses, blasted away steering wheels, and broke brake lines. Every piece of canvas on base was shredded and sandbags were ripped apart.

Artillery crews were driven under cover, infantry were driven into holes, the air control tower and radar were shut down and the base infrastructure was destroyed in minutes. The combat base had become a quivering target unable to respond or function.

Chapter 41

Almost immediately, two big artillery rounds hit the main ammo dump behind the Seabee compound and whole pallets of artillery and mortar rounds stacked outside the bunker exploded. The unbearable noise and concussion rose in a crescendo of cacophony and pain that wiped out what little conscious sanity Hank had left.

A POL was collocated with the ASP and was hit almost at the same time the ASP got hit. Burning oil, diesel fuel, and tar poured out of the POL and into the ASP, setting off munitions inside and underground.

Hank didn't know and didn't care, but a few minutes later the mess hall took multiple direct hits and it was no more. After months of probes, ranging rounds, and visual observation, the NVA gunners knew the exact coordinates of the most important targets on the combat base. Fog be damned. They kept firing and hit what they were aiming for.

How they were able to function lesser men would never know, but the combat base artillery began functioning again. Artillery batteries got their act together quickly and began firing counterbattery with shrapnel flying though their emplacements and explosions knocking down their revetments and parapets. Soon, Marine mortar outgoing added to the defense. There was no sign of a ground attack yet, but it was expected. Artillery to soften up defenses precedes an attack and the softening they just went through was devastating. The Marines put a wall of 81mm and 60mm on every pre-registered coordinate on their target card hoping to interdict and prevent a coordinated and massed attack. Even a battalion of massed enemy hitting the wire right then would probably get through the wire and wreak havoc on the base.

The ammo dump took another direct hit and the bunker contents began cooking-off. Massive explosions shook the base and knocked down aboveground structures. Later, it was hard to tell how long, a cache of C4 plastic explosives blew and the shock wave was so massive it blew sandbags off the roofs of bunkers at the other end of the base and collapsed the overhead on the Marine's combat operations center. People in the underground bunkers could only imagine what it did to the Marines in the trenches, mortar pits, and fighting holes along gray sector near the ASP. Were any defenders left at all? There was no question in anyone's mind, Marines were dying.

The main ASP wasn't the end of the disasters. Later the auxiliary ASP on the west end near the artillery batteries took a hit. Drums of powered CS stored there were exploded and cast into the air forming clouds of CS gas that spread out across the base. Mercifully, Hank and Stout didn't know much of what was going on. Constant concussion had driven their brains into defensive measures and they lost consciousness. It was whiffs of CS acting like smelling salts that brought them around.

The ground was littered with unexploded ordnance, flechette darts, and shrapnel three inches deep. Hank and Rawlins helped each other stagger across the moonscape ground between the hole and the main Seabee bunker. There were plenty of craters to take shelter in. Neither of them remembered the rounds hitting that close.

They didn't get far. Rawlins's trained and experienced mind recognized the sound of the diving rocket even in his dazed condition. He grabbed Hank and fell into a crater. The explosion that followed just a few seconds later bounced them both in the bottom of the hole. They were low enough so the shrapnel and force of the explosion passed over them, but the concussion felt like getting hit with a baseball bat and knocked them both out.

Hank regained consciousness slowly, but his brain wasn't working well enough to understand what needed to be done. Rawlins wasn't in much better shape, but he had the instinct bred of many battles to keep him moving. They had to get to the bunker. He shook Hank.

"Come on Tucker, we have to get to the bunker. Come on, damn it! We've got to move."

Hank didn't really understand the words, but the tone got him moving, sluggishly, but moving in the right direction with Rawlins's help. Just before they reached the dirt ramp down to the entrance, something big cooked-off in the ammo dump and knocked them both down.

Suddenly, Toby was there dragging both of them toward the ramp. They crawled down the ramp and into the bunker. Hands grabbed them and pulled them inside.

"Hank! Hank! Are you wounded?" Toby was in a panic seeing Hank senseless.

The voice was just a ringing sound from deep in the barrel hank seemed to be in. Hollow echoes bounced around in his head but he couldn't make any sense of them. He realized he was somehow away from the explosions and no longer feeling the sickening punches of concussion, but he couldn't focus his eyes to see where he was.

Then someone was passing something under his nose and his breath caught and he coughed. He jerked his head away and his vision began to clear. Sounds began to make some sense.

"I can't find anything wrong with him," a voice said.

A light shined in an eye and then in the other.

"His pupils are dilated, but they are responding to light. I don't think he has a concussion or any brain damage. He'll come out of it in a few minutes and he's going to have a badassed headache for a while. Let him rest until he gets steady. I've got to get out of here."

Hank watched the corpsman grab his unit-one and run to the bunker entrance. He listened for a moment and then ran out into the maelstrom Hank and Rawlins had just escaped.

"You back with us, Hank?" It was Rawlins.

"Yeah, but I don't feel so good. How'd you get me back here?"

"I don't remember much of it myself. I remember your brother helping. I think we got each other back here."

"Help me up," Hank said. "Where's Toby?"

"Right here. You sure you want to get up?

You don't look too good."

"I don't feel good. I have to move though. I'm starting to cramp up."

Suddenly he was on the deck and looking up again. Rawlins was next to him and groaning. Toby was still standing but holding on to a beam. Dirt was falling from the roof and the beams gave an awful groan. Hank curled into a fetal position and tried not to throw up.

"That was damn near a direct hit," Toby yelled. "The roof held!"

Rawlins rolled over and got to his knees. He shook his head and grunted then heaved himself up on his feet and stood there swaying back and forth.

"You okay?" Hank asked.

"Ask me in five minutes. Need some help?"

"No, I got it."

Hank sat up and braced himself on his arms behind him. Then he turned over on hands and knees. He reached up and Rawlins took his hand and heaved him up. They stood there grinning at each other.

"Can't be too bad," Rawlins said. "We're on our feet."

"I need some caffeine. I'll help you."

"She-it," Rawlins said. "You can't help yourself. Go on. I'll come behind you and catch you when you fall. Toby, you catch me if I fall."

"Hank," the Chief said. "You back with us?"

"Not all the way, but I can function."
"Relieve Jones on the radio. I need him.
Back to work, Hank thought.

Chapter 42

After the initial attack. there was only about 1800 feet of usable runway left and the entire runway lighting systems was knocked out. The electricians and steelworkers were out on the runway before dark. Every minute the runway was closed was a minute desperately needed supplies couldn't get in, not in the quantities needed, especially munitions. The big guns and mortars were firing counterbattery and interdiction missions constantly and most of the ammunition supply was destroyed.

The word circulating in the bunker was, the base was surrounded by a division of NVA, but no one had seen any. They were holding off their attack for some reason, but they were there, so they said, close to the base.

Marines and Seabees, punchy from exhaustion, manned the perimeter watching for the first signs of a ground attack. After working to restore the runway and base facilities for hours, Seabees had to man the bunkers and fighting holes guarding that scary opening in the perimeter where the runway came though. Sleep was a luxury grabbed in hour long stretches before another emergency called them away from their rest.

After the first big artillery attack there was a slight pause. Incoming resumed in the afternoon but not nearly with the intensity of the opening attack. The rounds, rockets and mortars came in more randomly and more terrifying because of it. You never knew when and where the next one was going to hit. You just knew it would be soon. Sometimes you could hear the artillery fire from a few miles away or the tubing sounds of a mortar firing in close, if you were away from the equipment and sound of diesels. Most often the Seabees just had to pray something unheard wouldn't fall on their heads. They had to keep working regardless.

With shrapnel still flying from exploding ordnance in the ASP and NVA incoming still hitting the base, equipment operators and steelworkers moved their equipment to the runway and began patching holes in the matting, rebuilding the rock bedding, replacing whole sections of matting, and dodging incoming. Everyone pitched in. Your rate didn't matter. You worked on the runway. The damage was overwhelming. There just wasn't enough Seabees or Seabee equipment to cover it all. The COC sent Marine working parties to help on the runway. The tankers moved their tanks out to assist and sometimes to just sit between the Seabees and whatever was out in the grass shooting at them. Seabees went to work in full combat gear with tools in one hand and a rifle in the other. Everyone was expecting the ground attack to start at any moment.

The electricians were able to get runway lighting working and C-123 short field cargo planes using the remaining runway were able to get in that first night to deliver limited but badly needed ammunition supplies. Other electricians began repairing the base electrical infrastructure. Almost all power and phone lines were destroyed.

Men woke up still covered in tar from the previous shift and went to bed with more tar on top of the old tar. The morning fog turned out to be salvation. The artillery still came in, but the NVA artillery observers couldn't see their targets to adjust fire.

Helicopters and a few short field aircraft were using a portion of the runway, but the base needed the big C130s landing to get the quantities they needed. A regiment can go through a lot of ordnance fast during an attack. By the 23rd enough runway had been repaired for C130s to get in.

Hank didn't know it, but his Civic action

work wouldn't be needed at Khe Sanh village. The district headquarters was attacked by the NVA while the ASP was exploding. Much of the artillery firing he heard from Khe Sanh's 105s was in support of the CAG platoon and the ruff puffs guarding the headquarters. The village was overrun while the ASP was cooking off. The CAG Marines were evacuated to the base and the Army advisors took Ruff-Puffs and refugees to the FOB compound.

The Chief got through the work assignments at morning quarters without assigning Toby but told him to hang back. After he dismissed the formation he pulled Toby aside.

"Tucker, see what's available for moving dirt and start clearing the camp of munitions. There's plenty of craters for burying the unexploded stuff littering the compound."

Toby drew flak pants to go with his flak jacket for some protection in case something exploded. Jagged pieces of shrapnel were everywhere. Huge pieces of enemy 122mm rocket warheads with razor sharp, serrated edges sat on top of the ground and made movement dangerous and difficult for any wheeled vehicle. Light caught the edges of smaller pieces of shrapnel in the dirt everywhere. Unexploded artillery, mortars, and small arms littered the landscape like a carpet in places. Closer in to the ASP, unexploded ordnance and shrapnel covered the ground in a carpet inches deep.

Eleven hundred tons of ordnance, some exploded, some duds, some unstable, some still smoldering, had to be blown-up or buried. It was like Dong Ha all over again. EOD blew the stuff that needed demolitions, but nothing was sure where munitions that have been through an explosion were concerned. Power generators and telephone wires were knocked out all over the base and men were working to restore power and communications around the clock and having to step around or over munitions that might explode at any moment.

Toby checked the yard to see what was available. A mechanic was working on a frontend loader.

"Is this all that's available, Hawk?"

"This is it. I have to replace a hydraulic line on this loader. It might be ready in about an hour. It hasn't got a seat and half the wheel is blown away, but it will run. The dozer you can take now. It's got a hydraulic leak too, but you can probably get a few hours work out of it."

"Either one will do. I've got to clear some of this ordnance away from the camp or bury it. I'll take the dozer for now."

It wasn't ideal, but everything else that

could still run was on the runway or already working jobs on the base. He figured he stood the best chance of surviving exploding ordnance on the dozer, and if the hydraulics failed, well, he'd just leave it where it was and get the loader.

The urgent task was getting unexploded ordnance and shrapnel that could cut tires away from the yards and bunkers so Seabees could move around safely.

Seabees had moved a lot of the scattered ordnance on the first day. Most of the unstable munitions had either exploded or were blown up by EOD. Men carried smoldering rounds, duds, and unstable stuff away from their working positions in their arms and even stacked or piled it at collection points. Those would be easy. The dozer blade could handle them. When that was done, he could use the loader to move the other stuff to a safe point to be buried or blown-up when the situation stabilized, but the equipment and materials yards had to be cleared.

There were plenty of artillery craters deep enough to hold the unexploded stuff and Toby made use of them. On the dozer he wasn't worried a whole lot about what was on the ground. It takes a lot to hurt a dozer, even a toy dozer. What truly worried him was what was still falling from the sky. The NVA were acting like they were here to stay and the base was still getting hit regularly, not like the first day, but still plenty, especially when something like equipment or armor moved on the base. They had to have observers in close and a pretty good map of the base.

There really wasn't any clear ground on the base except around the Marines positions. They had begun clearing even while the attack was happening. He moved the dozer out and used the blade just skimming the ground to clear a path out of the yard. So far, so good. Nothing blew up.

The weather was comfortable for a change. It was overcast with low, scud clouds. The temperature was in the mid-seventies. Hardly any wind. The day was dry. The heavy rains were beginning to slack off, sometimes leaving whole days with only a short downpour late in the afternoon. Toby worked steadily, moving spent ordnance into piles of dirt and metal, plowing out holes deep enough to bury the piles, and removing shrapnel in the process.

He kept his head swiveling so he could watch the Marines on the perimeter. He couldn't hear shit on the Dozer. As he was pushing a pile toward a crater near the back side of the Seabee camp, he noticed the recon marines out by the runway running and diving for their holes. *Crap!* He couldn't hear anything but the diesel on the dozer and didn't know what spooked them, but he wasn't taking any chances.

He disengaged the engine and let it idle. The first mortar hit near the perimeter as he jumped off the tread and crawled behind the blade. Another round went over Toby and hit in the scattered munitions and shrapnel closer to the ASP.

Suddenly the blade and dozer were peppered with shrapnel and a piece of metal sheared off the front of the dozer and slammed into his helmet. Toby crammed his body tight into the space next to the blade and pulled his helmet tight onto his head.

When everything quieted down he took his helmet off and checked it. The covering was ripped and the metal dented.

He did not want to get back on top of the dozer.

Before he climbed back to the seat, he checked around the machine. The dozer was scarred and scraped by shrapnel on one side and almost normal on the other. A carpet of shrapnel covered the ground on one side and the other side was almost clear. The damn mortar had hit in the carpet of shrapnel around the ASP and turned it into secondary shrapnel that then blasted the dozer. If he hadn't got behind the blade he'd be shredded hamburger now.

Then the incoming stopped. That's the way it had been all morning. Just random terror. He waited a few minutes and then climbed back on the dozer keeping one eye on the marines on the perimeter. They were moving around again filling sandbags and breaking out mortar rounds for their 81mm.

This is insane, he thought. Mortar attacks are just an interruption. He was amazed at how calm he was. Everything that was happening was so foreign, it just didn't seem real. He fingered the dent in his helmet. It was real.

From his dozer seat while pushing fallen ordnance near the back of the Seabee area, Toby watched in amazement as two Marines walked out to the ASP, or where the ASP used to be, and start raking shrapnel into holes with garden rakes. What was amazing wasn't that they were doing it, but where the hell did they get garden rakes?

He continued with the dozer across the shrapnel bed to the marines and shut the engine off. One of the Marines watched hm climb down.

"Man, we thought you were dead meat when that shit-storm hit your machine. Glad you made it okay."

Toby showed them his helmet. "Could have been worse," he said. "If I hadn't seen the recon jumping in their holes I would have been hamburger. Look, you guys get in cover. I'm going to be burying this shit and you'll just be in the way. Tell whoever the fucking idiot was that sent you out here what I said—not that he's an idiot, but I'm going to be working here."

Both Marines grinned. "We hear and we obey," the big one said.

They didn't waste any time getting back to their positions and under cover.

I don't know why I did that, Toby thought. I don't want to be out here when the next one comes in. But if those guys are out here without any cover, shit, they're fucked. He climbed back on the dozer and started the engine. First he used the blade to scrape out a trench and then started dozing scrap shrapnel, dirt, and munitions into it. The wide blade made quick work of the worst of it. He finished up by dozing about three feet of dirt over the whole mess and returned to the Seabee area to finish cleaning up the equipment yard. Not one round of incoming, artillery or sniper, came in while he worked.

As he was shutting the dozer down, he wondered about men who joined the infantry. They made it a point of pride that they had to endure the harshest living conditions as a normal part of their job, that they were expected to endure conditions that would destroy lesser men. He took it a step further. The infantry used that perverse sense of pride to create a feeling of exclusiveness, didn't they? A sense of being the elite, to get men to do things no normal human being would tolerate. Look at those guys out there with rakes.

He couldn't see anything elite about living day after day in the mud and cold, suffering malnutrition, their lives constantly at risk, digging holes to shit in, holes to eat in, holes to sleep in, and then spending time they ought to be resting burning the shit. There is nothing elite about working and sleeping in the same stinking, filthy clothes, often with fungus growing in their armpits. There is nothing elite about being pounded by artillery hour after hour, day after day, without any way to hit back. And there is damn well nothing elite about dying in those holes, but there it is. Conned by propaganda and seduced by status. I will fear no evil because I'm the baddest mother in the valley. Marines were proud of their status as men who could get it done regardless. Toby stopped and thought for a moment. And the fact is, exhausted and covered in dirt, they are magnificent sons-a-bitches. And then he looked around and had another thought. They? Shit, us Seabees are right here with them.

For just a moment as he climbed down across the treads, he felt that pride. Nothing else he had ever done or built gave him the sense of belonging to something special like the Seabees did. That was a good feeling, but it lasted all of ten seconds. Warning horns started blaring just before a

122mm rocket hit the middle of the base and he ran for the bunker. The fog was lifting.

Another battalion of Marines, 1/9, Landed at Khe Sanh and moved out to the Rock Quarry. The Seabees didn't know what the Marines were doing or where they would end up. So much was going on and they were only aware of their own small part of the battle. But hell, they probably knew as much as the grunts.

Chapter 43

Dreary, fatigue filled days full of fear and panic ended in nights filled with emergencies and mind-numbing explosions. Seabees worked two twelve-hour shifts on paper, but the shifts blurred into one another. In reality, they grabbed a few hours' sleep when they couldn't go any further, a meal on the run, and took care of bodily functions wherever and when the work and incoming allowed. Showers, even a quick wash under the spigot of the water buffalo, became a dim memory.

Hank woke up on the fourth morning after the ammo dump blew up with his eyes gummy and his mouth tasting like his body smelled. The day before, a helicopter and a fighter jet were shot down near the base. Strangely enough, those downed aircraft were more ominous than the artillery barrage. The base was totally dependent on air-support. If the enemy could shoot down a fighter jet, what was going to happen to the big, slow supply birds? If they couldn't get in, Khe Sanh was going to be in deep trouble quickly.

The ammo dump had finally stopped cooking off and the base only had to contend with enemy incoming. He was in the large bunker and took a moment to look around and remember where he was. No one worried about assigned bunks now. When they came in from the runway, they just flopped on anything available. Toby was nowhere to be seen. He had been there when Hank turned in, but equipment operators didn't get much downtime. If they weren't operating, they were helping mechanics repair the equipment.

All the civilians caught at Khe Sanh when the attack started tried to bribe their way into the Seabee bunker. The reporters were usually successful because they generally brought good booze with them, but many others were turned away. Helicopter pilots were welcome and not just because they usually brought great gedunk with them to supplement the C-Rats, but they were the only way out of Khe Sanh if you had to go. That's when they started calling the Seabee bunker the Alamo Hilton. The bunker was spacious and had good lighting, but most important, it was massively built with eight feet of wood, steel, dirt, rock, and sandbags over it. Only the Marine command bunker could compare, but it came in second place.

The Seabees on the runway had suffered two shrapnel casualties the previous day. No one was killed, but two Seabees earned purple hearts. The work was so hard and continuous he hadn't had the time or interest to notice what was happening to the Marines. A job fortifying Charlie Med changed that. It was the body bags lined up outside that drove home the price the Marines were paying.

Ten Marines were zipped into body bags waiting to be evacuated. He was shocked to realize that men were dying around him and he hadn't noticed. He didn't even know which incident had caused the deaths or if they were from the combat base or one of the outposts. Of course he knew casualties had to be happening. How could they not, but the endless demands of the work and his own survival didn't leave a lot of time or energy for looking outward. The body bags changed all that. It didn't matter that they weren't Seabees. It still hurt to see those body bags. Young men, hell, just boys, were wrapped inside those bags. One more vision to add to dead CIDG at Bu Duc and the blank staring eyes of Peanut.

When your very existence is threatened every minute of the day and night, your world becomes compressed. Tunnel vision becomes tunnel existence. You remain totally focused on surviving in your little corner of the world, and since that is where you must survive, it is the only corner that matters. Seabees and Marines alike often didn't know what was happening on the other side of the base, or care. The terror was so random and relentless, you could only worry about what was about to fall on you, and even though you put it out of your mind, you knew people were dying, were going to die, but maybe not you, and implicit in that thought was, maybe someone else, and because of your own fervent wish to survive, that thought, even if never rising to full consciousness, becomes, let it be someone else--then you see the body bags. Even if it isn't conscious, the logic is inescapable. Someone is going to die. Don't let it be me. *Let it be someone else.* And you walk away with a nagging sense of guilt and that is a shame because everyone else was thinking and feeling the same thing.

As the expectation of attack grew, the Marines quit sending out patrols like they used to. Some short patrols went out from the combat base but they stayed within 500 meters. The closer outposts like the one near the rock quarry patrolled further out but stayed close to their own camps. Rumors were flying about whole divisions of North Vietnamese preparing to attack the combat base and the perimeter Marines were on alert twenty-four hours a day. Seabees didn't have time to worry about North Vietnamese surrounding the base. The ones further out shooting rockets and artillery at the base were worry enough and the work had to go on.

Hank quit trying to get information about what was happening from the Marines when one of them tried to convince him the giant crater near the ASP was made by a 300mm artillery round. Now, he wasn't a military expert by any stretch of the imagination, but he was pretty sure that was bullshit.

In just four days the entire base and much of the surrounding territory was pockmarked with artillery craters. Except for shattered stumps and a few bare limbs, the trees were gone. Piles of trash that had accumulated before the attack and above ground buildings were turned into secondary shrapnel by incoming artillery and scattered across acres. From the top of the Seabee bunker looking southeast you could see the garbage dump before the attack. Now, the whole base looked like a city landfill—on the moon. Many tents still appeared to be standing, but they were actually rain covers for partially sunken bunkers recently dug. They wouldn't last long.

Chapter 44

While the Seabees toiled and ducked incoming, Marine battalions and companies were being moved around to block avenues of access to the base. To the south, the SF camp at Lang Vei blocked access from Laos on Route Nine, but nobody on the combat base expected 400 CIDG and a few SF troops to be much help in stopping regular NVA troops.

On the 27th a company of Vietnamese rangers moved in outside the wire on the east end of the base off gray sector. The Marines kept them outside the wire though. They didn't trust the south Vietnamese troops. Marines didn't seem to trust anybody.

After five days of intermittent bombardment, everyone was adjusting to underground living and keeping one ear open for the sounds of artillery in the distance and tubing sounds in close, that is, when diesel engines weren't growling in their ears. The incoming they feared the most was the NVA 152mm artillery. The damn things had eighty pounds of explosives in them and could punch right through a reinforced bunker. Worse, they were pinpoint accurate and had a much greater range than anything the Marines had at Khe Sanh. They stood off in the distance and pounded the base without worry of counter battery.

Staff Sergeant Rawlins was transferred from his job as military advisor for the Seabees to a platoon sergeant's job. He and Hank were taking a break in the bunker on the 28th and choking down some of the worst coffee either of them had ever drank.

"Keep your head down, Tucker. You guys don't need me now anyway. You've become pretty good defenders on the perimeter. I'd almost let you in my Corps."

"Hank grinned. "Almost?"

"Yeah. I'd say you're somewhere between being squids and marines. Almost."

"Where are they moving you?"

"Lima Company. I got first platoon on Red Sector."

"Have you been getting any word on what the hell is going on? Are they going to attack or not?"

"All I can tell you is there's a lot of them out there. Why they're holding back is anybody's guess. They should have attacked when the dump blew up. Hell, they could have walked right through the wire. If nothing else they would have used up what little ammunition we had left."

"There's a rumor that there isn't going to be any Tet holiday this year," Hank said. "You heard anything?"

"The ceasefire was canceled for I-Corps. Not sure what's happening anywhere else. With a division of North Vietnamese Army out there, it doesn't make any difference anyway. How do you like your revolver?"

"I like it fine, but the OIC wants it. He's a pretty good guy. I may end up giving it to him."

"Can't hurt to make the skipper happy. I've got to get back to being a Marine. You take it easy."

"Any way I can get it, staff sergeant."

Hank watched Rawlins pause at the bunker entrance and listen. Nobody moved outside without listening first now. He'd stop again near the top of the ramp to listen again. He would already have his next shelter fixed in his mind. That was another habit everyone was getting into. If you had to move on the base, first you thought about your route and figured out where each place was that you could dive into for cover and then you located your next shelter before you moved on. Incoming was less frequent now and random, but it could come at any time and hit any place. The detail Chief stopped to talk to Hank.

"Tucker, I need you to take a detail out to the water point. The pump is sucking air. We've already checked the bladder reservoir and the tower but can't find any leaks. Shrapnel or something may have damaged the dam and the water level in the pool is dropping. See what the hell is going on and get it fixed before the fucking Marines panic."

"Who do you have to go with me? If the dam is breeched, I'm going to need some help."

"Take Thompson and Clark. They were part of your crew before you got here. Take Holder too. Four of you should be able to handle it."

"Uh, Chief, you did get a Marine escort for us, didn't you?"

"What are you, some kind of candy-ass?" Then the Chief grinned. "Four Seabees should be able to handle a piddly little division of NVA." He laughed. "Of course I got you an escort. Get your men together. A team from Bravo Recon is taking you out there."

Most of the Seabees knew most of Bravo Recon. They were co-located on the runway perimeter. Recon were said to be the sneakiest Marines in Vietnam. They went out on recon patrols in six-man teams and often stayed a week in Indian country observing the NVA. Their job was to stay undetected and observe. They were experts at avoiding enemy contact. They were just what Hank wanted.

This would be a short, quick hike for them, but for the Seabees, it was a scary patrol into enemy territory. Hank took his M16, two bandoleers of magazines, and four frag grenades. He took his revolver too. Even though they would only be going a short distance, leaving the wire and a battalion of Marines behind was unsettling.

Chapter 45

Sergeant Abbot, the recon team leader gathered his team and the Seabees.

"My name is Abbot," he said. "I want the Seabees in the middle of the column right behind me. There will be three recons in front of the Seabees and three behind. I will be directly ahead of the lead Seabee. That will be you, Tucker."

"Right," Hank said.

"Keep your eyes on me and follow my signals immediately. Have any of you ever been on a combat patrol?"

"I've been out on patrol with the Army SF," Hank said. "Thompson and Clark were with me at Bu Duc and have some firefights behind them, but they haven't been on a patrol. Holder, have you ever been outside the wire?"

"I've been with Detail Bravo from the

beginning," Holder said. "This is my first time outside the wire."

"You will patrol right behind Tucker," Abbot said. "Keep your eyes on him. Being somewhere the enemy might target you individually has a different flavor than just being on a base that's getting hit randomly, so pay attention. We won't be far from help at any time, but we just don't know what's out beyond the hill. Let's move out. Keep your intervals and keep quiet. Remember, the idea is to avoid the enemy."

The water point was a pool created by damming a stream about 150 meters outside blue sector perimeter. That's not far, almost shouting distance, but there was a small hill and tall elephant grass between the perimeter and the reservoir, so the perimeter guards could not see the repair party once they were about a football field's distance away, and the repair party couldn't see the reservoir or who might be hiding there until they were right on top of it. Visibility was lousy that day. The fog had rolled back in and the day was overcast with the ceiling only about 500 feet with fast moving clouds, so the perimeter would lose visual touch with them even sooner.

The dam was earthen and about eighty feet wide and formed a reservoir about six feet deep behind it. Back during the heavy rains of September and October the river flooded and washed the dam out. It was rebuilt in the fall with old PSP matting from the runway to reinforce the sides and a deep pool was created in the stream by blasting to act as a reservoir if the river level ever fell. The rains had tapered off from the monsoon highs, so something else must be dropping the water level in the reservoir. Maybe a hostile something else. Maybe a stray mortar round. Rawlins had been surprised the NVA hadn't cut the water supply yet, so maybe they were getting around to it. It was only 150 meters from the base, but maybe, maybe, maybe.

These were the thoughts that were going through Hank's head as the small patrol was enclosed in fog and moved into the tall elephant grass. He wondered why the Chief hadn't requested a whole platoon, or maybe even a company. A mortar round hit inside the base as they left the wire via the runway opening near the gorge.

Hank and his crew had to sling their weapons so they could carry picks and shovels in case the breech in the dam, if that's what it was, was small enough to be fixed right away. No one wanted to make two trips outside the wire. They'd know soon enough.

They moved into the tall elephant grass near the hill. The recon guys seemed to flow through the grass hardly disturbing the foliage. Hank had slices on both arms and several on his legs before they had gone fifty meters. The long blades of the grass had razor edges and sliced right through the cloth of their greens. There was a path, but Abbot refused to use it. Recons were experts at staying alive in enemy territory. Hank was happy follow them.

It didn't take long to get close to the water point. The point man stopped the patrol and waved them down. He moved to the crest of the hill prone. As he squatted down, Hank discovered a new irritation. As if the grass cuts weren't enough, now there were things attached to his arms, worm-like things. Other similar things had found a way through the cuts in his trousers and were attached to his legs.

The recon guys had warned them to blouse their trousers and button their sleeves and neck, but that practice didn't do any good. If leeches were on his arms, they would be on his legs too. He tried not to think about where else they might be. They hadn't had much time to suck blood so far and were still small, not big enough to feel. The recon guys said they would fall off by themselves when they had their fill and not to worry about them. They had to be completely quiet on patrol and that's how they dealt with them, but the thought gave Hank the willies. Things were sucking his blood.

Abbot tapped Hank on the arm and waved the rest of the group up. He waited for everyone to close up.

"Spread out and move up to the crest. Be as quiet as you can."

He wasn't expecting precision maneuvering from the squids and he didn't get it, but he did get the quiet he wanted. The Seabees were out of their element and stressed out. Another mortar round hit somewhere on the base. A thought crossed Hank's mind. The enemy was close enough to hit the base with a mortar. They were at least that close. He tried but couldn't remember the range of a mortar.

Reaching the crest of the hill didn't reveal anything worth seeing, just more elephant grass and some scrub brush that hadn't been blasted away by artillery. He did find something that surprised him though. Munitions blasted out of the ammo dump had reached that far. He found two unexploded mortar rounds. The recon guys buried them to keep them from becoming VC booby-traps.

He wondered why the NVA hadn't targeted this area too. Not only had they not made a direct attempt at disabling the water supply, they hadn't even tried to hit it with artillery. The patrol started down the side of the hill toward the dam, but still couldn't see it. The recon guys stopped the Seabees and left one man with them while the rest went in to see what was there in their own stealthy way.

After a ten minute wait the Seabees were called forward. Hank spotted the problem as soon as he broke through the last of the elephant grass and he relaxed. This wasn't going to take long at all. Almost dead center in the dam something had blasted a PSP plank away and gouged out the dirt. Runoff was cutting the gouge deeper and had already lowered the water level in the reservoir enough to expose the top of the pump intake.

The dam looked like a beaver dam rather than something man-made. No, that wasn't right. It looked like a stream stopped up with trash. Drift wood and debris almost covered the inside slope of the dam and weeds and elephant grass had grown up on the walls. A large log had lodged in the breech and slowed the erosion. That happenstance had saved the water point from disaster.

The recon team spread out on both sides of the stream to provide security while the Seabees got to work. The inside slope of the dam ought to be reinforced with stone and boulders, but Hank didn't have enough men to handle that job. That wouldn't get done without equipment either. All he could do was patch the breech as best he could with his available resources and report what he found to the office.

After the breech was filled in with logs, rock, and dirt, he moved the PSP back over the patch and waited a few minutes to see if it would hold. The water level in the reservoir rose steadily and quickly submerged the intake. It didn't need to be watertight, just slow the flow and hold back the stream enough to maintain the water level in the reservoir without washing away. A better fix would have to wait for better resources.

“You guys about ready?” Abbot asked. “We need to get the hell out of here.”

Recon Marines were never happy sitting in one place.

“Yeah. That’s about all we can do for now,” Hank said and suddenly flinched and ducked. “Geeze! What the hell was that?”

A large machine gun had just fired several rounds. It wasn’t far away.

“Sounded like anti-aircraft to me,” Abbot said. “Let’s go. You guys keep your eyes on me and be quiet.”

The team moved out in the same order they came in, but Hank was sure they weren’t going toward the base. What the hell were they doing? It wasn’t long before he found out. The machine gun fired again and their direction became obvious. The recon team was taking the Seabees in the direction of the gun.

Chapter 46

The fog was thicker than on the way out. Hank kept his eyes on the sergeant and tried to suppress the excitement building in his chest. He kept waiting for Abbot to call a halt and get the Seabees in some kind of cover.

The gun fired again and Abbot waved the patrol down. He made hand signals to the point man and started crawling back to Hank.

"Form a wheel with your men."

"What the hell is a wheel?"

The sergeant just stared at him with a look of disgust on his face. He waved the other Seabees up. When they were all there, he showed them how to form a wheel. He had the four Seabees form a cross facing outward at the four cardinal directions with their toes touching inside.

"Stay right here and don't panic. You'll be

fine. We're going to have a look and get some coordinates for the mortars on the base. We'll come back on the same path we go out. Don't shoot at noises. Just stay quiet and you'll be okay. They don't know we're here."

Hank couldn't even talk. His throat had dried up and he could hardly swallow. It wasn't as much fear as it was excitement. He just nodded. Then he heard an aircraft low overhead in the fog and the machine gun fired again. They had to be firing blindly at the sound.

The recon team moved out in a crouch and the jungle got quiet.

"Hank! What the fuck are they doing?"

Thompson's voice was raspy and high pitched.

"Keep it quiet. They're just locating the gun for our mortars. It must be sitting right under the runway approach. Keep your eyes open. They'll be back soon. We're good."

The next twenty minutes were the scariest in Hank's life. What if the recon couldn't find them again? What if they got in a fight with the machine gun? Should he move his team up to help them? How the hell was he going to get his men back inside the base if the recon didn't come back? Where the hell was the base? All he could see was fog. Panic began to set in as all sorts of wild thoughts took over. He didn't fear any man on earth, but guns were a different matter. A gunfight was the only time his size was a disadvantage. He was gulping hard to quell the excitement when he heard a voice and almost pissed himself.

"Hold your fire. We're coming in."

Relief flooded through him. "I hear you," he said in a loud whisper.

Abbot came first and went prone facing the jungle he just left. Then the others came in one at a time.

"Good job," he said. "Fall in like before."

"What's happening?"

"A platoon is coming out to take that gun. It's not going anywhere. I've got to get you guys back to the wire and bring them back out here. Let's move."

The trip back to the wire was slow and cautious with the recon sergeant talking on his radio all the way. The fog was too heavy to depend on pop flares for identification, so he had to talk to the perimeter all the way in. Finally it was time to part ways with the recon about a hundred feet from the opening at the end of the runway. The sergeant sent the Seabees in one at a time and continued to talk with the perimeter bunker until they were all safe inside the wire. Each of them was told to take cover in the first bunker on the line.

As soon as Hank, the last man in, was in the bunker, a platoon of Marines left the wire with the platoon commander talking to the recon on his radio.

Thompson turned to Hank.

"I wanted to be a Marine before joining the Navy. What the hell was I thinking?"

"You weren't. Let's get back to some sanity. You guys report back to your crews. I'll let the Chief know we got the job done."

It was a hell of an adventure and one Hank didn't want to repeat. The recon were able to get the platoon back to the gun and they attacked the position an hour after Hank got back. They captured the gun and one of the gunners after killing the rest of the crew. Taking the gun out was a successful maneuver but the success of the NVA at getting an anti-aircraft gun so close and almost under the runway approach scared the hell out of the pilots and the Marines. Air was the only resupply option open with Route Nine closed. If the NVA could shut the runway down, the base was in a world of trouble.

Chapter 47

The Tet holiday came and went and nobody at Khe Sanh noticed, well, the Seabees didn't notice. From the reports they were getting, the rest of the country seemed to be falling apart with attacks on all major population centers, but Khe Sanh started January 30 with an artillery barrage, not much different than what had been happening every day since the 22nd.

February came in with fog and cold temperatures, both welcome as the runway crew repaired holes in the matting put there by a couple 122mm rockets.

Arclight strikes woke everyone up twice during the night. While the B52 carpet bombing put their nerves on edge, it was also reassuring. That awful rumbling in the ground was making life miserable and short for the NVA.

On February 3rd, the Marines had a water

shortage on base and Hank got nervous waiting for the call to go back to the water point. It seemed to him he was getting more than his share of those kind of jobs. He relaxed when the report came that shrapnel had pierced the large rubber water bladder reservoir that fed the water tower and the water points on base went dry. Marines had to haul water in five-gallon cans on mechanical mules until the repair was made. The water buffalos in the Seabee camp were full and careful management avoided a crisis.

Constant repairs had depleted the crushed rock stockpiles on base and Hank was drafted to accompany two dump trucks out to the quarry. He was getting a little tired of catching these one-off details, but he was an augmentee and not part of the permanent detail, and he was available more often than guys on a regular crew. Nothing to do but suck it up. Everybody was doing all they could and nobody's job was easy or safe.

Most of the runway repairs had to be done quickly with temporary patches, but at some point the bed would have to be rebuilt and the repairs made permanent or the bed would begin to wash out and the matting would sag. If that happened, a new runway had to be built.

Getting dump trucks out to the Quarry and back was a hairy operation. The road close to the combat base was reasonably secure and patrolled and once near the quarry, First battalion, Ninth Marines was close by and providing security. Large numbers of enemy couldn't get by 1/9, at least without them knowing it, but individuals could, so "reasonably secure" didn't mean a walk in the park. A division of NVA were out there somewhere still trying to get close to the base and the trucks had to cover a mile of territory between the combat base and the quarry.

Back in Dong Ha the security platoon would be providing convoy escorts, but the whole Detail at Khe Sanh hardly made up a full platoon and had to make do. Hank and a couple other men were how the Detail was making do. They didn't have to go alone though.

Combat engineers with a platoon of Marines led the way sweeping the road for mines early in the morning. Hank was relieved when he found out the trucks would be escorted by two Marine tanks. First in line was a tank, then the two dump trucks, then another tank. Hank was riding shotgun in the first truck. The first danger they had to face was getting the trucks out of the equipment yard.

"Hey, Hank. Are you riding shotgun?"

"Looks like it, Tony. Is this thing going to run?"

EO3 Tony Valente was the driver for this mission. He was inspecting the tires before departing. Tony looked exhausted and strung out. His eyes darted around as he talked and his hands had a slight tremor in them. Hank wasn't in much better shape. Everybody in the Detail was a little shell shocked. Hell, everybody on base was shell shocked after more than a week of random artillery.

"It don't look like much, does it," Valente said. "Beat all to hell. It will run though. All the damage is to the body. Looks like the rubber is good. Climb in and let's get this show on the road. The tankers don't like sitting still."

The seats were shredded and the windows were either missing or full of spider web cracks. The windshield had three star-cluster holes in it with cracks extending in all directions.

"Can you see well enough to drive?" Hank asked.

"Just. I can see well enough to see the tank. I'm following him."

"The driver in the other truck is waving. Time to crank it up."

"Hold on to something. Soon as we get outside the revetments, the incoming is going to start. I ain't stopping for nothing."

Valente got the diesel cooking and slipped the clutch in. The old dump truck, probably left over from WWII, started moving ahead. It was built before turbo diesels came on line and was slow, plenty of torque, but geared so low it needed a mile to get over fifteen miles an hour. That wasn't a problem at Khe Sanh. They wouldn't be riding down any highways.

"This shit is getting to me, Tuck."

"What? The incoming?"

"Yeah."

"It's slowed down a lot since the dump blew up," Hank said.

"It's not the volume. It's the pure damn random way it comes in. You just never know when that shit is going to fall on your head. You know it's coming, but you never know when or where. Can't even use the shitter without worrying. It's getting hard to squeeze one out."

Hank laughed, but the sound didn't have any humor in it. "The tank is moving through the gate. Are we supposed to fall in behind him?"

"That's the plan. So far, so good. Maybe those little fuckers in the hills are going to let us get off the base without blowing us up this time."

Hank was watching the perimeter closely for signs of incoming and no sooner than Valente got his bad luck words out of his mouth, he saw what he was looking for, Marines jumping into their fighting holes.

"Incoming is on the way! Move this thing."

Valente was already getting all he could out of the big bucket on wheels. There wasn't any use in weaving or trying any evasive maneuvers. They were already moving targets and the best they could do was keep moving. Suddenly a shock wave smacked the truck and rocked it. Hank was watching the cracked mirror and saw the eruption of dirt and debris behind them. His view of the second truck was obscured for a moment, but then he saw it emerge from the dust cloud.

"That was too damn close," Valente said. "Is our other truck okay?"

"Yeah. The round hit between us. Probably a mortar."

"I don't even want to think about coming back with a full load of rock onboard. Think it was just a lucky shot?"

"Hope so," Hank said. "I'd hate to think they can do that any time they want."

Valente had the old truck moving pretty good and holding on was getting hard. The springs in that thing were designed to cushion twenty-ton loads, not Seabee asses. The tankers weren't wasting any time and Valente was having a hard time keeping up.

They took their first sniper round through the windshield two hundred meters outside the gate and Valente could no longer see well enough to keep going, but he had to. They were expecting incoming, but the reality so close was a shock. They couldn't stop. Stopping was just what the enemy wanted, a stationary target.

"Kick the windshield out, Tuck!"

Hank was big enough to reach the windshield from his seat and lifted his legs to get a good shot at it. He jackhammered the heels of his boots forward and hit the glass, but all he managed to do was create a thousand new spiderweb cracks and eliminate what little visibility was left. Valente started braking. He couldn't see at all now.

"Hit it again, Tuck. I can't see."

Hank cranked his legs back and shot them forward again. This time his side of the windshield popped out of the frame.

"Come on, Tuck. Stop fucking around."

Valente was bent outside the driver's window and driving with one hand.

Hank moved to the center of the seat and wound up again. This time the whole windshield popped out onto the hood. Valente got back behind the wheel and started increasing speed again to catch up with the lead tank. Hank looked in the big side mirror. The mirror glass was gone.

"Can you see behind us?" he yelled. "Are they still with us?"

"Yeah. They're coming up fast."

A sniper round punched right through the hood of the truck.

"We have to go back," Valente yelled. "They're attacking us."

"Keep going. Don't stop this thing. We're closer to the quarry than the base. There's a thousand Marines at the quarry."

The Tank had slowed and was using his coaxial fifty to provide some cover for the trucks while they moved forward. If Valente had stopped, the convoy would have been sitting ducks for RPGs. They kept moving and got past the sniper. Soon the quarry was in sight.

Chapter 48

Back in September before any of the serious enemy activity began, three 15-ton rock crushers were flown in and assembled at the quarry about a mile southwest of the base. The tonnage of the crushing machines referred to the amount of rock the machine could crush in an hour, not to the weight of the machine. The OIC had led a patrol out into the boonies around the base and found a hill of basalt rock suitable for a quarry to supply the bedding needs for the runway.

The quarry operation was primitive by modern construction standards. Most of the drilling was done with hand drills and sledge hammers and the blasting was done with C4. The Seabees came through though and produced a bodacious amount of rock crushed and sorted to the right size, but 3000 feet of new runway bed and constant repairs had depleted the stockpiles on the base.

There wasn't much of interest to the NVA at the quarry, at least not of enough interest to waste any artillery on, and the crushers and quarry equipment were still in good shape. Fortunately for Hank and the drivers, the crushers weren't needed. The quarry crew had sufficient rock stockpiled to load the trucks several times over.

The first loads were onboard quickly and the tanks prepared to lead the heavily loaded convoy back to the base. Just as the lead tank started moving, a Marine from the platoon providing security for the quarry ran out and flagged him down. Hank could hear artillery explosions from the direction of the camp.

"What now?" Valente asked.

"We'll know soon enough. Here he comes."

The tanks started moving away from the trucks and the Marine stopped by the driver's window.

"Put your trunk back by those rock piles. The base is taking incoming and red sector has a firefight going on. You'll have to wait for clearance to return."

Two piles of crushed rock separated by 30 feet made a good revetment for the trucks. Not knowing what might be coming their way, Hank and Valente got under the truck to wait for clearance to return to the base. Neither of them were looking forward to the trip back. If red sector was having a firefight, NVA could be occupying territory they would have to pass through to get to the gate. Hank double-checked his rifle and wondered again what the hell a carpenter was doing playing John Wayne in Vietnam. Oh yeah, he thought, I'm avoiding the draft, and laughed out loud.

"What?" Valente asked.

"Nothing. Just a crazy thought."

"Care to share it. I could use a laugh."

"I joined the Seabees to avoid the draft and getting sent to Vietnam."

Valente barked a laugh. "How'd that work out for you?" he asked and laughed again.

"Well, as you can see, I did avoid the draft and here I am plying my trade in this tropical paradise."

"What's that tank doing?"

"Looks like he's getting ready to go. Back to work. You won't mind if I sit on the floorboards, will you?"

"Sit wherever you want. Probably won't matter to an artillery round."

"You're just full of sunshine and joy, aren't you? Let's get it cranked up. He isn't waiting."

Hank could hear small arms through the open windshield hole as Valente got the big truck full of rock moving. It was so damn slow and Hank felt so damn vulnerable sitting there with nothing but a hole where the windshield used to be. A windshield wouldn't make any difference to even a rifle round, but open air just left you feeling naked and vulnerable. The tankers were impatient, but Valente was getting all he could get out of the old diesel. They were presenting a moving target, but it was a slow-moving target.

A firefight was going on somewhere west of them. That wasn't a bad thing since they were heading east, but Hank wondered what the Marines had found. If it was the expected attack they'd have to abandon the trucks. The best they could get was about ten miles an hour on the rough road. Infantry could run faster than they were going.

The turrets on the tanks were moving constantly. The lead tank covered one side of the road and the following tank covered the other. The M16 in Hank's hand didn't give him a lot of comfort.

Looking forward, he saw the tank veer to the left and move past what looked like two little kids standing on the side of the road. As the truck got closer he saw they were a little boy holding the hand of a smaller little girl. He was maybe six or seven. She couldn't have been more than three, just a toddler. They were both crying. Memories of Peanut came back and his breath caught in his throat.

"Stop the truck!"

"What? Fuck that. I'm not stopping until we're inside the fence."

"I said stop the fucking truck. Those kids need help."

"Tuck! What the fuck is wrong with you. We can't stop out here."

Hank had a good view of the kids now, just a few feet in front of the truck. He saw the red running down the outside of the girl's leg.

"Stop the damn truck! It won't take me a second."

"Fuck!" Valente screamed. "You're going to get us killed."

"Just slow down then. I'll grab them and be back in the truck before you can shift."

Valente was pissed, but he slowed the truck next to the kids and Hank was good to his word. He was out of the cab in a flash and had the children scooped up in his arms before the truck was ten feet away. Then it happened. They wanted the tank, but the big slow truck was the easiest target.

Hank saw the flash of the RPG igniting from the corner of his eye and dropped to the road with the kids in his arms. He only got one quick roll to the side, almost crushing the little boy, before the RPG hit the engine compartment of the truck. The front of the truck exploded, but it continued rolling in slow motion to the side of the road. Even an RPG couldn't stop the momentum of 20 tons of stone.

"Oh, Jesus, no," he screamed. Valente! Valente!"

He let go of the kids and jumped up looking around wildly for help. The little boy just laid there, limp. The lead Tank had stopped and his turret was swinging toward the direction the RPG came from. The other truck was still moving forward and the following tank's main gun fired. He was facing the right direction and must have seen the RPG fire. A second later the lead tank's machine gun fired.

Hank ran toward the burning truck.

"Tucker! Get the fuck down. There might be more of them out there."

Valente was in the middle of the road crawling toward Hank. Both tanks were stopped and firing. The second truck was still moving slowly forward. Hank ran forward and jerked Valente to his feet. He had to scream to be heard over the tank guns.

"Get in the other truck! I'll get the kids."

"Leave them. They were bait."

"I'm not leaving them. Go! Get in the truck.

The rear tank was moving forward again with his turret turned to use his machine gun. When Hank grabbed the kids, the little boy fell limp across his arm. The little girl clutched his other arm. He started running for the second truck, the lead tank started moving toward the base again. The truck was speeding up, but the door was open. Hank tossed the kids, one after the other into the cab and jumped up on the running board. The boy slipped off the seat onto the floorboards. The driver double clutched into a higher gear and the truck picked up speed. Hank pulled himself into the cab and reached for the boy. Valente had the girl.

"What's the matter with the kid?" Valente asked.

"I don't know. He was okay on the side of the road."

Hank held the boy and shook him a little. He was unresponsive.

"We better get him to Charlie Med."

"We can't take kids onto the base," the driver said.

"The hell we can't. Just keep moving."

The girl was silent in Valente's lap. Hank didn't know what or who the kids were, or what happened to them, but he wasn't going to leave them out there alone and bleeding. They might have been used, but it wasn't their fault. The baby seemed scared to death. The boy was like a rag doll. He had to help them.

"What are you going to do with them, Hank?"

He cradled the boy in his arms. He was so

still.

"I'll take them to Charlie Med. The docs will know what to do. How'd you get out of the truck?"

"I saw that fucker."

"The guy with the RPG?"

"Damn right. I was looking out the door for you and looked right at him when he stood up. I couldn't have been doing more than five miles an hour and I knew it was all over. When I saw the flash, I jumped out and let it roll. Glad it was full of rock. Even an RPG couldn't move it much."

"Man, you got our asses in big time trouble," the driver said. "You should never have slowed down. I'll drop you by the bunker. You tell the Chief. I was just following you."

"It's my problem," Hank said. "Don't worry about it. If anybody asks, just tell them I ordered you to slow down. I did."

Valente and the driver were quiet then. They were pissed and scared, but the Detail was a team.

"Aw hell, man," the driver said. "I'm not going to hang you out. Just get the kids taken care of and try to figure out how you're going to get them back to their people. Is that kid okay? He don't look so good."

"I don't know. Can you go faster. I need to get them both to Charlie Med. I know some guys in the FOB. Maybe they can help."

"How are you going to contact them?"

"The Marine Communications room has to have communications with them."

"Good luck with that. The Marines find out you brought natives on the base they'll be looking for your scalp—if there's any left when the Chief gets done with you. We needed that dump truck."

"They're just kids, for god's sake. What were we supposed to do?"

"The tank drove right by them and didn't stop. That's what the hell we were supposed to do. Wait till he makes his report."

"Screw that. We're going to help them. If they want my scalp for that, screw them."

Hank wrapped his big arms around the boy and held him tight against his chest. He was a skinny kid, probably didn't weigh forty pounds. He didn't seem to be breathing. Hank put the thought out of his mind as a vision of Peanut's eye flashed into his mind.

"Can't you go faster?" he yelled. "The kid needs a doctor."

The little girl snuggled tight into Valente's arms. Hank hugged the boy and tried to will him to breathe. He tried to decide if he should be doing mouth to mouth or something but didn't know how to do it anyway. The kid was such a fragile little thing, he'd probably do more damage than help if he tried. He wondered how he was going to handle getting them taken care of. He'd worry about his own ass later.

As they approached the base, he started feeling better. Red sector was quiet. He couldn't see any incoming hitting anywhere in front of them. The Marines were working on their fighting position. That was always a good sign. He kept his eyes on them hoping they didn't start jumping in their holes. That was the craziness of this damn place. A half hour before the trucks had been held up because of a firefight on red sector. Now the Marines on red sector were out and digging like nothing unusual had happened.

The lead tank passed through the wire and Valente followed him a minute later. The little boy remained limp in Hank's arms. The tank didn't wait around and headed for his revetment on the west end of the base. Valente and the driver headed for the runway to dump the load. He dropped Hank, Valente, and the children off by the equipment yard and went on to finish his task. Hank held the boy and went straight to the Charlie Med. Valente followed with the girl.

Chapter 49

A corpsman was putting med supplies inside a unit one just inside the entrance. By that time most of the corpsman knew most of the Seabees and everybody on the east end of the base knew Hank. He was the biggest man around and always willing to help when something needed fixing or built.

"What have you got there, Hank?"

"He's hurt, doc. I don't know what's wrong with him. The little girl is bleeding."

"Put her on the cot and give me the boy. Oh shit! Go inside and get a doctor. Where the hell did they come from?"

"I found them on the road out to the quarry. They were just standing there and crying. There was a firefight going on not far from there. I couldn't just leave them there, Doc."

She didn't want to let go of Valente. Hank

remembered Peanut again and tried hard to put the picture of her dead eyes out of his mind. He spoke to the child softly and sat her on the cot. The Corpsman bent over the boy and started mouth to mouth.

Between breaths he yelled. “Get a doctor.”

Hank went looking for doctor. He found one in the part of the tent they called the ward.

“Doctor, the corpsman asked me to find you. We have a couple wounded children out there. Can you take a look at them.?”

“Children? How did children get on the base?”

“Doc, He’s not breathing and she’s bleeding. Can you look at her now?”

“Where are they?”

“Follow me.”

As Hank and the doctor entered the exam room, the corpsman stood up. His distress was obvious.

“I tried, Doctor, but he’s not responding.”

The doctor felt for pulse and lifted an eyelid. He didn’t need to look further. The eyes were already changing. He examined the body for wounds and stopped with his hands feeling the back of the child’s neck.

“How long has he been unresponsive?” he asked.

“Since just after we were attacked,” Hank

said. “Probably twenty minutes.”

The doctor pulled a sheet over the kid’s head.

“He has a broken neck. Do you know what happened to him?”

Two Corpsman ran in.

“The bird is five minutes out,” one of them yelled. “Get the medevacs ready.”

The doctor looked for the corpsman. “You can handle the girl. Take over. I’ve got to get our medevacs ready.”

He got up and ran back inside the tent.

“Hank, pull my unit one over here. She just has a cut on her thigh. I just need to clean the wound and bandage it. She’ll be okay.”

Hank was in shock. He felt dizzy and his face turned white. The corpsman saw it and pushed him down on a cot.

“Put your head between your knees. Bend over, damn it. Breathe. Deeper. Breathe in. Now out. Deep breaths. Keep doing it.” He grabbed his unit one and found the smelling salts. Hank jerked his head away from the smell and stared wide-eyed at the Corpsman.

“Feel better?”

“I . . . think so.”

“What happened?”

“I . . .I . . . oh Jesus. The little boy. He’s dead.”

"Yeah, it's tough when kids get hurt. Sit there for a few minutes while I fix the girl up. She just has a gash on her thigh. What are you going to do with them? Somebody has to claim the body."

"Can they stay here for a few minutes? I've got to find a way to reach the FOB and see if they can take care of it."

"Go on. I'll move the body and give her some C-Rats. That will keep her busy for a while."

"Thanks, Doc."

He was dreading telling the Chief about the kids more than telling him about the truck, but he had to. The Chief could probably get a connection to the FOB through the Marine communications center.

A helicopter had just landed and everyone was diving for cover. The Marine cargo handlers knew artillery or mortars was on its way when a bird landed. Hank and Valente had to take cover too. The bird landed and moved immediately into the revetments near the apron. A mortar hit thirty seconds later.

He waited a full minute without incoming, Maybe they were done.

"I'll handle the Chief," he said. "You can report back to your crew."

"Okay," Valente said. "I'll go with you if you want."

"No, I'll take care of it. Thanks for taking

care of the girl."

"Forget it. What happened to the boy?"

"I don't know. He seemed to be okay when I picked him up before the RPG came in. Maybe he wasn't. Let's go while we can."

Hank jumped up and started running for the Seabee Bunker.

The Chief was bent over a stack of materials orders and looked up as Hank entered the bunker.

"How the hell can you wreck a damn dump truck?"

Oh crap. He already knew.

"I don't think we better do a second trip today," Hank said. "It's pretty bad out there."

"A patrol got ambushed west of the quarry," the Chief said. "First Battalion sent out a platoon to reinforce them. Nobody is leaving the wire. You didn't answer my question."

"Chief, I got a problem."

"Oh how I hate to hear those words. What's the problem, Hank?"

Hank explained about the kids and asked if the Chief could get a line through to the FOB.

"Hank, sit down."

The Chief took a sip of coffee and turned to Hank.

"I am already aware of the truck. How did kids get involved?"

"They're little kids, Chief. They were all alone. I couldn't leave them there."

The Chief watched Hank for a moment. Hank was pale and looked like he was ready to come apart.

"How little?" he asked.

"Oldest is maybe six. A little boy and a little girl. She's maybe three. Her leg was bleeding and they were all alone out there on the road to the Quarry. The Marines went right by them and left them standing there."

"Okay, settle down. How did the kid die?"

"I don't know. When I picked him up after the attack, he was limp. I brought him in so the Docs could look at him."

The Chief relaxed back into his chair.

"You were damn lucky Valente didn't get killed. We couldn't afford to lose that truck either . . . but hell, no faster than you could move anyway, I don't see how the truck could have been saved. They were going to get one of you. I'll have to see what the Boss says."

"Chief, I did what I though was the right thing. There's not much else I can say about it. We have to do something about the little girl and the body.

"Why do you need to contact the FOB?

"I know a couple guys there. They work with the Bru. They'll know what to do."

"Where are the kids?"
"Charlie Med."
"Okay, hold on."

Chapter 50

Zanh came over from the FOB with a terp and took the girl and the body back with him. The FOB was hosting a large group of refugees from the village anyway and the kids were most likely from the refugee group. After talking with Hank, Zanh said he would handle it. Hell, it was the fog of war. Shit happened that couldn't be explained or fixed all the time.

Hank felt better after the little girl was taken care of, but something was nagging at the back of his mind, something he didn't want to remember or think about.

The lull in the incoming didn't last long. The NVA began shooting their big 152mm artillery from Co Rock in Laos and no amount of air support or friendly artillery could stop them. If the 175mm guns the army had tried to bring in back in September had made it, they might have been able to put enough pressure on the NVA in Laos to force them out of range, but the 175s didn't get to Khe Sanh and neither the 105s nor the 155s on base had the range to challenge the artillery at Co Rock. They weren't very effective with counter battery on the smaller artillery the NVA had inside Vietnam either. Besides the big rounds coming in from Co Rock, NVA howitzers hit the base regularly from the valleys and hills around the base. 120mm and 82mm mortars still added their devastation to the artillery and NVA infantry got close enough to hit the perimeter with B40 rockets. Add in 122mm rockets and the base faced a deadly stew of munitions that continued to drive everyone underground when the fog cleared.

Sleeping was a luxury. Rockets and mortars hit at night and artillery hit during the day, not constantly, but periodically the NVA would coordinate an attack and hit the base with time-on-target barrages of a hundred or more rounds. It would get quiet again and just as the crew started moving again an artillery round would come in and shut everything down. Add to that terror and noise from Arclight carpet bombing sometimes just a couple klicks from the base and fighter-bombers dropping snake and nape (250lb snake eye bombs and napalm) within sight and sleeping became impossible even in the bunkers.

The rubber bladder reservoir on base was punctured by shrapnel again and a lot of Marines got very thirsty before the repair was made and water restored to the water points. Strangely though, the main water source at the creek outside blue sector remained untouched.

Hank became quieter than usual. He didn't have much to say during bullshit sessions, which was unusual. His whole demeanor was more stressed and even depressed. Toby tried to get him to loosen up and talk about whatever was bothering him, but he didn't improve.

Hank and Toby were taking a break with coffee on the evening of February sixth when the volume of outgoing from the 105s and 155s on base suddenly picked up. Hank was quieter than ever.

"They must have found something to shoot at," Toby said. "That's a lot of rounds going out."

He stood up and looked out across the bunker.

"The tanks are moving down to gray sector. I wonder what's going on."

Hank listened and watched for a few moments.

"The guns are shooting south," he said. "The village is pretty much abandoned. Can't be that. What's south of the village?"

"Your buddies," Toby said.

"Lang Vei! I wonder if the SF are in trouble."

"Aren't the Marines supposed to back them up?"

"I guess they are, if that's what the artillery is firing at."

"Tucker!"

"Here!" Hank and Toby yelled.

The Chief wants the Tuckers in the bunker."

"Got it," Hank yelled. "On our way."

The Chief was working on a message in the radio room and looked up when Hank and Toby walked in.

"You two pack your sea bags. Murphy wants you on the first flight that can get you out of here."

"Back to Dong Ha?"

"That's your first stop. He's got another detail to fill. Damn near every population center in I-Corps was hit during Tet and he's got temporary details trying to put things back together from Dong Ha to Da Nang."

"Can we even get out?" Hank asked. "Nothing got in today."

"A C-one-twenty-three is due in as soon as we have minimums in the morning. He isn't going to shut down, so you'll have to load on the run. Look, other than you losing a damn dump truck, the

OIC and I appreciate the work you guys did here. I tried to keep you, but Murph needs men for details and we've already kept you two months longer than we were supposed to. Pack up and try to get a few hours' sleep. I doubt you'll get any downtime in Dong Ha."

In the morning. Hank and Toby waited at the apron for the fog to clear. Toby worried about Hank. Getting out of Khe Sanh should have cheered him up, but it hadn't yet.

A lot was going on around the base. Hank found out from the Marines at the tower that the SF camp at Lang Vei did get attacked and as far as they knew had been overrun. There was a commotion at the south gate and Marines were being moved down there. Right then though, the Tucker brothers were more concerned with how they were going to get out of Khe Sanh than with what was going on at Khe Sanh.

Trying to get out of Khe Sanh was more hazardous than staying. The NVA started shooting as soon as a helicopter or plane appeared in the approach, sometimes when they could only hear them in the fog. Neither of them was looking forward to the ride out. Most flights to Khe Sanh left with more holes in the aircraft than they had when they got there.

They had made a few friends in the

permanent detail but weren't able to say goodbye to many. Those who weren't working were sleeping or trying to. The Tuckers were learning departures without any fanfare or farewells was the military way. Since the CBMU was homeported in Da Nang, individuals rotated in and out as their tours started or ended, not as a unit, and even though strong friendships were formed in the unit during the year an individual served, the cohesiveness of a Mobile Construction Battalion that rotated as a unit was never formed. Still, Toby hoped he'd get to see those guys again. They had been through a lot together.

But that was another thing about the military. It wouldn't be long before Hank and Toby would just be "those brothers that were here back in the fall," and then just a dim memory of a couple of guys lumped into the group of men who came in to augment the Detail to finish the runway. The permanent Detail had to stay right where they were and the horror they had to face and would continue to face was bonding them into a very tight group. The Detail was there for the duration.

Some nostalgia set in as Hank waited and relieved the melancholy that was haunting him. Fact was, he admired the hell out of every man in the Detail. The OIC was just a Lieutenant JG, but he led a Seabee Detail in about the worst conditions any Seabee unit had faced since WWII. He not only had to lead the Detail, but he was the principle engineer for the entire base also. The Chiefs were the backbone of the whole effort, drawing on every ounce of experience from long careers to solve problems that simply couldn't be left unsolved and doing it with material and manpower shortages under life threatening conditions. Every man in the unit gave everything they had. Hank's time with them wasn't long, but he would always be proud to have been part of what they accomplished. And he knew it wasn't over for them. He could hear artillery while he waited for his plane. Detail Bravo had a lot more hurt on the way and no end in sight.

Toby heard the sound of aircraft engines in the fog and nudged Hank. At ground level he could just see the runway where it went through the fence on the east end. Minimums at Khe Sanh would be no-fly conditions anywhere else. It wasn't long before NVA AA guns started punching holes in the cloud and fog. That sound produced a thrill of pain in his stomach he had to squeeze down hard on to keep from pissing himself.

A Marine cargo handler waved Hank and Toby over to him.

"When he turns onto the apron start moving toward him. He's going to lower his ramp and dump his pallets on the move. You've got to keep up. Toss your bags onboard when the crew chief signals you. Don't hesitate no matter what happens. Get inside as soon as your bags are on. He won't wait for you. Get up and over the ramp and fast as you can. It's going to come up even if you are on it."

"Where should we follow him?" Toby asked.

"Next to the ramp. Don't get behind it. Those pallets will be coming down fast. You'll be able to keep up with a slow jog. He won't increase speed until the cargo is off. Once it's off you have to jump. He knows he has about thirty seconds before the mortars come in."

"Damn!"

The Marine grinned. "You got it. Get ready. Here he comes."

The C123 isn't a big plane compared to the C130 but suddenly appearing out of the fog it looked huge. He touched down just a few hundred feet down the runway and continued a fast rollout. Almost to the apron he decelerated quickly with the ramp already coming down and turned onto the apron.

"Go! The Marine said.

Chapter 51

Hank and Toby threw their sea bags over their shoulders and ran. Both of them were big enough to carry them like overnight bags. They let the plane pass and fell in next to the ramp getting buffeted by prop wash. A pallet rumbled off the back. They had to jog to keep up. Another pallet rolled off the back. The Crew chief waved at them and they tossed their bags on the ramp, waited for the back of the ramp to come by and jumped on. The pilot was already pushing his throttles forward.

Hank had to grab Toby and help him forward against the acceleration. They grabbed their bags and pushed their legs toward the crew chief who was still waving them on. The plane picked up speed and the ramp started to lift. The plane turned east onto the runway and accelerated back toward the east end. A mortar hit the apron just as the ramp closed.

The crew chief pointed at net seats along the fuselage. Hank and Toby dropped their bags under the seats and flopped in the seats. The crew chief talked on a head mike and signaled them to strap in.

They were thrown sideways as the plane made a fast U-turn at the end of the runway and the engines went full military power. Assist rockets on the wings fired and he was airborne before it seemed possible and the nose lifted into a climb that scared the hell out of Hank. The plane leveled off but the pilot kept the engines screaming. The crew chief shuffled back to the Seabees.

"Stay strapped in. We'll be landing at Dong Ha in 20 minutes."

Hank and Toby let out a long breath of air they had been holding in while the plane got out of range of NVA anti-aircraft guns.

Landing at Dong Ha was a lot more peaceful than taking off at Khe Sanh, but all arrivals and departures anywhere in I-Corps were exciting. The approach was so steep it felt like you were falling out of the sky, nose first. No pilot made long approaches over enemy territory.

After Khe Sanh, Hank wasn't sure how he would adjust back to the normal Seabee six-and-a-half-day work week with Sunday morning inspections and training lectures and Sunday afternoons off. Having a half day off on Sundays was a luxury he had forgotten. He needn't have worried. Since Tet, no one was working a normal schedule.

"Seems a lot quieter than the last time we were here," Toby said.

"After Khe Sanh any place would seem quieter. I heard they got the new runway south of here done and most of the big stuff is going in there now. Let's cut through Camp Barnes."

At the gate they found out MCB 11 was gone, rotated back to their homeport, and MCB 7 had replaced them. Hank and Toby cut across the camp and parted ways at MCBU 301's gate. Toby had to report in to Alpha Company and Hank continued on to Charlie Company and the builder's shop. Seeing the base camp again eased some of the depression he was fighting and he cheered up to almost normal, but he couldn't shake the feeling that something awful had happened. He shrugged it off and tried to enjoy a little peace.

Chief Murphy was chewing out a SWF3 when Hank got to the shop. He spotted Hank but continued with his "motivational lecture" until the kid's face was red and then dismissed him.

"Hank, how the hell do you do it? You've been out in the boonies eating C-Rats for almost six months and you're as big as you ever were. What the hell is your secret?"

"Righteous living and a pure heart," Hank said. "My old daddy used to say . . ."

"I'm sure he did," Murphy said, interrupting. "He was probably as big a bullshitter as you. Toby get back okay?"

"Sure. He's checking with Alpha Company."

Tubby ran into the shop.

"Hank! I heard you got back. Good to see you, man."

"You too Tubby. How's the legs?"

"Good as new. I'm back on a full work schedule."

"Let's hold off on the terrible trio reunion for a while," Murphy said. "You'll have plenty of time to catch up. Operations has a job for you three. Get a coffee and take a break until Toby gets here. I don't want to go over this more than once."

When Toby arrived he was a bit agitated.

"What the hell's going on? I checked in and the boss sent me right over here. Hi Tubby. You're looking good."

"Hey Toby. I'm ready for some work. I've been sitting on my ass long enough.

"Murph has a job for us somewhere," Hank said.

"What kind of job?"

"We'll find out soon enough. Get some

coffee. It tastes like diesel fuel, but it's got caffeine in it."

Murph finally got away from whatever was holding him up and waved the trio over.

"Besides being the only people available, you three have worked together so I'm sending you out to Con Thien. It's a small job and I don't anticipate you'll be there more than a couple weeks. You'll be TAD to MCB Seven and work with their detail already out there. They need you to convoy a loader and some materials out to the hill and help reconstruct an observation post. They're taking a lot of incoming but the hill is well fortified and you guys know how to handle that. Toby, you'll take the frontend loader and Hank and Tubby can bring the six-by and whatever building materials you need. The security platoon will take you out to C2 and the Marines will pick you up there and escort you to the hill."

You said it's a small job," Hank said. "That don't tell me much. What kind of materials do we need to take?"

"It's a fortified bunker. You've done this before. Load up with heavy beams, planks, and fasteners. I'd take some AM2 matting too. Those guys use up anything they can get their hands on. Stay flexible. You're taking a six-by, so take anything you think might help. You were at Khe Sanh. The situation at Con Thein isn't much different except it's been going on a lot longer. Plan accordingly. I told them I could supply one builder, one equipment operator, and one steelworker and they were happy to get you."

"When do we leave. I'd like to get a shower and a decent night's sleep before we go," Toby said.

"That's about all you'll get. You'll leave at 0500 tomorrow."

Chapter 52

Seabees just had to suck it up and go where the work was and get done what needed to get done. Hank was glad there were people like that who chose to make a career of it, but knew he wasn't one of them. He was proud of his Seabee service and always would be, but he wanted to get home, build a house for his wife on that vacant lot he purchased, and start working toward starting his own company. He and Toby had been in the Navy for twenty-seven months by then, but they were still civilians in uniform, working for scab wages.

"Do you guys realize we only have about three months left on active duty?"

Toby counted on his fingers for a moment. "Three months and two weeks," he said.

"Have you started your short-timer's calendar yet?" Tubby asked.

"I can't remember the last time I had a place to hang one," Toby said.

"I'm thinking about extending," Tubby said.

"In Vietnam?" Hank and Toby said in unison.

"Well, yes. Where the hell else would I be talking about?"

"That's crazy talk, Tubby," Hank said. "Why the hell would you want to go and do a thing like that? Kids get killed over here."

"What?'

"Why would you want to . . ."

"No, what did you say about kids?"

Hank stopped and stared at Tubby for a moment.

"Nothing," he said. "What the hell has kids got to do with anything? Why would you want to stay in this place?"

Tubby looked at Hank a little strangely but then dropped the thought.

"I don't know," he said. "I like the Seabees and this war isn't going to last forever. I'll be making second class in June. I passed the test. If I reenlisted in the regulars, I could probably retire as a Chief when I'm forty and I'd still have my trade. Shoot, I'd be on easy street and still a young man."

"Think about that carefully, buddy," Hank said. "I don't see any signs of this mess slowing down anytime soon. You got to be alive to retire."

"That's true, but if I ain't, I won't know about it."

Hank couldn't argue with that logic and didn't have time anyway. The Security Platoon LPO was waving him to the truck.

Tubby couldn't sit quietly and watch the bush passing. Hank would rather not be distracted. His depression was nagging at him again. He wanted to watch the escort for any signs of trouble, but there was no denying Tubby when he wanted to talk.

"Hank, when did you start learning your trade?"

Hank let go of the unformed thoughts and emotions that were driving him back into depression. Tubby was asking about something much more pleasant.

"Probably when I was a kid. The old man had a shop set up in the basement where he could build cabinets. I used to sit on the cellar steps and watch him for hours. I became his, "get me one of those" assistant. I think I learned more about tools and how to use them watching him than from anything else in my career. The old man was a master carpenter, but cabinet making was his love. He turned out some beautiful work in that basement shop. Built my mom a knotty pine kitchen. How'd you get into metal work?"

"I helped a neighbor out one summer. He

did mostly duct work, but he was a good all-around metal man. He gave me the best advice I ever got."

"What's that?"

"He told me to get my trade first, then worry about other things. Once you have your trade it's one of the few things in this life nobody can take away from you. If you want to go on and try something else later, go for it, but you'll still have your trade if it don't work out, and with a good trade, you can make a living anywhere."

"Smart man," Hank said. "Didn't he have any advice about working for companies that do business where they shoot at you?"

Tubby just grunted.

Their first stop was a Marine camp called C2. The convoy from Dong Ha to C2 was mostly uneventful, but that's not to say it was boring. All the area along the Main Supply Route (MSR) out to Con Thein was Indian country and anything could happen. They had to pick up a platoon of Marines leaving C2 for Con Thein that had two tanks with them. The Marines had swept the route for mines between Con Thein and C2 that morning and would be returning to the firebase with the Seabees. They would provide the escort for that section of the journey.

Hank had asked why the Marines didn't just fly the equipment out to the hill and was told the flying cranes were no longer allowed to fly into that firebase after one had been shot up while it hovered over the LZ. Neither the Army nor Marines were willing to risk those big multi-million-dollar heavy-lift flying-machines. The situation was further complicated by artillery. Firing missions into North Vietnam and in support of ground forces in the DMZ by the big guns back at Camp Carroll and the Rock Pile had to be stopped while a helicopter was in the shell trajectory area. The coordination required to use even the smaller medium-lift birds was overwhelming. The only sure way to get heavy equipment out there now was by convoy on the MSR and that had its own risks.

Toby was driving the big heavy-duty frontend loader. He had some protection to the front by carrying the bucket high, but Hank worried about him all the way out and would continue to worry until he was off that machine. Toby had perfected the Khe Sanh crouch though and could hardly be seen behind the controls. The loader looked like it was operating itself.

The day was clear and dry for a change. Visibility was good and the temperature was comfortable in the high seventies. That kind of day had both advantages and disadvantages. A clear day meant they could get help from the air if they got in trouble, but it also meant they were visible to NVA forward observers.

After a short stop at C2 to hook-up with the Marine patrol, the Seabees moved out in the middle of a four-vehicle convoy with a tank in front and another in the rear. The lead tank commander got with Hank, Toby, and Tubby to get the show on the road.

"Once we're moving, don't stop for anything," he said. "Any vehicle that sits in one place for more than a minute will become a target and endanger the rest of the convoy. If you stop, you can expect artillery or RPGs almost immediately."

When they moved out, both tanks were covered with the Marine infantry platoon and combat engineers that had walked and swept for mines on the way to C2 that morning.

"Hank, besides at Bu Duc, have you fired your rifle except on the range?" Tubby asked.

Hank had to think for a minute. They had been through a lot of incoming, but it was mostly artillery or rockets. Firefights were rare.

"Can't say I have. Bu Duc was kind of unusual too."

"How about on perimeter duty at Khe Sanh?"

"Once. I fired that machine gun I used to have. Other than that, I can't remember having to use my personal weapon."

"It would be nice to get a job in public

works when we get back to Dong Ha, and not even have to carry it," Tubby said. "Even better, public works down in Da Nang."

"Don't hold your breath, Tubbs. We might not get into any firefights, but there aren't many places the CBMU has details that doesn't get some kind of incoming. I doubt we'll see Da Nang again until we catch our flight home."

Chapter 53

Hank was feeling pretty good about the job as they progressed along the MSR without any incoming or any sign of trouble at all. Crossing a bridge, he saw the Marines guarding it turning-to and moving around. That was always a good sign. The convoy slowed and stretched out to cross the bridge one at a time without having to stop but resumed speed and closed back up on the other side.

The hill was visible in the distance. Con Thein was famous at Dong Ha for the amount of incoming they took. Standing in Dong Ha and looking north, a person could watch and hear the artillery hitting the firebase just visible in the distance. The Marines called it a meat grinder. They all dreaded their turn in the barrel. That's what they called the thirty-day rotation on the hill. The duty was so hazardous with unrelenting artillery attacks and primitive living conditions thirty days was about the maximum men could stand. Hank was surprised and relieved he hadn't seen or heard one round hit Con Thein since they left C2.

The closer they got the more the ground began looking like Khe Sanh after the big attack on the first day. Huge craters from Arclight bombings, smaller craters from both American and NVA artillery, and even smaller craters from mortars dotted the moonscape land around Con Thein. Craters overlapped older craters. This place had been at war for a long time. But it was quiet as they passed through the south gate at speed.

The Marines dismounted on the fly and wasted no time taking cover while the tanks moved quickly to their revetments. Looking around, Hank thought he had driven into the middle of a city landfill. This place was a mess with churned up dirt roads and trash and wreckage everywhere. It was hard to tell the road from the torn and blasted landscape. Hell, it was hard to tell there was a base there.

He had a problem. No one had told him where to go or what to do once they got to the base. That was normally not a problem. There was always someone to ask when you got to your destination, but not here. No one was in sight now that the tanks and infantry had disappeared.

He had to stop and try to figure out what to

do next. That got a reaction. Two guys in greens stood up a hundred yards up the dirt road and began waving at him wildly. They were shouting something, but he couldn't hear them. He got the truck moving again right toward them.

They kept waving and one of them was jumping up and down. It was obvious they wanted him to go faster. He shifted down and kicked up the speed. Toby was right behind him.

As the Six-by drew next to the guys waving, something big exploded a hundred meters up the hill.

"Down there!" one of the wavers yelled. "Get it in a revetment. Move man! You're drawing incoming."

Tubby pointed. "There, get this thing in there."

Hank spotted the revetments made from fifty-five-gallon drums as he turned onto the side road that went down the hill to a small compound with equipment and bunkers. He went straight for the first opening he saw. Toby bounced the big loader down the hill and put it in another vacant revetment. He was off the machine and into a bunker before Hank and Tubby could dismount.

Another incoming round hit on the other side of the hill as they ran for the bunker. The two wavers were already there with Toby.

"What the hell were you guys doing

stopping out there?"

"We didn't know where to go," Hank said. "I couldn't just wander around."

"Somebody should have told you before you left. We need that loader."

"Well, fuck you," Toby said. "I was on that fucking equipment."

"Shit. I didn't mean it that way. It's just we're getting pounded and can't get enough work done without it and can't get the fuck out of this miserable place until we're done. We have a backhoe, but it won't do the job and we're exposed up there at that damn OP. Sorry, man, I didn't mean you aren't important too."

"Forget it," Hank said. "I'm Hank. That's my brother Toby and the little guy is Tubby."

"Fuck you, Tucker," Tubby said.

"Is it like this every day?" Toby asked.

"Pretty much. I'm Jenkins, equipment operator. It's not all the time, but something is going to hit the hill three or four times a day unless they get a hair up their ass. Then they might hit us with thirty or forty. Snipers too. They get in close and try to make some casualties with B40s. Always keep one ear open for artillery sounds. You can hear it fire from across the river. Always keep your eye on someplace you can use for cover. Don't go anywhere without knowing where your cover is. If you hear artillery, dive for cover. You don't get much warning here."

"And watch the Marines," Tubby said. "If they're jumping in holes, take cover."

"You got it. You sound like you've been here before."

"No," Hank said. "We just got back from Khe Sanh. It wasn't much different out there."

Jenkins just shook his head. "Out of the fire. Into the frying pan," he said. "Come on over to the bunker. I'll introduce you to the detail."

As you might expect, the Seabee bunker was well built, but it was small, just enough for the MCB7 detail. They hadn't expected any reinforcements and since they didn't expect or want to be there any longer than necessary, they built well but quickly and without any extra space. Jenkins introduced the MCBU Seabees to the MCB 7 Seabees. The LPO, a first-class EO named Thatcher sat down with Hank.

"What kind of materials were you able to bring with you?" he asked.

"Six by six beams, four by twelve planks, some AM2 matting, a crate of galvanized six by six fastening brackets, and assorted other lumber and fasteners. I would have brought bigger timbers, but they were the biggest the materials yard had left."

"The AM2 is welcome. We didn't bring any. What skills did you bring?"

"I'm a builder. Toby is an equipment

operator. Tubby is a good metal man."

"Did you bring a torch?"

"Yep, extra tanks too."

"Okay. Let's work out a schedule. I assume Toby will operate the loader."

"That was the idea."

"Good. The job site is exposed as hell and the enemy has it zeroed in. They've knocked out that damn OP four times over the last two years. The Marines want something that will survive a direct hit from artillery with time delay fuses."

"Fat chance," Hank said. "If we had a batch plant out here, we might be able to pour enough concrete to build them a reinforced concrete bunker and bury it under six feet of dirt and rock. Other than that . . ."

"That's what our engineers said too. Well, we have to give them the best we can do with what's available. The AM2 will help create a fuse buster layer. First job is to clear the wreckage and prepare the hole. Toby's loader will make fast work of that and reduce the amount of time the crew will be exposed. Let's get them together and work out the plan."

Chapter 54

The requirements for the observation bunker were impossible to meet. On the one hand, protection from time delay artillery required deep fortification with either concrete or several feet of dirt, rock, and metal over and around the occupants, preferably, both, but concrete wasn't available. On the other hand it was an observation post and the occupants had to be above ground with a clear view of the area they were observing to do their job. Hank and Thatcher met with Marine engineers, forward observers, and battalion operations officers to come up with a compromise design that would meet at least some of the contradicting requirements on each side of the equation.

While the LPOs were meeting with the Marines, Toby, Tubby, and the rest of the detail cleared wreckage and prepared for construction.

Each time Toby took the big loader up the hill, the NVA fired from across the river. To compensate for Toby's inability to hear over the sound of his diesel, one Seabee was stationed a hundred yards down the hill in a position Toby could keep an eye on. When the artillery fired he'd wave and Toby could jump for cover. The artillery was so damn close he didn't have but seconds to get off the machine.

Toby dumped another load over the side of the site and started to turn the machine for another scoop. He did a quick visual check of his sentinel man down the hill and he was waving.

He neutraled, locked the brake, and jumped. He just made it to the hole before the round came screaming in. It hit two-hundred feet away. Thank God it wasn't one of the big ones. He didn't want to get back on that machine. Fact was, he wanted to get the damn loader off that hill. A big Marine ran to the site and was pissed.

"Get that fucking machine off this hill. You're drawing fire."

He had subdued gunny stripes on his collar.

"Find an officer to approve that and I'll be down that hill faster than you can say do it, Gunny. I sure as hell ain't doing this shit because I like it."

Toby climbed back on the loader with his eye on his sentinel. The gunny took off running. Toby turned the machine back into the hole and scooped up another load. He got two loads dumped before the waving started again. He had the machine stopped and locked in record time this time.

It was a smaller round again. They were probably using 105s and not wasting 152mm rounds on a piece of construction equipment. Every round had to be hauled down a long trail and carried in by laborers and the NVA didn't waste the big and accurate rounds. They would probably wait for the bunker to be completed and then blow it all to hell. Thank God for little favors. He, Hank, and Tubby planned to be gone by then.

This time the gunny had an officer with him. The officer ran up to the loader and slashed his hand across his throat, telling Toby to shut down. Toby was happy to comply.

"They're not going to stop until you're done here and get that thing off the hill. How long is this going to take?"

"Lieutenant, give me an order and I'm gone, but those guys over there with the telescopes won't have any cover until we get this bunker finished."

The lieutenant and gunny looked where Toby was pointing. Forward observers were working their trade out of sandbagged fighting holes without overhead cover. The officer and gunny just turned around and walked back down the hill.

Crap! Toby thought. I was hoping you'd tell

me to leave anyway. Me and my big mouth. He turned the machine and went back into the hole for another load. To his pleased surprise, it was two hours before another round came in. He would only need one more trip to the hill to finish the clearing. It was true he'd need the loader up there again later and it would also be needed to move materials to the site, but that was later. Right then his nerves were shot. He was not going back up that hill again that day. Maybe never, he thought, but knew he would, even as he thought it.

He took the loader to the revetments and parked it next to the backhoe and went to the Six-by to get his clothes and stuff. There wasn't room in the cramped Seabee bunker so Toby, Hank, and Tubby were in an abandoned Marine bunker not far away. It was the pits, but they had plenty of room. The bunks were spider holes in the walls leaving the floor space open. Well, it would only be for a couple of weeks and the spider holes were dry at least.

Hank came in later and said the Marines had settled on a compromise design and the building could start as soon as the hole was prepped. That was good news. The sooner they could hook up with the morning minesweeping platoon and convoy the equipment back to Dong Ha, the better.

Chapter 55

The Marines on the hill had learned lessons about getting underground early on, long before the terrible trio got there. The bunkers were dark, dank, plagued with bugs, rats, and mold, and damp, but they were well built with plenty of overhead cover. The only thing they were missing was runway matting to add some steel between the artillery and the Marines, but they made up for that with artillery casings. Everything on Con Thein was underground and fortified with multiple layers of sandbags and needed to be. North Vietnam was only a few miles to the north across the Ben Hai river.

The artillery over there was hitting Dong Ha nine miles further south so it had no problem reaching Con Thein with amazing accuracy. Every Marine Hank saw on the hill looked shell shocked. The Tet offensive, still going on in many parts of the country, was hardly noticed at the strong points on the DMZ. The NVA hadn't tried to invade across the DMZ, so Tet was more business as usual than anything else. The firebases at Con Thein, A3, and Gio Linh got pounded regularly anyway.

No lights were allowed on the hill at night so there wasn't any reason to stay awake if you didn't have to, not for the Seabees anyway. Hank hated to go down into the stinking hole to sleep, but he liked it better than staying topside.

"You guys can sit around and shoot the shit if you want. I'm going to get a few hours of sleep if the NVA will let me."

"Go on," Toby said. "I'm putting it off as long as I can so I can pass out before the stink gets to me."

"Suit yourself," Hank said. "Oh four-hundred comes early."

The hole in the ground was built well when it was built, but years had passed since this one was constructed. Countless wet and dirty Marines had sheltered on those worn-out racks. Three inches of wet mud seeped up into the cracks of a couple pallets used as a floor to keep wet boots out of wet mud. So far Hank hadn't seen any rats or other creatures of the night, but he had been warned about them.

Previous Marine grunt occupants trying to

improve their living conditions had branched out horizontally by digging spider holes in the sides of the bunker, just man-sized slots about seven feet long, a couple feet high, and about three feet deep in the sides for sleeping and freeing up floorspace for other uses like poker and craps. The spider holes were dryer than the floor and provided a bit more cover from artillery, so he chose to sleep in one.

He ran the butt of his rifle around the inside to make sure no rats were there before him, then flicked his lighter to see inside. It looked pretty good and reasonably dry. Hank didn't smoke, but everybody had a lighter. There was always need for a fire starter or fast light.

The canvas from a broken stretcher had been placed in the spider hole for sleeping and that would provide some protection from the damp earth. Hank left his boots and greens on and climbed in with his rifle alongside him. Living in filth was becoming normal. He couldn't wait to get back to Dong Ha and return to living a life that at least resembled civilization.

The earth was packed from countless butts pressing it in the past, but overall the hole was kind of cozy. The top of the spider hole was held up with planks supported by pieces of 4x4 at the four corners, so there wouldn't be any dirt falling in his face. Having all that earth around him provided a comforting sense of security. He squirmed until his butt found some comfort and then closed his eyes.

Toby and Tubby remained above ground in a sandbag fortified fighting position next to the bunker. In reality, it was just a ring of sandbags three high and two wide with a dirt, now mud, bottom. Lying flat in the mud they might find some protection from shrapnel or small arms, but it was only bare minimum protection from mortars and no protection at all from artillery.

Two Seabees from the MCB 7 detail stopped at the position and invited them to the Seabee bunker for a Coke. They said they had light in the bunker and it was more comfortable than sitting outside in the dark.

"Hell, yeah," Tubby said. "Come on, Toby. Let's get a Coke. These guys can give us the straight skinny about this place."

Like most places the Seabees made their home, the Seabee bunker was probably the best one on the base. They weren't a permanent detail, but they made life as comfortable as possible for as long as they were going to be there. No unit on Con Thein was permanent. Battalions, companies, and supporting units rotated to the hill for thirty days and then were relieved by another unit for their turn in the barrel. Somewhere down the line after the Seabees left, a Marine squad would commandeer the Seabee bunker and the cycle would go on.

The bunker had a double entrance so they could close the outer entrance before opening the entrance to the interior of the bunker. That way they could have light inside at night without it shining outside when someone came in or went out. Show a light on Con Thein at night and the NVA wouldn't be your only worry. Some Marine might shoot you.

The MCB7 boys were there on a one-time detail to rebuild the observation post on one of the hills on the base. Con Thein was actually three hills. Each of the hills had an observation post, OP1, OP2, and OP3 for observing NVA movement along the DMZ. OP1 had become an obsession with the NVA gunners across the river and had taken a direct hit from 152mm artillery more than once. The Marines wanted it rebuilt to withstand a direct hit from one of those massive shells. The Seabees were skeptical it could be done but were doing their best to get it done. The problem was no one really knew how massive it had to be to withstand that kind of firepower with delay fuses. Even duds punched four feet into the ground.

Toby and Tubbs had a good conversation with the MCB 7 guys but didn't have a whole lot to contribute. About 0130 they decided to get back to Hank and the bunker and try to get some sleep. Toby pushed open the second barrier and stepped outside with Tubby right behind him. They didn't make it two steps. A massive shockwave hit them and knocked them back into the entrance tunnel.

"Damn!" Tubby yelled. "What the hell was that?"

"Artillery!" one of the MCB 7 guys yelled." "Get in here."

Chapter 56

With his eyes closed and no sound to distract him, the memories came. He couldn't shut the movie in his head off. The dump truck rolled along. The tank swerved. Two little kids on the side of the road. Out of the truck. He grabbed the kids up in his big arms. The flash of the RPG. Diving to the ground. The little boy under him when he hit the ground . . .

Hank didn't know what had happened. He was sleeping and then something hit him like the wrath of God and suddenly he could hardly breathe. There was no light at all. He remembered where he was and tried to slide out of the spider hole but was blocked by dirt. Was the opening on the other side? He tried that side but was blocked there too. He panicked. What the hell had happened?

His heart began to pound and he gasped for air. He got a lung full but it was foul and made him cough. Panic was rising higher. He had to get out of there. He felt all along the bottom of the spider hole. Dirt and rubble had encroached into the hole. When he touched the dirt higher up some of it fell into the hole. He froze. He squeezed his eyes shut and closed his fists. Quiet down, he thought. This is not a nightmare. This is real. Figure it out.

I'm trapped! He started to panic again. He tried to gain control but the thoughts were coming too fast to make any sense. He wanted to run, dig, scream, anything to relieve the fear. And then he knew. A deep primal fear made all his muscles rigid. I'm buried. I'm buried alive.

He started to dig at the wall of dirt that sealed his small tomb but stopped when the packed dirt crumbled and fell in on him. Air! The word screamed inside his head. I'm going to run out of air. He gasped. It was getting hard to breathe. I'm suffocating. The panic took over and he screamed.

The scream helped. Breaking the total silence made the total dark seem less threatening. He took shallow breaths. That's better. It was just panic. I've got plenty of air. The dirt itself has air. No need to panic. His hands were shaking and he couldn't stop them.

The ground shook and dirt fell on him. In total dark Hank reached his limit. He started screaming and couldn't stop.

Only two rounds came in that night. Toby and Tubby waited for a few minutes and then went back into the night.

"That sucker was close," Tubby said. "Where'd it hit?"

Toby didn't answer. He was staring into the night—right at where the bunker was supposed to be, but instead of the sandbagged roof all he could see was three Marines standing in a shallow hole and throwing sandbags and broken planks out.

"Oh shit, Tubby. The bunker. It hit the bunker. It's gone."

Tubby was already running toward the disaster and shouting Hank's name.

Toby got over the shock and knew what to do. He ran to the backhoe.

The rumble of the diesel could be heard all over the base as Toby ran it to the bunker. Tubby was in the hole tossing debris out and still shouting Hank's name. Toby could see the roof had collapsed and one side of the hole was blown in, filling the bunker with debris.

"Tubby! Get the Marines out of there. You stay and guide me."

"He might be buried in the rubble."

"That's why I need you in there. Watch where I'm putting the shovel."

More Marines and an officer showed up but stood back and let Toby work.

How long would the NVA hold off? Toby wondered.

"This isn't working," Tubby yelled. "I can't see shit."

If he turned the lights on, he, the machine, and Tubby were going to be mortar bait. Screw it. Hank was in there. Toby switched the lights on.

Marines scattered and disappeared into the dark. Hell, a lit cigarette at night would draw enemy fire and a fifty-foot-wide circle of dark around the bunker had just turned to day.

Tubby started signaling for Toby to drop the shovel right away. He stood right next to it and watched the teeth dig in. Toby took a scoop of rubble out, dropped it and swung the shovel back into the hole. He drew the shovel into the rubble slowly with Tubby watching every inch and then lifted another scoop out of the hole.

The work seemed like it was taking forever. They had to be so careful and go slow. Hank could be anywhere in that mess. Was he even still alive? Tubby tried not to think about what he was going to find. The explosion that caved the bunker was big. He wondered why the NVA were holding off and then thought, they're probably shocked out of their gourds at seeing this patch of light suddenly appear. It won't last long though.

Twenty minutes into the clearing one of the Seabees yelled, "Incoming!" and ran for cover.

Tubby looked up at Toby but he just waved his hand to keep on going. Strangely enough with all that light at the bunker, the round hit up near OP1.

"Toby! Go careful. I see the floor pallets. Hank has to be in this mess."

The work slowed down even further. Finally, Toby couldn't chance using the bucket any further and shut the engine down. He climbed down and into the hole now eight feet deep. He and Tubby cleared the last of the rubble from the roof.

"He's not here," Tubby said "Toby, he's not here."

"Where the hell is he? I know he went in the bunker to get some sleep before we went over to the Seabee bunker."

They both turned slowly at the sound of dirt falling from the side of the hole. Hank rolled out of a hole in the side and fell to the bottom of the bunker.

"Grab him!" Toby yelled. "Let's get him to the Seabee bunker."

Toby grabbed one side and pulled Hank's arm over his shoulder. Tubby grabbed Hank's belt and tried to help Toby lift him. Two Seabees jumped into the hole and helped them get Hank up the slope of rubble. Hank was a bank page. He just stared straight ahead, his face slack.

"Hank! Hank! Are you okay?"

Not a sound. Hank went slack and Toby had

to hold him up.

"Come on, Hank. Let's get under cover. Help me out. Walk."

Hank seemed to perk up a bit but Toby had to get the Seabees to help again. Hank's mind was somewhere else.

Then Toby heard what he feared most. The big round sounded like a jet fighter diving in on top of them. He pulled Hank to the ground and covered him with his own body. The explosion came, but it was just a lot of noise to the Seabees. It hit on top of the hill shooting streamers of fire in a hundred directions. One of the Seabees started yelling.

"Get him up! Drag him if we have to. Run."

All four of them grabbed a piece of Hank and started running for the Seabee bunker hoping they would make it before the next round came in. The NVA seldom fired just one of the big 152mm guns. The next one could hit anywhere.

"Toby, you left the lights on the tractor! They're going to draw incoming right on top of us."

"Get Hank in the bunker. I'll get the lights off."

Toby let go of Hank and ran to the backhoe. He only had time to flick off the lights before he heard the rumble from across the river. Somebody in the dark screamed, "Incoming!" He started running for the bunker listening for the fighter jet sound of another big round. He heard it coming just before he dove down the entrance ramp. He hit the dirt just as the round exploded not far away and the shockwave bounced him back into the air and knocked the air out of his lungs. Hands grabbed his shirt and dragged him through the outer entrance. A second round hit and knocked dirt off the walls of the bunker and made the overhead bounce.

It was pitch dark in the bunker. Toby gasped to catch his breath and tried to look around. When he looked up, dirt fell in his face. He spat and wiped his eyes.

"Where's Hank?" he yelled.

"Over here," Tubby yelled back.

Toby moved toward the sound and stepped on somebody's leg. "Get the fuck off me. Watch where the fuck you're going."

"Tubby!"

"Here."

"How's he doing?"

"I can't find anyplace he's wounded, but he hasn't said anything yet."

"All right. Keep talking. I can't see shit."

"Keep coming. Keep coming. Keep coming. Fuck! Stop. That's my leg."

"Fuck! Don't we have a damn light in here?"

"Yeah. Hold on," Thatcher said. "Let me relight it."

"Brilliant fucking idea," Toby yelled. "Wish

I'd have thought of that."

Chapter 57

Hank looked up when the light hit his eyes.

"Hank, are you okay?" Tubby said.

His eyes moved to find Tubby.

"Hank, what's the matter?" Toby asked. "Are you hurt?"

Hank looked at Toby and then his eyes looked around the bunker. He started shaking and his eyes opened wide. Suddenly he screamed and jumped up. He looked around wildly and ran for the entrance. He was outside before anyone could stop him.

He moved so fast and everyone was so shocked by his scream it was a few seconds before anyone could react. Finally, Toby jumped up and ran after Hank. He pushed through both entrances and ran up the ramp.

Hank was just standing in the night and

looking at the sky.

Toby touched his shoulder and Hank jumped. He looked at Toby and settled down.

"There was no light at all," he said. "I was sleeping in one of those spider holes and woke up buried alive. I started screaming and couldn't stop."

"The bunker took a direct hit from a mortar," Toby said. "We got to you as soon as we could."

"I couldn't stop screaming."

"I would have too."

"I died in there."

"No you didn't."

"You don't understand. I died in there."

"Hank, you're right here. You're okay."

"I know. I'm here, but I'm not okay."

Hank took a deep breath and shuddered as he let it out. "God, that was awful. I can't go back in there, Toby. You go ahead and get some sleep."

"What are you going to do?"

"I'll sit in a hole. I can't be covered again. I might not make it the next time."

"I'll sit up with you. Tubby will too."

"No. Leave me be for a while. I've got to deal with this."

Toby knew Hank wouldn't relent. He'd been that way his whole life. When he had to work out something inside, he had to be alone.

"Me and Tubby will check on you. Try to

get some rest."

"I will. You go on back in there and tell them people to leave me be for now. I'll work this out."

When Toby returned to the bunker everyone inside looked up.

"He's spending the night in a hole. Leave him be. He knows what he's doing."

Toby sat against the wall with Tubby and was quiet.

"Do you think he's okay?" Tubby asked. "I've never seen him like that."

"He just needs some time to work through it. He was buried for almost an hour, Tubbs. Man, I can't even imagine what he went through."

"Shouldn't one of us be out there with him?"

"No. Leave him be. He has to deal with this himself. You'd just make it harder for him."

"Okay. You're his brother. You know him better than I do."

Hank picked his way across the hill away from the Seabee bunker. One of them was sure to think they could help and come outside and he didn't want to be found. He found an abandoned Marine fighting hole that was reasonably dry and climbed in. The incoming had stopped, but it was sure to start again.

He sat back against the side of the hole and

looked up at the sky. He wished there were some stars out. As he looked skyward, the tears started down the side of his face. He didn't want them to start and he couldn't stop them.

He had never been truly afraid of anything in his life, not even as a little boy, but sealed in that hole he had completely lost it. Losing it like that shook him, but he was dealing with a bigger problem and wasn't sure he could handle it. The little boy at Khe Sanh. The memories had finally broke through his desire to escape them and he knew. He killed that little boy. Two hundred and fifty pounds of Hank Tucker landing on him broke his neck.

Chapter 58

In the morning no one could find Hank. The Seabees all set out in different directions checking every hole they could find. No Hank. Toby went to a company command bunker and asked for the company commander's help. He checked by radio with all his platoons and the Marines checked their own areas, but one by one, they reported back negative.

Toby was about to panic. He agreed to take the loader up to the worksite before continuing his search. Maybe he could see better on top the machine.

When he parked the loader and shut down, he heard noise in the observation bunker hole. Thunk, thunk, thunk. He walked to the side of the hole and looked in.

Hank was stripped to the waist swinging a

pick squaring up the sides of the hole. He was covered in sweat and dirt and every muscle in his torso stood out.

"Hank, what the hell are you doing?"

Hank stopped and looked over his shoulder at Toby.

"What's it look like?"

"Everybody on base is looking for you."

"Nobody looked here. Get your loader down her and get this rubble out."

"I've got to let the Marines know we found you. I'll be right back."

"Go on. Tell the crew to get their asses up here. I ain't getting this bunker done by myself."

One by one the rest of the crew came up the hill and started working. None of them said anything to Hank and he didn't offer to make any conversation. Toby got back and moved the loader in to remove the rubble. Tubby picked up a pick and worked alongside Hank. He didn't have the patience of the rest though.

"You okay, Hank?"

"Yeah, Tubbs. Just needed a little time to get my head straightened out."

Tubby worked a few minutes more. He felt better. Seeing Hank shook up like he was really got to him.

"You ready to move the timbers up here?"

"Soon as we get the base leveled. Another hour."

"I'll tell thatcher."

"Go on."

They used the hill itself for fortification as much as possible, but the observation deck had to be exposed to the north. They compromised on a two-level design with the lower level completely underground and the observation deck on top with its own overhead protection and fast access to the fully fortified lower level. It was a pretty good compromise. The observation deck not only served as an observation platform it also became the defense against time delay artillery. The fortified roof of the deck would cause the fuse to detonate in the observation space and the space would dissipate the blast to the sides protecting the observers sheltering in the lower bunker. The MCB 7 engineers and the Marines were happy. The Seabees building it just wanted to be done with themselves out of there.

The NVA kept them motivated. Working the lower level kept them below ground and out of sight most of the time, but when Toby had to bring the loader up the hill, it was like one of those carnival shooting galleries. Sometimes it was just snipers. Other times NVA mortars would have a try. For some reason though, the big guns across the river remained silent. That was a good thing because neither the mortars or the snipers were very accurate and usually only got a single round off before the Marines responded and suppressed fire.

The lower level was complete at the end of the first week and work started on the observation deck. The roof of the lower level was supported with a double layer of 4"x12" planks cross-laid on 6"x6" beams and posts. A layer of rock and sand bags topped the planking, and a layer of AM2 runway matting topped the sandbags and provided a floor for the observation deck.

Building the observation deck was more exciting. The idea was to build a low fortified bunker on top of the lower shelter level. The roof would be fortified like the lower level, but it would conform to the slope of the hill making it harder to see and harder to target. The problem for the Seabees was they were no longer working in a hole and all the materials had to manhandled. Toby couldn't keep the loader or any equipment on the hill without drawing incoming.

The weather was improving by the day. The monsoon season was petering out with daytime temperatures in the mid-seventies and cold nights. The day and week-long downpours of the season were becoming just hour-long events. Overcast and low clouds were common, but an hour or two of sun in the afternoon could be expected.

With the lower level finished, the Seabees working the upper level had a place to shelter from incoming and were able to pick up the pace. Hank supervised cutting the posts and roof timber for the slanting roof off-site in some cover and reduced the time builders had to spend on the hill.

As soon as the posts were set and the planking laid on the roof, the Marines provided a work detail to fill sandbags and the fortification progressed quickly. Toby put the finishing touches of rock and dirt on with the loader. The observers inspected the bunker and gave their approval. It was the best protection any of the observation posts ever had.

At the end of the second week the crew gathered at the bottom of the hill near the Seabee bunker and looked at their work from a distance.

"You can't even tell there's a bunker there," Thatcher said.

"That's the idea," Hank said. "It's hard to hit something you can't see."

"Are you guys going back with the morning platoon sweep of the MSR?"

"Yeah. Toby's making arrangements now. Can't say I'll be sorry to see this place in the rearview mirror."

"We'll be heading back in a couple of days," Thatcher said. "Where are you heading next?"

"I hope just Dong Ha. We've been on off-

site details since we got here. I'm hoping for . . ."
Hank was interrupted by a loud rumbling from across the river.

"Incoming! Incoming!"

Chapter 59

Everyone made it to the Seabee bunker before the incoming hit. It was the big stuff this time but it wasn't close to the Seabee bunker. Still, it shook the ground the bunker sat in. Hank counted three large explosions. Silence followed the third. They waited five minutes before emerging from the bunker.

"Where'd it hit?" Tubby asked.

Hank was staring up the hill with Thatcher.

"You got to be kidding me," Thatcher said.

The hill looked flatter than before. The place where OP1 was supposed to be was just a large notch in the hill instead of a sloping dirt covered roof. More debris were scattered around it than usual.

"Looks like a direct hit," Toby said. "Crap, what now?"

"Come on. Let's see how the lower level

held up."

The entire upper level was gone, roof, sides, and all the supporting timber. Many of the timbers had survived but they were fifty feet down the hill. They wouldn't remain there long. Marines would have them in their bunkers as soon as they could get up the hill. The round had penetrated the sandbags and rock but detonated above the roof of the lower bunker. The AM2 matting that formed the top layer of the lower roof and the floor of the observation deck was perforated and holed in several places, but the roof to the lower bunker had held. The design worked. The blast was dissipated to the sides inside the observation deck.

"Let's find the Marines and figure out what we do now," Hank said. "I know one thing. Unless they get operations to extend this project, we're out of here in the morning. This is a fucking waste of time."

"My detail won't be far behind," Thatcher said. "This top bunker is going to get blown away no matter how well we reinforce it and the fucking gooks are just going to keep doing it. I doubt our operations shop will put a permanent detail out here just to keep replacing the upper level. Glad I ain't a Marine."

"I've had that very same thought myself," Hank said. "Toby, get your loader checked out for the trip back up the MSR. Tubby, get the tanks on the six-by topped off. Come on, Thatch. Let's talk to the Marines."

After inspecting the damage, the Marine S3 agreed replacing the upper structure was a waste of time and materials. The design had worked the way the engineers had expected. It protected the lower bunker but replacing it over and over was time consuming and dangerous. Hank and his team were released to leave in the morning and Thatcher starting wrapping up his project.

No one celebrated that night. Rather than feeling a sense of completion, they all just felt frustrated. They had worked hard in horrible conditions and it had all been for nothing. It was just frustrating as hell and disappointing to have gone through all that and to leave without any real accomplishment to look back on. The MCBU Seabees crowded into the MCB 7 bunker for their last night and everyone was asleep early, except for Hank. He found a hole outside and spent most of the night staring into the dark trying to reconcile his own survival with the death of a little boy.

Hank, Toby, and Tubby with the six-by and the loader met the security platoon escort at C2 in the afternoon the next day and returned to Dong Ha without incident. It was the 21st of February but it seemed like it ought to be March or April. Hank was tired. He was tired of small camps in the boondocks where people shot at you. He was tired of building stuff only to have it blown away. He was tired of Vietnam and tired of the Navy and he was tired of memories that would no longer go away.

When Hank reported to the builder's shop, Chief Murphy was looking at a message and shaking his head.

"We're finished at Con Thein," Hank said.

"Glad you're back. Hold on a minute."

Murphy continued reading the message and shaking his head.

"Damn, damn, damn," he said quietly.

"What's going on?"

Murph looked up and he had tears in his eyes.

"We lost a man at Khe Sanh today. I sent him out there."

"A Seabee?"

"Yes. A First-Class Builder. He didn't even get on the ground. His helicopter was shot down. Hank, hang loose for a while. Grab a meal and a shower. I've got to handle this."

Murph didn't wait for a reply. He was out the door before Hank could ask who the builder was. The detail at Khe Sanh had suffered several wounded, but as far as Hank knew, this was the first fatality. Not knowing who it was didn't lessen the shock. A Seabee had been killed in action. Coming so soon on top of his own near-death experience, the shock took a few moments to sink in but when it did, it was like a kick in the stomach.

And then he had another thought. If Murph sent a First-Class Builder out there he was going to need a replacement. I'm a BUL1 and I just finished up an assignment. Damn! I do not want to go back to Khe Sanh. Then he felt ashamed. A man had just died and he was thinking about his own ass. Damn right! He thought. I did my time in Bu Duc and Khe Sanh and Con Thein. Me and Toby only have a couple months left over here. I do not want to go back to that place.

Hank was sitting in the shop mulling over his future when Murph returned.

"Did you get something to eat?"

"Didn't feel like eating," Hank said. "Who was it on the helicopter?"

Murph told him who it was and Hank tried to picture him in his mind. He knew him of course, but they had never been close friends or even worked together. That didn't make the death any less tragic. Murph was dealing with it and controlling his emotions. "He was taking the mail out there," he said. Then he squared up his shoulders and looked at Hank.

"Hank, I've talked it over with the company commander and we're going to use you as a rover."

"Here?"

"Yes. You'll pull a lot of temporary jobs to fill in where I need you, but it will all be here on Dong Ha or close by."

"Chief, you are talking music to my ears."

"It will just be for sixty days. We'll send you back to Da Nang for your last week so you can check-out, get your pay caught up, and get your uniforms squared away."

"How about Toby?"

"Alpha company is reassigning Toby. I don't know what he is getting."

"What's going on with Tubby?"

"I've got enough fabrication work to use him here in the shop. Look, I've got to get with the old man to make some arrangements. Take some time to get squared away. You look like hell."

"Thanks," Hank said. "I need a shower."

Chapter 60

Toby caught up with Hank at their hooch. He had a fresh shave, a haircut, and a brand-new set of greens and boots on.

"You missed a good meal," he said. "I forgot what a hot meal tasted like."

"I had to meet with Murph. We lost a man at Khe Sanh this morning."

"I heard. I didn't know him. He's not sending you out there is he?"

"No. He's keeping me and Tubby here in Dong Ha. How about you?"

"Same. My Chief assigned me to the transportation crew for the next sixty days. Looks like I'll be driving the base bus and filling in on equipment when they need me until we're ready to go home."

"I'm in the shop and roving. Murph is

keeping Tubbs in the builder's shop too. I better get a shave and a shower. I think I got mold growing in my armpits."

"Catch you later," Toby said. "I've got to help the mechanic with the frontend loader. It got some dings out there on the hill. You better write Eva. We're getting short."

Hank hadn't written his wife while he was at Con Thein. It was hard to believe he would be home with her in just a few short weeks. He tried to conjure up her face but couldn't get a clear mental picture. It had been almost a year since he was with her. He took his wallet out and retrieved her picture. He sat like that for a few minutes just looking at her image.

It had been a long hard year with experiences and people he would never forget—and memories he wished he could forget. He put the picture away and grabbed his towel and shaving kit. It wasn't over yet. He still had sixty days to get through. Time to get with it.

Most population centers in South Vietnam were cleaning up and rebuilding after the offensive launched by the VC during the Tet holiday while Hank, Toby, and Tubby were at Khe Sanh. By all accounts it had been an unmitigated disaster for the VC and the level of enemy activity across the whole of the south was dropping off sharply. They did a lot of damage, but their losses were so great they ceased to be an effective fighting force. Some said that's exactly what Ho Chi Minh wanted. He planned the operation and let the Americans eliminate the only effective fighting force in the south that might oppose him in the future.

Dong Ha, being close to the DMZ, still received occasional incoming artillery or rockets, but not nearly as much as they received during the fall. The 122mm rockets were rare now since it was the VC, not the NVA, who launched them most.

There was still fighting in Hue and in hamlets around Saigon, while Marine and Army units cleaned out remnants of the forces involved in the offensive, but most of the republic was experiencing more peace than they had seen in years.

Seabee details were being sent out to district and hamlet headquarters to help rebuild all around the country, sometimes just two or three men to see what they could do, because there just weren't enough Seabees to meet all the construction needs.

Hank got his shower and his first hot meal in two weeks. He didn't complain. The men out at Khe Sanh wouldn't taste a hot meal for a long time. They were calling it a siege now. The combat base was surrounded and cut off and the Seabees of Detail Bravo were there for the duration.

Hank was a good finish carpenter and could make his living as a cabinet maker if he chose, but the Navy didn't always give you a choice. Besides, he liked seeing a building going up. Murph kept him in the shop for a few days doing some joinery and then sent him down to Phu Bai for a week to fill in on a detail building hardback hooches for Marine aviators. That assignment turned into a two-week job and when he got back to Dong Ha, he and Toby were true short timers.

"Six weeks, Hank," Toby said that evening in the hooch. "What are you going to do when you get back?"

Hank took a pull on the beer he was nursing and laid back with his arm behind his head.

"I've got a little money in the bank," he said. "I think I'll take Eva down to Dewey Beach for a couple weeks. Then . . .well, I'm not sure. I'd like to start building on that lot I bought. I'm tired of paying rent and paying off somebody else's house. But I got to earn a living. Maybe I'll make the jump and start my own company. I know a lot of contractors and can probably get sub-contracts to get started."

"I think that's a great idea. I'm going back with Paolucci and sons. I wrote to the old man and he said he has work for me. There's a lot of highway building going on."

Tubby rattled the screen door and walked in.

"Well, I did it."

"Did what?" Hank asked.

"Extended six months. It took a while since I'm a reserve, but the paperwork came back today. I go on leave for thirty days starting tomorrow."

Hank wanted to question Tubby's sanity, but hell, he'd already did the deed. And he was a buddy. No sense beating up on him.

"Hope it works out for you, Tubbs. Where are you going on leave? Back to the states?"

"Hell no. There's nothing back there for me but a bunch of drunks where I come from. I finally got out of that shithole and I don't plan to go back. I'm going to Hong Kong for thirty days on the U.S. Navy. I have six months' pay on the books and a hard-on. I plan to get rid of both."

Toby chuckled. "You better watch them Hong Kong whores, Tubbs. One good screwing and you'll be falling in love."

"You never know. They say them Chinese women really know how to take care of a man."

"Till his money runs out," Hank said. "Well hell, have good time. You'll probably never get another chance to see Hong Kong. You say you leave tomorrow?"

"I fly down to Danang in the morning. Then the first flight to Saigon. Then the first commercial flight out to Hong Kong. Let's get drunk."

"I'll have a couple with you," Toby said,

"but let's hold the drunk for when you get back. Me and Hank will only have two weeks left and we can have a real party. Besides, you don't want to be flying with a hangover."

Tubby kicked at something on the floor.

"Yeah, I guess you're right. What have we got to drink?"

"Whatever is in the club. Remember? They blew our stash up at Bu Duc."

"I know that," Tubby said. "Ha! I got you." He pulled a flat bottle out of his back pocket.

"It's not enough to gets us drunk, but it's enough for a buzz. Where's the cups?"

With Tubby gone and Toby driving in twelve-hour shifts Hank had a lot of time to think. Way too much time. Shop work wasn't the kind of mind-numbing work he needed. Sitting alone and staring out at the southern rice fields by the south perimeter was getting to be too much of a habit. He knew he ought to find something to do and quiet the thoughts that came without wanting them in his mind. Still, there he sat trying to remember and trying to forget.

The dead baby's eyes at Bu Duc was a sharp memory, but the rest of that day was just jumbled impressions. The firefights at Bu Duc seemed like memories he should be able to bring back clearly, but he couldn't. When you're in a fight you only know what is right in front of you, and even that is most often a confused jumble of loud noises, shouting, orders, and emotions that jump between excitement and terror. You remember the terror. They seem like something substantial until you try to nail them down in your memory, and then you feel cheated because all you get is flashes of impression, but the pain of something awful happening, the pain of something lost is still there.

Trying to remember that first day of the attack on Khe Sanh was even more confusing and terrifying and all jumbled up with bombardments that came later. It was hard to remember what happened when, but not hard to still feel the terror of just having to wait for it to end with no way to stop it, wondering every minute if the next one was going to fall on you. It was a terror he would never forget.

His memories of body bags and wounded Marines and Seabees and Tubby's legs when the steel fell on him combined to drive his mind to the same place every time—waking up in a dark hole and realizing he was buried alive. He didn't want to go there, but he couldn't resist the perverse need for reliving that horror again and again, and each time he did, the terror threatened to overwhelm him again. He would never be able to talk about the things he learned about himself in that hole. Finally his mind always returned to the little boy he killed. He didn't mean to. Oh God, he didn't mean to, but that thought made it even worse. Sometimes things you break can't be fixed and it didn't matter if you didn't mean to break them. He was sure he'd give his own life to bring that little boy back, but he couldn't. Nothing could bring him back. He was dead and nothing could change that and that made it even more horrible. It couldn't be fixed!

What is it with the human brain that makes it such a perverse beast? Need to lose some fat? The frigging brain will burn lean muscle and protect fat. Need sleep? The frigging brain will start firing on all cylinders torturing you with every humiliation or frustration you've ever experienced. Need to remember something desperately? Forget it. You won't be able to find it in the perverse son of a bitch. Need to forget horrible experiences? The frigging brain will bring them back in a jumble of impressions that leave you exhausted and wanting to scream and refuse to answer your one question. Why?

Hank sat in the dark not even seeing the dim moonlit rice fields. The tapes in his head were playing again. Right then he needed someone to interrupt him but no one was there. He'd seen to that. Another perversion of the brain.

Chapter 61

As March moved toward April, the weather got better and Hank got quieter. Toby was worried. Hank had always been the big brother, Toby's hero. Toby had been a late bloomer physically. He didn't start his growth spurt until he was sixteen. He never had to worry about bullies in school though. They knew if they messed with him they had to answer to Hank. Hank had always been confident and outgoing, always ready to stick up for the little guy.

Hank had changed after he was buried in that bunker. Fact is, he had been changing all year long, both of them had, but after that mortar hit his bunker he got quieter and more withdrawn. He didn't socialize much with anyone now. Even with Toby his conversations had become mostly one-word responses. He was spending way too much time alone down by the south perimeter, but Toby didn't know what to do about it. Maybe there wasn't anything to do about it. They both had been in some bad places and been through some bad times in Vietnam, but Hank's experiences were worse. Even at Khe Sanh he seemed to get the short end of the stick more than anyone else. Maybe because he sought it out. Who knows? That's the way Hank was. He'd step up to keep someone else from having to.

They were under thirty days now. Getting back with Eva would be good for Hank. She had always been good for him. But Toby wondered. He knew he, himself, had changed in ways that wouldn't change back, but those changes were probably good changes, changes he felt good about. The quiet, withdrawn person Hank was becoming was not a good change though, not in Toby's opinion. The old Hank was the good Hank, the indestructible Hank, the Hank that stood up for little guys, the Hank who just naturally took over on every job.

Now the indestructible Hank was having horrible nightmares and they were always the same. He'd wake up screaming, and then he would be embarrassed and confused and go off somewhere by himself. Toby just didn't know what to do.

The month wound down slowly. Tubby returned from leave and the terrible trio had their party, but

Hank wouldn't drink. He had reached the point where he would sleep in the hooch again, but his nightmares continued. Toby remembered his mother after their father died. That's how Hank was acting. He acted like he was in mourning, but Toby couldn't figure out why. As the days wound down to departure, Toby could feel the stress lifting from his own shoulders and could enjoy the almost intoxicating anticipation of getting on that plane and flying home. Hank didn't seem to be looking forward to it at all. Chief Murphy sent for Toby and Hank at the start of their last week before they were scheduled to return to Da Nang to process out.

"I have one last job for the Tucker boys," he said. "You guys are so short I can't send you out on anything that's going to take any time, so you can do a little project for me just outside of camp."

"In the ville?" Hank asked.

"Exactly. There's a little Catholic orphanage in Dong Ha village. We've been promising the sisters there we'd help them put up a little chapel. It's not a big job and you probably won't get it done, but you can make some progress and I can send a crew out later to finish it. The slab is already poured and set-up. See if you can get it framed."

"Kids?" Hank asked. His voice sounded almost frightened.

"Well, yes. It's an orphanage, Hank."

Hank was preoccupied while they loaded studs on the six-by. Again Toby was reminded of his mother's mourning when their father died.

"Hank, what's going on? You've been moping around since we left Khe Sanh."

He almost told Toby about the little boy then but stopped before it could get out. He couldn't burden Toby with it.

"Yeah, I guess I have," he said. "Just a lot of stuff catching up with me, I guess. It will get better in another week."

"You want to talk about it? Sometimes it helps to talk it out."

Again the temptation to spill his guts almost won. But no. This was something he had to live with. No one could really understand. It was done and he couldn't change it or fix it. It would fade in time.

"Nothing much to talk about," he said. "Help me with that keg of nails. Let's get this show on the road."

Kids hawking Coca Cola, Ho Chi Minh sandals, silk Vietnam jackets, and pot and other assorted and unsavory items including their virgin sisters if they were to be believed, lined almost the entire road into the village. Tin sheds held their wares and the adults supervising them. Military vehicles and Marines on foot were the primary traffic and

Americans had money and were mostly generous with kids. Every boy looked like the kid at Khe Sanh.

The orphanage was small, just twenty-five kids tended by six nuns. One of the nuns was a white woman, Sister Angelic. She spoke good English and told them she was French. Toby went with her to meet the kids, but Hank refused the invitation and set about unloading the truck. The framing job wouldn't take long. It was good to get his mind off kids and onto the job.

Toby would make a good helper. He'd been doing that since he was a kid. Hank looked around for his brother but he hadn't got back from wherever the nun took him. He set about laying out the base and top plates and studs to frame the sides of the building. Whoever had poured the Pad set anchor bolts so he just had to tap the base plates on the bolts to mark them and then drill on the marks. The Chief hadn't given him a plan, but he didn't need one. The concrete floor gave him all the information he needed for dimensions except height. That was easy too. The studs were precut for hardback hooches. The chapel was going to look very much like a big hooch.

Toby returned and they began framing the walls. By the end of the day the walls were framed in. They would return the next day and put the rafters up.

"Let's see if we can shake Tubby loose for a day," Toby said. "The three of us can roof this sucker with tin in a day."

"I was thinking the same thing. Why don't you load the tools up on the truck? I'll let the nun know we'll be back tomorrow."

He could hear the kids playing on the other side of a hedge. The nuns would probably be there. Hank found the opening in the hedge and stopped to watch the kids. Their ages ranged from toddler to teenager. The big ones were helping the little kids. The nuns weren't around. Hank watched the kids. He wanted to leave but he couldn't.

The longer he watched the more depressed he got. Several of the boys in the group were about the same size as the kid at Khe Sanh. Each of them was watching or helping a smaller child. Just like the kid at Khe Sanh. He couldn't help it. Tears welled up in his eyes, but he didn't cry. He couldn't.

"You are troubled," a soft voice said. "I have been watching you. Why do the children trouble you so?"

She was French, but she was petite French. She couldn't have been more than five foot three. Hank towered over her. She was also plump, probably in her fifties, maybe older.

"Bad things happen in a war, sister. The

children remind me of one."

"Would you like to talk about it? Your heart is heavy."

"I'm not Catholic, sister."

"Does that matter?"

The temptation came again and this time he couldn't resist it. She was a nun. When he left here, he would never see her again. He couldn't stand it any longer. He had to tell someone.

"I killed a little boy," he said.

Chapter 62

Toby watched Hank talking with the French nun. He started to join them, but something about Hank's posture caused him to hold back. Something intimate and private was going on between them. He watched for a few moments and then returned to the truck. Whatever was going on Hank would work it out. He always did.

The light was starting to fade and Toby was getting nervous when he finally saw Hank coming down the path. Not just Hank, but Hank and five Vietnamese kids. That was surprising. He hadn't wanted anything to do with kids since Khe Sanh.

"Who are your friends?"

"Just some of the kids at the orphanage. Are some of those C-Rats still in the truck?"

"A couple."

"Give them to the kids. They don't get a lot

of protein."

The children waited with their hands folded in front of them while Toby climbed in the truck and got the boxes of C-Rats. He handed them to Hank. Hank handed one each to each the two largest boys.

"Go on now. You share with the little ones. We'll be back tomorrow."

No smiles. They all seemed so serious. They turned as a group and started back down the path.

"It's amazing how they take care of each other," Hank said. "The sisters are doing a good job."

Toby just stared at Hank amazed. He was seeing and hearing the old Hank.

"So what were you and the French nun talking about?" he asked.

Hank watched the kids until they were out of sight and ignored Toby's question. Toby was about to ask again when he finally spoke.

"A lot of things, Toby. A lot of things. We talked some about responsibility and war and what it does to people. Did you know she's a very educated woman?"

"I figured so," Toby said. "I know she speaks three languages."

"Yeah, and more than that. She has two university degrees. One in divinity and one in psychology. Amazing isn't it? I mean her being out here in this little orphanage and everything. It was good to talk with her."

"Well, yeah, I thought she was interesting too. You ready to go back? We don't want to be outside the gate after dark."

"Let's git. Probably ought to load the truck with the lumber and tin for the roof tonight. That way we can get an early start and maybe get the chapel under roof by tomorrow night. And don't let me forget. Let's steal a crate of C-Rats. The kids love them."

Toby kept glancing at Hank out the corner of his eye all the way back to the gate. Hell, he looked okay. Fact was, Hank looked better than Toby had seen him since Khe Sanh. He wondered what the hell that nun had done to him.

They loaded the truck before turning in and checked with Murph to get Tubby shook loose for the day. Murph worked it out and said he would tell Tubby to meet them in the equipment yard at 0700. Hank slept through the night with only a single interruption and no nightmares.

Sometime around 0300 a single rocket exploded without warning. No sirens and the explosion wasn't close. Hank and Toby woke up but since the sirens hadn't sounded they went back to sleep.

Tubby was waiting at the equipment yard with a

canteen cup of coffee when they arrived. Toby and Hank had to wait while Tubby checked the building supplies on the truck to make sure they had everything he would need to tin the roof.

"Tubbs, will you get your ass in gear?" Hank said. "We need to get the building under roof today. Me and Toby have to check out tomorrow."

"You fucking short timers are always in a hurry. You're sounding awful chipper for a change, and I mean awful. It's too damn early to be so cheerful."

"Seven days and a wake up," Toby said. "We'll be in Da Nang processing out day after tomorrow. If that's not something to get happy about, I don't know what is."

"Get in the truck," Tubby said. "Let's get this job done. They're sending me down to Phu Bai tomorrow and I want to get some sleep tonight."

They got as far as the gate and were turned back. No one was allowed into the village.

"What's going on?" Hank asked the Marine on the gate.

"Some kind of explosion in the village last night. EOD and AFPs are on the scene and the ville is off limits."

"What blew up?" Toby asked.

"Got me. I know there were casualties, but they didn't tell me anything else."

"Shit!" Tubby said. "Let's go back to the

shop. Maybe Murph can find out when we can go."

"I hope it didn't involve the orphanage," Hank said quietly.

"Don't let your imagination run away with you. Murph can find out."

All the way back to the shop Hank was sinking into a very dark mood. It can't be them, he thought. It just can't be them. Please don't let it be them.

Murph wasn't at the shop and Hank couldn't sit still. He paced back and forth.

"Hank, sit down," Tubby said. "You're driving me crazy."

"All those kids, Tubbs. They already lost everything. Damn! Where the hell is Murph?"

"That's Chief Murphy to you fucking short timers. What the hell are you three doing here on your asses. Aren't you supposed to be roofing the chapel at the orphanage?"

Murph came in with a set of plans under his arm and a cup of coffee in his hand.

"Chief! We've been waiting for you. The gate is closed. They won't let us into the village. What the hell happened?"

"Oh, that. The district headquarters got blown all to hell. EOD thinks it was a satchel charge. The gate should be open now."

"Not the orphanage?" Hank asked.

"The orphanage? What gave you that idea?

No. I told you. The district headquarters got blown up sometime last night."

"I heard it," Tubby said. "Must have been a big damn charge. I thought it was a rocket."

Hank wobbled a little and sat hard into a chair.

"I've got to get the hell out of the fucking place," he said.

"Then get your asses in gear and finish the job. Go on. Get the hell out of my shop. I've got work to do."

Chapter 63

When the World Airlines jet left the runway at Da Nang and leveled off high over the sea everyone on the plane let out a collective sigh. It was silent for a moment and then the cheering started. They were on their way home.

Since Toby and Hank were ending their thirty-month active-duty obligation, They got physicals at Da Nang and personnel did their final paperwork. Their pay was brought up to date and they were paid for unused leave and given travel pay back to their home of record from the west coast. They converted their MPC back to dollars. They each had a satisfyingly fat roll of U.S. dollars in their pockets. They still had a reserve obligation, but they were effectively civilians as soon as they could ditch the uniforms and get into civvies.

They did get the chapel under roof before

leaving for Da Nang, but they didn't get to see it finished. The French nun was away on some errand and Hank didn't get to see her again. So much was left undone when they caught their flight to Da Nang, but that's the way a tour in Vietnam went. Damn few left with any feeling of closure. You arrived in the middle of projects and left in the middle of others. There was always another project to do and someone else to take over for their tour. That lack of closure was more noticeable for the Seabee Maintenance Units, but even the Mobile Construction Battalions rotated back to their homeports with miles of road still to be constructed by others, airfields half finished, and multiple projects turned over to their reliefs.

The flight was long and anticipation was high. Many have made that flight and all remember the moment when the plane crossed the coastline of the United States. Hank and Toby had one more flight to Philadelphia, the closest airport to home, then the slow car ride down to Wilmington.

Two days after coming home, Hank knocked on the door of the old green trailer on Tenth Street.

"Pops, are you in there?"

"Where the hell else would I be? Who is it?"

"It's me, Pops, Hank."

"Hank:? Are you back, boy? Want a beer?"

Popeye was crossing the kitchen to the

fridge when Hank came in. He looked older. but then, so did Hank.

"Take a load off and tell me about the Seabees of today. I've been wondering how things have changed."

Hank and Popeye talked about the service generally, carefully avoiding the things Hank didn't want to talk about. Popeye had his own demons that haunted him and respected Hank's. The conversation slowed after a couple hours and more than a couple beers.

"Was getting back home everything you expected?" Popeye asked.

"No."

"It was the same for me too. I guess we just expect too much. They don't understand. They can't understand, Hank. You figure that out after a while."

"Probably," Hank said. "I guess I was kinda disappointed that things seem to be as much out of control here as they are over there. I expected more."

"Give it time. It gets better. Tell me something. Would you do it again?"

Hank took a long pull on the bottle and thought for a moment.

"Do it again the first time? Yeah, if it was with the Seabees. Do it again now? No. I wouldn't go back there. Nothing good is going to come out of that mess."

"Are you doing okay?"

"Better than I was. Not sure if that will last. A fat little nun helped me put some things in perspective, but perspective don't change what happened. Stuff still creeps up on me sometimes. You been there, Pops. You know what it's like."

"I do," Popeye said. "Can I tell you something?"

"What?"

"It gets better."

END

Made in the USA
Middletown, DE
21 August 2023

37085016R00245